521 453

Z
Shawn O'Brien

SHAWN O'BRIEN
MANSLAUGHTER

BC

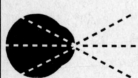
This Large Print Book carries the
Seal of Approval of N.A.V.H.

SHAWN O'BRIEN
MANSLAUGHTER

WILLIAM W. JOHNSTONE
WITH J. A. JOHNSTONE

WHEELER PUBLISHING
A part of Gale, Cengage Learning

GALE
CENGAGE Learning·

Farmington Hills, Mich • San Francisco • New York • Waterville, Maine
Meriden, Conn • Mason, Ohio • Chicago

LIBRARY OF CONGRESS CATALOGING-IN-PUBLICATION DATA

Names: Johnstone, William W., author. | Johnstone, J. A., author.
Title: Shawn O'Brien manslaughter / by William W. Johnstone with J. A.
  Johnstone.
Description: Large print edition. | Waterville, Maine : Wheeler Publishing, 2016. |
  © 2015 | Series: Wheeler Publishing large print western
Identifiers: LCCN 2015050974| ISBN 9781410486462 (softcover) | ISBN 141048646X
  (softcover)
Subjects: LCSH: Large type books. | GSAFD: Western stories.
Classification: LCC PS3560.O415 S526 2016 | DDC 813/.54—dc23
LC record available at http://lccn.loc.gov/2015050974

Published in 2016 by arrangement with Pinnacle Books, an imprint of
Kensington Publishing Corp.

Printed in the United States of America
1 2 3 4 5 6 7 20 19 18 17 16

SHAWN O'BRIEN
MANSLAUGHTER

CHAPTER ONE

"Now those folks were what I'd call downright unfriendly," Hamp Sedley said. "And they were frying salt pork in possum grease. I recollect that smell from when I was a younker."

"Good smell," Shawn O'Brien said.

"And they had cornbread, too. Got me a whiff of that."

"Too mean to share, I reckon," O'Brien said. "Either that or they didn't want to kill us in their cabin and make a big mess."

"Huh?" Sedley said.

"Four of them behind us. They've been dogging our back trail for the past hour."

"How the hell do you know that?"

"Because I look and you don't."

O'Brien turned in the saddle and stared at the gambler, his left eyebrow lifting.

"How many towns sent a hemp posse after you for playing with a marked deck? Didn't you take a glimpse behind you then?"

Sedley's face stiffened. "My dear sir, I was never run out of town for cheating at cards. Well, there was that one time down Tucumcari way when vigilantes tarred and feathered me. But that was all an unfortunate misunderstanding."

O'Brien grinned a question and Sedley said, "The playing card company made a mistake and put six aces in the same deck. I've never trusted the Bicycle brand since."

"Ah, that's understandable," O'Brien said. "Them slipping in an extra ace or two tends to get folks riled."

"Those four rubes still behind us?" Sedley said.

"Yup."

"That's bad news."

"For somebody, I reckon," Shawn said.

The two men rode across the western edge of the badlands of Wyoming's Great Divide Basin, following the meandering course of Big Sandy Creek through timbered hill country. Ahead of them the peaks of the Wind River Range scraped a blue sky tinted with the red and jade of the coming evening.

"How do we play this, Shawn?" Sedley said.

"We make camp and head for Broken Bridle at first light."

"I was talking about those four following us."

"Strange-looking rannies," Shawn said. "That's what happens when sisters can't outrun their brothers." He shook his head. "Too bad."

"They looked mean."

"And crazy."

"What the hell do they want?"

"Well, I'd say our horses, guns, and everything else we have of value about our persons."

"I need to be close, Shawn. I mean across a card table close."

"I know. But I don't think that's going to be a problem. It will be close."

Sedley's handsome face was set and grim. "They're not gentlemen," he said.

"The very opposite, I imagine," Shawn O'Brien said.

"Pity," Sedley said. "I always enjoyed swapping lead with a well-born fellow. Made a man feel classy, like he's stepping up in the world."

"You ever hit any of those fine gentlemen?"

"Well, I shot the riverboat gambler Jean Francois St. John in the thumb one time in New Orleans after he called me out. It was only a grazing wound, but he said his honor

9

was satisfied and we parted friends."

O'Brien smiled. "Very civilized and all that."

"Indeed it was. A minor dispute between sporting gentlemen."

"The shooting scrape we're about to get into won't be civilized and it won't be minor, depend on it," O'Brien said.

O'Brien and Sedley rode in silence for ten minutes, then Shawn suddenly drew rein.

"All right, they've pushed us far enough," he said. "I want this done before the light fails."

He drew his Colt and fed a round from his cartridge belt into the empty chamber under the hammer, then did the same with a second revolver he retrieved from his saddlebags.

"What are you doing?" Sedley said. He looked worried. "Do we dismount and bushwhack them?"

"Something a mean old reprobate by the name of Luther Ironside taught me when I was a young man at Dromore, my father's ranch."

O'Brien let the reins drop and held up both Colts.

" 'When all else fails, take the fight to the enemy,' Luther said. 'Charge with guns

10

blazing and unholy hellfire in your eyes.' "

Sedley drew his gun. His mouth was a tight, hard line under his trimmed mustache. "And what do I do, Mr. Hellfire?" he asked.

"Shove the nose of your horse into my sorrel's ass and keep it there."

Before Sedley could react, O'Brien kicked his startled horse into a gallop and let rip with a wild rebel yell . . .

Just as Luther Ironside had taught him.

Isa Cranston and his three sons had killed men before, but always at a distance. They were highly skilled riflemen who used the ambush and the head shot to great success, and usually their victims were dead when they hit the ground. At least the lucky ones were. Others endured a long, drawn-out, much more painful death.

"They'll make camp and that's when we bring them down," Isa told his sons, illiterate, inbred cretins he'd named Joshua, Abraham, and Moses.

Despite their mental limitations, the Cranstons were confident, in command, and planned what were routine murders the like of which they'd done many times in the past, killings that would land them a windfall of guns, money, clothing, boots, and two

11

fine horses.

But they'd never encountered a mounted revolver fighter before, trained by Luther Ironside in the ways of the great and heroic cavalry commander Colonel Turner Ashby, the incomparable Black Knight of the Confederacy, the Centaur of the South, a leader of hallowed memory.

Putting into effect what Ironside had taught him, Shawn O'Brien hurtled into the Cranstons like an avenging windstorm.

Colts bucking in his fists, he hit Isa and the man next to him in a single hell-firing moment of mayhem.

Then O'Brien was through them.

He turned the rearing, battle-maddened sorrel with his knees, his face to the enemy.

Hamp Sedley, a man with sand but no revolver skill, slammed his big American stud into the mustang of a lanky towhead with small, tight eyes and a thick beard down to his belt buckle. The little mustang went down hard, but with considerable skill its falling rider snapped off a Winchester shot before he slammed into the ground.

The bullet burned across the left shoulder of Sedley's frockcoat and ripped broadcloth, drawing blood. He cursed, fired at the man on the ground, and missed.

But then battle-maddened Shawn O'Brien

descended on the two surviving Cranstons like the wrath of God.

The man who was still mounted battled his frightened paint pony and tried desperately to get his unhandy .56 Spencer rifle into the fight.

O'Brien ignored the man and concentrated on the greater danger — the Cranston brother who'd been thrown from his mustang.

The towhead was on his feet, a Winchester to his shoulder. O'Brien charged, both guns blazing, and he and the rifleman fired at the same time. The towhead went down, shock and disbelief on his face, and was dead within seconds.

In a gunfight a man who's used to one thing but gets another can easily be unnerved.

Moses Cranston had killed three men and shared five more, but he'd never been in a gunfight. He'd shot at men from a hundred yards and watched them topple over like ducks in a shooting gallery.

Suddenly the big man on the tall horse galloped out of his worst nightmare. Moses fired too quickly and his bullet threw wild.

He didn't have time to think about it.

Four .45s dead-center chest will drop any man, and Moses Cranston drew his last breath before he hit the ground.

The man on the paint wanted out of it. He threw down his Spencer and yelled, "I'm done."

O'Brien would have let it go. But Hamp Sedley, shocked by how close he'd come to death, was not in a mood to forgive and forget.

He two-handed his Colt to eye level, aimed, and fired.

Coldly, dispassionately, he watched the man take the hit, then fall and lie still.

Sedley looked into Shawn O'Brien's widened eyes. "Serves him right," he said. "Trying to kill good Christian folks like that."

"You don't believe in turning the other cheek, do you, Hamp?" O'Brien said.

"The other cheek of my Texas ass, maybe," Sedley said.

A woman walked through the pines and drifting gun smoke.

She wore a dress made from a J.J. BAXTER & SONS flour sack, and her feet were bare and her horned toenails looked like bear claws. Her hair, once auburn, hung in dirty gray tangles, framing a face that was covered in wrinkles so deep they seemed to have been cut with wire. Her eyes had long since lost their luster and were the color of mud.

She had no teeth, good or bad.

Shawn O'Brien took the woman to be in her late seventies, worn down by a lifetime of hard work and deprivation.

In fact Molly Cranston was thirty-eight that summer.

The woman didn't spare O'Brien or Sedley a glance. She stumbled to her husband's body, rolled him onto his back, and crossed his arms over his chest. Her face showed no grief, no anger, no emotion of any kind, as though she wore a Nipponese face mask of the starkest white. The woman moved to her dead sons, at one point heedlessly brushing against O'Brien's leg, and began to arrange them in the same way.

Shawn moved to dismount, but Sedley stretched out a restraining hand.

"She doesn't need your help, nor would she appreciate it," the gambler said. "She's known for years that this would happen one day."

Clouds had gathered and a light summer rain fell, ticking through the branches of the pines. There was no wind, and gun smoke drifted through the still air like a mist. Crows cawed in their tattered finery, attracted by the smell of dead men.

"The old woman can't carry home her dead," O'Brien said.

15

"She won't," Sedley said. "She'll lay them out and stay with them. Then she herself will die very soon."

"So we just ride away and do nothing?"

"Yeah, that's exactly what we do."

Anger flushed in Sedley's throat and face. "Damn it, Shawn, we just killed four men and now you see the result."

"Consequences have no pity. All a man can do is accept them for what they are and move on."

Sedley swung his horse away. "Best we camp for the night far from here," he said. "The lady doesn't want us around."

Later that night by the campfire, Shawn O'Brien dreamed of his murdered wife, her naked, outraged body spread over a moss-brown boulder on England's swampy Dartmoor plain.

Deep in uneasy sleep he whispered her name . . .

"Judith," Hamp Sedley said, staring at O'Brien through the flimsy morning light. "You said Judith over and over again."

"My wife," O'Brien said. He blew on his smoking-hot coffee.

"I know," Sedley said. "I don't have the words, Shawn."

O'Brien nodded. "It's all right, Hamp," O'Brien said. "Neither do I."

CHAPTER TWO

Broken Bridle was a hot, dusty little settlement built on the ragged edge of nowhere, clinging for its existence to a slender thread of rail, a spur of the Fremont, Elkhorn & Missouri Valley Railroad.

A teeming Chinese tent city sprawled close to the track, the men anticipating more rail-laying work if the Irish didn't come in and take it all. Their womenfolk, children, and old people were content to follow along and add their voices to the constant cacophony that was characteristic of every hell on wheels town in the west.

But Broken Bridle itself was a cow town. It looked and smelled like a cow town, and its extensive cattle pens provided its bona fides, backing up its claim to be the "Dodge City of the Northwest."

Whether that was true or not, when Shawn O'Brien and Hamp Sedley rode into the town it was obvious the burg had snap.

The wide boardwalks of Main Street were crowded with people, and in the town's four saloons dusty cowboys rubbed shoulders with bearded miners, pale card sharks, painted girls, prosperous businessmen in broadcloth, pickpockets, and the usual assortment of hangers-on, dance hall loungers, shell game artists, and young men on the make.

"Yup, Broken Bridle has snap all right," the old man at the livery said. "She's a-hootin' an' a-hollerin' an' a-bustin' at the seams. She's ready to blow night or day, and we got the oldest whiskey and youngest whores north of the Picketwire."

The old man winked a faded blue eye. "What we ain't got is parsons or school ma'ams, and now Burt Becker an' them are in town, them two things is even less likely."

"Burt Becker?" Sedley said. "I heard he'd been hung down Texas way."

"Maybe you should listen with two ears to what folks say, sonny," the liveryman said. He was a dry, stringy old coot with a voice like a creaky gate. "How it came up," he said, "Burt was gonna get hung for a bank robber, but he turned things around an' hung the hangman. One time I made the acquaintance of that hangman, a traveling feller by the name of Hemp Rope Harry

19

Perry. Nice enough cove when he was sober, but a demon in drink, an' because of the whiskey he bungled many a hanging an' spoiled them fer folks."

"How did Becker manage to get the drop on his executioner?" O'Brien said.

"Easy. His gang was in the crowd. They stormed the gallows, like, and cut down ol' Burt. Then Burt hung Perry, the town sheriff, and the parson. The preacher was still holding on to his Good Book when he swung. After that Burt and his gang shot up the town, killed a poor Swede boy an' a hundred-dollar hoss at the Gallant Custer Saloon hitching rail. One time I made the acquaintance of that hoss —"

"What's a big gun like Burt Becker doing in a burg like this?" Sedley said. "Hell, it would normally take a dozen strong men with crowbars to pry him out of East Texas."

Suddenly the old man's face was guarded. "You'd better ask him that your ownself, sonny," he said. "But around these parts it's best not to be a questioning man."

"Pity that because I have one more to ask," O'Brien said.

"Then ask it. Just don't ask me about Burt Becker."

"Is Jeremiah Purdy still sheriff here?"

The liveryman's expression blanked, then

he said in an odd flat voice, "Yes, he is."

Those three words put an end to the old man's talk, and his attention moved from conversation to the horses.

"Let's go talk with Purdy and find out what ails him," O'Brien said. He felt uneasy. That ancestral sixth sense born to the Irish whispered a warning, and Shawn knew it would give him no peace.

"My father is mistaken," Sheriff Jeremiah Purdy said. "I need no help from you, Mr. O'Brien, or from any other."

"Then I wasted a trip," Shawn said.

"It would seem so."

Purdy was an earnest-looking young man somewhere in his midtwenties. He sported a thick shock of yellow hair that he constantly and somewhat nervously shoved back as it tumbled over his forehead.

Of medium height and slender build, he wore a pair of round spectacles behind which owlish eyes peered out at the world with a permanently startled expression, as though he couldn't quite believe what was going on around him.

On Purdy's desk lay a Smith & Wesson .32-caliber army revolver in a soft leather pouch designed for discreet carry in the pocket.

The belly gun and its mode of carry told O'Brien that the young man was either very confident of his revolver skills or he placed little emphasis on arms and their use. He suspected the latter was the case.

Hamp Sedley, who looked like somebody held a dead fish to his nose, said, "College boy, ain't you?"

"Yes. I'm a Yale graduate," Purdy said.

"Well, that's sure going to impress Burt Becker," Sedley said.

"I think you gentlemen should leave now," Purdy said.

He looked strained, like a man does when he hides a secret illness from a loved one.

But, to Shawn O'Brien's considerable irritation, for some reason Sedley had taken a dislike to the young sheriff and was on the prod.

"What is Burt Becker doing in Broken Bridle?" he said.

"He hasn't broken any laws," Purdy said.

"Not yet."

"A man can go where he wants. It's a free country."

"Your pa told us you needed help, young feller, and I think Becker is the reason," Sedley said.

"My father told you wrong. I've already said that."

"Becker wants something this town has," Sedley said. "What is it?"

Purdy rose to his feet. "Nothing. There's nothing in this town Becker wants. Now go, both of you."

"You've pushed it enough, Hamp," O'Brien said.

"He's hiding something, Shawn."

"You heard the man. He doesn't want our help."

"But —"

"We're leaving, Hamp. Now."

Sedley nodded, then stared hard into Jeremiah Purdy's face. "Take my advice, college boy," he said. "Buy yourself a bigger gun."

CHAPTER THREE

"So how's the steak?" Hamp Sedley said.

"Fair to middling," Shawn O'Brien said. "Yours?"

"Can't do much to mess up bacon and eggs. You eyeball those two by the door?"

"Yeah. As soon as we walked into the restaurant."

"Texas?"

"You bet."

"Guns?"

"Damn right they are. The older one is June Lacour; the one next to him with the mean eyes is Little Face Denton." Shawn smiled. "They're both acquaintances of my brother Jacob, so that ought to tell you something."

Lacour, a tall, loose-geared man in fine broadcloth and white linen, heard his name and rose from the table. He crossed the floor, his spurs chiming. He wore two Colts but countered any possible threat he might pose with a smile.

"Howdy, Shawn," he said. "It's been a while."

"Two years, maybe three. Last time was when you and Little Face brought Jacob home to Dromore. He was shot through and through and cussin' up a storm."

"How is Jake?"

"Good, last I heard."

"He still play on the piano?"

"I reckon. He likes Chopin too much to quit."

"He's a rum one is Jake. He should be back East playing in one of them big orchestras. He's not here with you, is he?"

"No."

"Me and him, we had times."

"I know. He told me." Shawn laid down his fork. "This here is Hamp Sedley. He's a friend of mine."

"Any friend of Shawn's . . . you know the rest."

"Right pleased to meet you, June," Sedley said, smiling.

He rose to his feet, extended his hand, and Lacour took it.

"Little Face isn't feeling sociable, huh?" Shawn said.

"Yeah. Some days he just don't talk to people, says it's too much of a chore to think up conversation."

But Little Face, a snake-eyed man with a double shoulder holster rig, saw Shawn look at him, smiled, and touched his hat. He made no move to get up.

Shawn returned the compliment.

"Little Face is right partial to Chopin's Nocturne in C Minor," Lacour said. "Says it makes him feel sad."

"And Jake played it for him?" Shawn said.

"Sure did. That is until it made Little Face so sad he killed a man. After that Jake refused to play it. I don't reckon he's played it since." Lacour gave Shawn a long look, then said, "What brings you to Broken Bridle?"

"Just passing through, June, seeing the sights."

"This isn't a passing-through town. It's a long ways from nowhere and there's no sights."

"Well, it doesn't matter. Hamp and me are drifting, blown here and there by the wind."

"Blow back to the New Mexico Territory where you belong, Shawn. There's nothing for you in this town."

"June, if I didn't know you better I'd consider that a threat," Shawn said.

"No threat. Just advice."

"To whom are you and Little Face selling your guns?"

Lacour grinned. His teeth were very white, the canines large, like wolf fangs. "Damn it all, Shawn, you always said things real nice. I mean, 'To whom . . .' That's grandstand talk."

"Is it Burt Becker?"

"Yeah, it's Becker. He pays top dollar."

"Why is he here?"

"Protecting Broken Bridle from bandits," Lacour said, his face empty.

"What bandits?"

"I don't know. There could be some around."

"June, if prostitution is the oldest profession, then the protection business is the second."

Sedley said, "What in God's name does this one-hoss burg have that's valuable enough to protect?"

"Why don't you ask Becker?" Lacour said, his voice without tone or inflection. "Now I have to go." The lanky gunman made to walk away, then stopped. "Shawn, you ever hear tell of a gun by the name of Pete Caradas?"

"Can't say as I have."

"Step wide around him. He's poison," Lacour said.

27

CHAPTER FOUR

"What is that?" Hamp Sedley said.

"I don't know," Shawn O'Brien said. "But it's enough to spook a man."

"Drums. It sounds like drums."

"Well, there are no Indians around."

Sedley shot out a hand and grabbed the arm of a plump, fussy-looking man before he passed him on the boardwalk.

"Hey, what is that noise?" Sedley said.

"What noise?" the plump man said.

"A sound like drums."

"I don't hear a thing."

"You don't hear that?"

"No. Now give me the road, if you please."

Sedley let go of the man's arm. The noise was still loud above the quiet of the noonday street, the dim throb of distant drums.

"Watch how it's done in polite society," Shawn said.

He stepped in front of a prim matron with a shopping basket over her arm. She carried a plucked and dressed chicken partially wrapped in blood-stained white paper and a small sack of Arbuckle coffee.

Shawn smiled and touched his hat, but the woman looked alarmed.

"Sorry to trouble you, ma'am," he said. "But my friend and I are trying to identify the drumming sound."

"There is no drumming sound. Now let me pass, young man," the woman said.

She seemed so frightened that Shawn didn't push it. "Sorry to have troubled you, ma'am," he said.

The matron sniffed, said, "Why, I never!" and brushed past, her starched underskirts rustling as her high-heeled ankle boots thudded on the boardwalk.

"Seems like everybody in this damn town is deaf," Sedley said.

"Or scared," Shawn said.

He and the gambler stood tall on the boardwalk, two men dressed in fine broadcloth, both sporting the large dragoon mustaches then in fashion. They looked confident, prosperous, and in command, though at that moment, both were very much lost.

"The young sheriff was scared; I could see it in his eyes," Sedley said.

"Something to do with Becker?" Shawn said.

"Could be. That would be my guess. A man like Becker doesn't ride into a town without causing trouble for the local law."

"And what about the drums that nobody in this town hears except us?"

"Becker again? I don't know."

Shawn's blue eyes reached into distance. "According to the map I got from Connall Purdy those are the Rattlesnake Hills to the east," he said. "The drumming noise seems to be coming from there."

Sedley was silent for a few moments, then met Shawn's questioning eyes. "Ah hell, all right, I got nothing else to do," he said.

Shawn O'Brien and Hamp Sedley were a mile from the Rattlesnake Hills when the drumming abruptly stopped.

"Somebody saw us coming, huh?" Sedley said, drawing rein.

"Seems like," Shawn said. "Makes a man think he's not exactly welcome to these parts."

Ahead of him rose ramparts of volcanic rock, their windswept slopes lightly covered in bunchgrass, sage, and scattered stands of stunted fir and aspen. It was grim, unwelcoming country with nothing to offer but isolation and, now that the drums had stopped, brooding silence.

In all that vast landscape only the sky was not still, small white clouds gliding across its blue surface like lilies on a pond. Insects made their small sounds in the grass, and the air smelled of dust and decaying rock.

Shawn slid the Winchester from the boot under his knee and led the way into a narrow canyon where the lava walls rose sheer on both sides. The trees that rimmed the canyon were stunted and twisted into grotesque shapes that leaned in the direction of the prevailing winds, like a bunch of very old, bent men who'd wandered off and lost their way. The day was as hot as an oven and there was no breeze.

Both he and Sedley had removed their frockcoats and placed them behind the saddles. Sweat stained their shirts, and the air was thick and hard to breathe.

After a thousand yards the canyon narrowed and the walls became close enough to touch. Some of the rock was heavily crusted with black and gray lichen, like ancient tombstones in an abandoned graveyard.

Despite the tranquility about the hills, they were part of a wild, terrible landscape that made Shawn uneasy in his mind, and when he realized he was riding stiff and tense in the saddle he had to force himself to relax.

"Damn it, Shawn, these hills are no place for honest men," Sedley said. He, too, felt the remoteness of the hills and a strange sense of impending danger.

"How about dishonest men?" Shawn said.

Sedley didn't answer because he wasn't listening. His eyes were fixed on the trail ahead of him. "Oh my God," he said finally.

Shawn then saw what Sedley had seen. A man, or what was left of him, blocked the way. He'd been hung with ropes onto a T-shaped cross, his entire naked body crusted with dried, black blood. His beard and long hair, both gray, were also matted with gore and saliva, and heavy iron nails had been driven into the palms of his hands.

Sedley turned to Shawn, a question on his horrified face.

Shawn swallowed hard, then said, "Looks to me like he was worked over with a bullwhip, then nailed up there to die."

"His eyes are gone," Sedley said.

"Crows probably. Or ravens."

Sedley looked behind him and then, as though he couldn't help it, back to the crucified man. "Who the hell was he? What was he?"

Shawn said, "Judging by his hands and arms I'd guess he was a miner of some kind. He sure doesn't look like a puncher or an outlaw. At times in his life, that man did work and lifted loads that were way too heavy for him."

"Hell, what's that?" Sedley said.

He swung out of the saddle and stepped to the cross. "Damn, he stinks," he said.

"What did you see?" Shawn said.

"Only this." Sedley gingerly held a cardboard sign by a corner.

He carried the sign back and laid it on the ground. "There's a lot of blood on it and I can only see some of the letters," he said.

Shawn dismounted and pushed the sign with the toe of his boot and read: ST AW OR IS WIL PEN O OU.

He studied the letters for a while, then looked at Sedley. "What the hell does it say you reckon?" he said.

Sedley studied the letters for a moment, then said, "STHAW . . . STRAW FOR . . . hell, I don't know what it says."

"It reads, STAY AWAY OR THIS WILL HAPPEN TO YOU," Shawn said. He scouted the ground around the base of the cross. "No tracks."

"Summer rains, I guess," Sedley said.

"Becker?" Shawn said.

33

Sedley thought about that. "It could be him, but I doubt it."

"Me too. This killing is evil. It has no style," Shawn said. "Becker has style of a sort and he's a shooter, not a" — he waved a hand in the direction of the dead man — "whatever it is you call a man who kills like that."

"A lunatic? Madman?"

"Seems like," Shawn said. Then, "There's plenty of loose rock and shale around. We could take him down and bury him."

"No, we couldn't," Sedley said, horrified. "Hell, the body is rotten. Once we got him free of the nails we'd have to bury him a finger and toe at a time, and I'm not ready for that."

Shawn remounted, measured the distance between him and the cross, and grabbed his rope. He shook out a loop, tossed it over the T-beam, and jerked it tight.

He took a couple of turns around the saddle horn, then backed the buckskin. The rope shivered straight as the big horse took the strain, and after what seemed an eternity the cross finally pulled free and toppled over. The dead man landed facedown on the grass.

"Now we can bury him," Shawn said.

"There?" Sedley said.

"Yes, there. Right where he lies."

"Shawn, there ain't enough damned rock in the territory to bury that," Sedley said. The skin covering his cheekbones, bronzed from unaccustomed sun, was taut, like a man ready to set spurs to his horse and make a run for it.

"There's plenty of rock," Shawn said. "It's just a matter of finding it."

"Hell, my hands."

"Don't worry about your hands, Hamp. I have a feeling you won't be shuffling cards again anytime soon."

Sedley glanced at the dead man, then said, "Two feet of rock ought to do it."

"I don't know who he was, but a pile of rocks isn't much to show for a life," Hamp Sedley said.

Shawn O'Brien crossed himself, then said, "Well, whoever he was may he rest in peace."

"Then that's it," Sedley said. Then, as though a thought had just struck him, "Are you in good with God, Shawn?"

"Maybe. I don't really know."

"Had an old gambler die in my arms one time. Feller by the name of Patrick Murphy. He got shot across a card table in Fort Smith by Long Fingers Dawson. You heard of him?"

"No, I haven't," Shawn said. "And I'm not catching your drift, either."

"I'm circling up on it. Just be patient. Well, Pat Murphy was a mick, just like you, an' before he croaked he said, 'Humphrey —' "

"Humphrey?" Shawn said.

"Yeah, that's why I call myself Hamp. Anyways, he says, 'I'm a goner so mind an' say a prayer for me to Saint Bernardine of Siena, the patron saint of gamblers.' "

Sedley let a silence stretch and Shawn said, "So? And then what?"

"And then he died."

Sedley swung into the saddle and looked down at Shawn who was not yet mounted. "The strange thing is, from what I read later, ol' Bernardine was down on gambling. He said playing cards and dice were tools of the devil and gamblers should be burned at the stake."

"Odd kind of patron saint, huh?" Shawn said.

"Seems like. But in any case, all gold miners are gamblers, so say a prayer to Bernardine for the poor feller we just buried, him being a tinpan an' all. But use my name, like. So Bernie thinks it's coming from me."

"I'll see what I can do."

"And say one for me when you're at it,"

Sedley said, his face stiff. Then, "Behind us."

His eyes flickered in that direction and Shawn followed them.

About a hundred yards away six mounted riflemen were strung out across the valley floor. Silent. Alert. Watching.

Slowly, moving carefully, Shawn mounted. He slid the Winchester from under his knee and propped it on his thigh.

"Showdown time, I reckon," Sedley said. His mouth sounded as though it was full of dust.

"Seems like," Shawn O'Brien said.

CHAPTER FIVE

The sun burned like a red-hot coin and there was no breeze in the canyon. Heat shimmered from its rock walls and cast a pall over everything.

Sweat beaded on Shawn O'Brien's forehead and trickled down his back. The sorrel was restless and tossed its head, the bit chiming.

Minutes ticked past . . . the riflemen made no moves, still as equestrian statues in a museum, but Shawn felt their eyes on him.

"Maybe we should just ease on out of here," Sedley said. "Kinda like we were just visiting."

"They see us break, they'll come after us," Shawn said.

"Why are they just standing there, doing nothing?"

"Figuring the odds, I guess. Wondering how many of them we can drop before they get to us."

"Hell, I can't drop any."

"They don't know that."

"Yet," Sedley said.

A moment later the drums started again, a steady *tom-tom-tom,* primitive, incessant, and ominous.

"Hell, it's all around us," Sedley said.

"Get ready, Hamp," Shawn said. "Now those boys are on the prod."

The horsemen milled around and yelled back and forth to one another, as though working up the courage to charge.

Since he did most of the shouting, their leader appeared to be a black-bearded man astride a tall, rawboned bay. He carried two Colts in shoulder holsters and a Winchester booted under his knee. His lips were pulled back from his teeth in a savage grimace.

"They're going to come in on us," Shawn said. He tossed his Winchester to Sedley. "Do what you can with that."

He drew his Colt and a second from the waistband.

Shawn fought down a sudden spike of fear and forced himself to steady for what was to come. A defiant rebel yell surged in his throat, but he let it choke into a whispered question: "Now what the hell are they doing?"

Sedley's lips were pale and dry. A man

who can't shoot has no business being in a gunfight against odds, and he knew it well.

"Having second thoughts?" he asked. His voice creaked.

Shawn followed the eyes of the horsemen. Their heads were tilted back and they seemed to stare beyond him, but high up, to the top of the canyon wall to his right.

Sedley had also read the signs. He turned in the saddle and his eyes widened. "What the hell?" he said.

A man with long, white hair to his waist sat a huge dappled gray, a powerful animal with the muscular confirmation of a medieval warhorse.

Despite his ivory hair the rider did not seem aged.

The way he sat the saddle, poker-backed as an armored knight at the lists, suggested enormous vitality without a hint of weakness. Adding to his gothic mystique, a black cloak fell elegantly from the man's shoulders and draped across the hindquarters of his horse. His right hand rested on top of a battle-ax with a massive steel blade, a vicious skull-cleaver Shawn had seen only in history books.

The mysterious rider removed a foot-long, S-shaped pipe from between his teeth and used it to motion to the horsemen in the valley.

A moment later Sedley said, "They're quitting, turning round, and pulling out."

"That's what it looks like," Shawn said. "But I'm not counting on it."

He reached behind him into the saddlebags, found his field glasses, and trained them on the white-haired man.

Shawn was stunned. Shaken. Disturbed as a condemned getting his first glimpse through the portal of hell.

The white-haired rider's face was turned to him, shadowed slightly under a black, floppy-brimmed hat. He had a wide, cruel mouth, eyes as cold as gun sights, and his every feature twisted into a demonic mask of hate. This was a man who knew nothing of love or kindness, only avarice, greed, pride, anger, lust . . . the scars left by deadly sins etched deep in every line and wrinkle of his face.

It was the face of a savage.

Shawn remembered his father, Colonel Shamus O'Brien, telling him once that the deadliest desires spawn the deepest hatreds.

The rider on the great horse seemed to possess both desire and hate in equal measure.

Now the man's gaze was fixed on Shawn's

41

face, and he felt as though the skin was being flayed from his skull.

The rider raised the battle-ax above his head, and a thunderous voice that echoed around the canyon roared, "Get out!"

The pounding drums had been silent since the other riders left, but now they reached full crescendo as the man on the ridge turned his horse, slowly rode over the crest of the hill, and disappeared.

The drumming abruptly stopped, replaced by a brooding, echoing silence.

"What the hell was that?" Sedley said. Under a recent sunburn, his pale, gambler's face was a shade paler.

"A gent who obviously doesn't want us here," Shawn said.

"He'll cut his finger on that damned tomahawk, and it will serve him right," Sedley said.

Shawn smiled. "One time my brother Patrick brought an ax like that home. He was hunting butterflies and found it in a cave."

"An O'Brien hunting butterflies?"

"Yeah. Patrick's head is always full of strange notions. Anyway, he said the ax had been left there by the old Spanish men who explored the New Mexico Territory hundreds of years ago. Patrick said they called it a *hacha de guerra,* or war hatchet."

"Damn, that thing could put a hurt on a man," Sedley said.

"Yes, it could split his skull wide open. And that's why we're getting out of here while we still can."

Sedley shook his head. "A crucified miner, a man with a meat cleaver, there's something mighty strange going on here, Shawn, and I don't like it."

"Me neither. Let's go talk to Sheriff Purdy and ask him what he makes of it."

Sedley made a face. "Him? All he'll do is piss his pants and run to mama."

CHAPTER SIX

"Yeah, when a man is tied to a cross and nails driven through his hands, I'd say he was crucified all right," Shawn O'Brien said.

He wondered if Sheriff Jeremiah Purdy was stubborn or just plain stupid.

Beside him Hamp Sedley's disdainful face revealed that he harbored no such doubt. He obviously believed the latter.

"Savages?" Purdy suggested. His voice was weak.

"Indians don't crucify their enemies. Only white men do that," Shawn said.

"We saw them," Sedley said. "Who is the ranny with the long hair, a battle-ax, and a bad attitude?"

Purdy shook his head and his pleasant young face shut down. "I don't know what you're talking about," he said.

A brewer's dray trundled past the sheriff's office, and when it was gone, Shawn said, "You heard the man. Who is he?"

"And didn't he hear me? I don't know what he's talking about."

"There are men in the Rattlesnake Hills and they scare you," Shawn said. "Why?"

Purdy tapped the Smith & Wesson on his desk, his eyes defiant. "I stopped being scared around the time I got this," he said.

"Damn it all," Sedley said. "That's a two-bit, tinhorn answer to a fair question. Now tell us why the white-haired man scares you."

For a few moments Jeremiah Purdy looked like a trapped animal seeking a way out. He found none such and in a small voice said, "His name is Thomas Clouston. *Doctor* Thomas Clouston."

"He's a sawbones?" Sedley said.

"A psychiatrist, and once a highly respected, though from all reports, an exceedingly humble, one."

"He didn't look too exceedingly humble up on that hill with an ax in his hand," Sedley said.

Purdy ignored that and said, "When I was at Yale the professors talked admiringly of Dr. Clouston's early work with the insane. But his downfall began after he gave a series of lectures in Berlin, Rome, and Paris. When that was concluded he crossed the Channel to study under the famous psychiatrist Dr.

Edwin Strait at his hospital in London."

"So what happened?" Shawn said, happy to finally draw Purdy out of his shell.

"Dr. Strait believed that in most cases insanity was caused by too much alcohol and other pleasures of the flesh and a lack of self-discipline. To restore patients to mental health all a doctor needed was a firm hand and a strict regimen of sternly worded lectures, fresh air, and exercise."

Sedley said, "Too much booze and pleasures of the flesh, huh? Then I've been nuts for years."

"I know. But I never wanted to mention it to you, Hamp," Shawn said, his face empty.

Sedley growled something about people in glass houses, but Shawn wasn't listening.

"So Clouston returns home, buys himself a battle-ax, and camps out in the Rattlesnake Hills?" he asked.

Purdy managed a smile. "Not quite. He opened a mental hospital in Philadelphia and put Dr. Strait's treatments to work. But he took them too far, administered beatings, ice-cold baths, and confinement in underground bread and water cells, all in the name of instilling the notion of self-discipline."

"I guess he killed a heap of loco patients that way," Sedley said.

"He did. Too many. In our modern hospitals, using the latest treatments, the tuberculosis death rate among patients is about sixty percent. In Dr. Clouston's clinic the rate was closer to ninety percent. At one point he was burying three or four a day."

"Cut to the chase, Sheriff," Sedley said. "How did this Clouston feller end up king of the hills, and how come he didn't try to kill Shawn and me?"

"I'll answer your second question first. No matter his past crimes, Dr. Clouston is a fine psychiatrist and he can read people. He studied Shawn, and maybe you, Mr. Sedley, as men who live by the Colt's gun. He knows your breed and probably figured on that particular day his butcher's bill would be too high."

"So he decided to let us go?" Sedley said.

"That would be my guess."

Purdy's chair creaked as he sat back. His eyes flickered to the street, almost opaque from yellow dust kicked up by wagons, horses, and foot traffic, then back to Shawn.

"As the death toll at Dr. Clouston's clinic rose, the Philadelphia authorities finally took notice and raided the place. They removed a hundred dead or dying patients, and Clouston was warned never to practice medicine in any form again or face hanging."

Purdy looked up from the cigarette he was building and said, "Perhaps Dr. Clouston could have weathered the disgrace, but his beautiful young wife couldn't. Suddenly cut dead by Philadelphia's high society, she lay in her bathtub and cut her wrists."

"And Clouston?" Shawn said.

"From what I was told, he headed west and wandered for a couple of years. They say he shot a man in Kansas City, another in Denver, and was involved in a whore cutting in a saloon in Cheyenne." The sheriff lit his cigarette and spoke from behind a blue haze of smoke. "Then, about a month ago, the doctor showed up in the Rattlesnake Hills with a gang of hardcases."

"Why?" Shawn said.

"Nobody knows."

"What's up there?" Sedley said. "Gold? Silver, maybe?"

"All you'll find in those hills is a fine crop of rock, cactus, and rattlers," Purdy said.

"Has Clouston threatened the town?" Shawn said.

The sheriff shook his head. "No. But he's warned a few people off, hunters and the like. He's pretty much staked out the Rattlesnake Hills as his home range."

Shawn watched Purdy's owlish eyes grow guarded as he asked, "What about Burt Becker? Could he be in cahoots with Clouston?"

"No, he's not," the young sheriff said. "After his wife died, Dr. Clouston declared war on the world. He blames the medical profession and society, especially the upper classes, for his wife's suicide and his own disgrace. He's a man eaten up by hate. It rots him from the inside like a cancer."

Sedley smiled slightly. "Shawn, maybe it's just as well Clouston didn't know that your pa is the richest man in the New Mexico Territory."

"And one of the richest in the United States," Shawn said. "Just to keep the record straight."

"There you go," Sedley said. "That's the only excuse he needs to chop you up into little pieces."

"The Colonel is rich, not me," Shawn said.

"I don't think the mad doctor will make that distinction," Sedley said.

Shawn grinned and shook his head. "Hamp," he said, "sometimes you're a real pleasure to be around."

He rose to his feet and Purdy said, "I guess you'll be moving on now. Nothing to keep you boys in Broken Bridle."

"Except a promise I made to look out for you," Shawn said.

"I can look out for myself, Mr. O'Brien. I'm in no need of your protection, I assure you."

"You're hiding something, Sheriff," Shawn said. "And I aim to find out what it is."

"Then I'll stop you," Purdy said.

Shawn was surprised by the glint of steel he saw in the young man's eyes.

CHAPTER SEVEN

"Why did blood and brains splatter all over the doors of the Iglesia de los Santos Martires? Is that what you're asking me?"

"Only making conversation is all," Little Face Denton said. "No offense intended."

"The fool was seeking sanctuary," Pete Caradas said. "He thought he'd be safe in the church. Instead he should have seen to his guns."

"Blood and brains all over a three-hundred-year-old door brung all the way from Spain," Denton said. "I bet that was a sight to see."

"If he'd gotten inside I would have spared him, I think," Caradas said. "It's bad luck to kill a man in church."

Denton picked up the bottle of rye they shared and poured into his glass. The whiskey glowed warm, like ancient Baltic amber.

"Was Sergio Mendoza as fast with the iron

as they said?"

"In Mexico and parts of Texas he was a famous *pistolero.* But he knew I could kill him."

"And it was over a woman?"

"A man needs a reason to fight."

Pete Caradas's eyes moved to the saloon bar where a tired-looking woman in a bright red dress smiled and laughed at every word a skinny young clerk in a high celluloid collar said.

"Little Face, look to the bar. Would you fight for what that woman has to offer?"

Denton glanced over his shoulder, then turned back to his companion.

"Nah. She ain't hardly worth it."

Caradas nodded. "Mendoza's woman was worth it."

"They say you washed the blood off the door by yourself," Denton said.

"Yes, with a bucket." Caradas's smile never reached his strange eyes, gray as graveyard mist. "And all the time I was doing it a priest beat me with a willow switch as thick around as his little finger."

"Why did you clean the door?"

"Because it was a great sacrilege to defile the Church of the Holy Martyrs with blood. I knew that and the priest made me do penance. That's why he made me wash the door and beat on me with the willow switch."

"In Mexico? Did anybody care?"

"They cared. I wanted to live in that town for a while longer. I had Mendoza's woman in my bed, remember?"

Caradas stretched his long legs, elegant in gray broadcloth. His boots were black and fine, made on a narrow Texas last.

"There was a buzzard squatting in the plaza that day," he said. "It stared at me until the job was done, then it flew away. The priest said it was a sign."

"What kind of sign?"

"He didn't know."

Little Face Denton could not meet Caradas's eyes for long. They reflected no light.

When his eyes had died, Denton had no way of knowing. He guessed a long time before. Many kills ago.

"It was my understanding you didn't like talking to people, Little Face," Caradas said. He had a slight Cajun accent born of the Louisiana bayous where he spent his boyhood with his widowed mother.

"I don't, but I like talking to you, Pete."

"Why?"

"You've killed eighteen men. Folks say that."

"Folks say a lot of things."

"Why do you suppose Shawn O'Brien is

53

in town?"

"Passin' through, the man said."

"Is that all?"

"His wife was murdered a while back. She was an English aristocrat, and beautiful, I was told. A man does some long riding to forget a thing like that, trying to leave it behind him."

Caradas reached for the whiskey bottle, but Denton intercepted him and poured his drink. "His brother Jake would be bad news."

Caradas smiled. "Yes, he would. Jake is a sight meaner than Shawn, but he can't match his speed on the draw and shoot."

"You don't say?"

"I do say."

"Is he faster than you, Pete?"

Caradas shook his head, his face unsmiling. "No, Little Face, he isn't. Shawn O'Brien isn't near as fast as me with a gun. No one is. Not now, not ever."

He held his glass to the light of an oil lamp over the bar. "Damn," he said. "I've got a fly in my whiskey."

CHAPTER EIGHT

"Hey waiter, I've got a fly in my coffee," Hamp Sedley said.

"I'll bring you another cup," the man said. He sighed. "There's a herd in town and cows bring flies." The waiter, a sleek-headed man wearing a white apron, leaned close to Sedley and Shawn O'Brien. "See the young redhead acting tough over there?"

"Uh-huh, with the two-gun rig. Looks like he's on the prod, don't he?" Sedley said.

"He is on the prod. He's one of the drovers brought in the Rafter-L herd this afternoon and he fancies himself a shootist."

"He's got no quarrel with us," Shawn said.

"You're right, he don't. But later you might care to wander down to the Streetcar Saloon. The kid says he'll brace Pete Caradas there tonight. Says by midnight Caradas will be dead and he'll be cock of the walk in Broken Bridle."

"Or he'll be dead himself more likely,"

Shawn said.

The waiter left and returned with a clean cup. He winked at Shawn, smiled, and said, "Remember, don't miss the fun."

Speaking around a mouthful of pork chop, Sedley said, "Think the kid can shade Pete Caradas?"

"I don't know either of them, so I can't say," Shawn said. "But I reckon the redhead's on the brag and he'll make a play just like he figures."

Shawn gave up on his tough steak and fried potatoes and let his knife and fork clatter onto the plate.

As he expected, the red-haired kid jerked in his direction, scowling.

Shawn smiled at Sedley. "Red's on the prod all right," he said.

Maybe it was Shawn's smile that did it. Or the ivory-handled Colt in his holster. Or the way he wore his hat. Or maybe it was nothing at all. Often a man on the prod doesn't need an excuse to brace somebody.

"You seein' enough, mister?" the kid asked, loud, so it would carry across the crowded restaurant.

"I reckon I've seen all I want," Shawn said.

"What's that supposed to mean?" the redhead said. He had a round, pugnacious face, and it looked like his nose had been broken a time or two.

"It's supposed to mean nothing at all," Shawn said, smiling.

"Suppose I come over there and wipe that smile off your face with my fist?" the kid said, getting to his feet.

"Suppose you bring a couple of your friends to carry you back," Shawn said.

"Here, that won't do," the restaurant owner said, a stout man with hairy forearms the size of hams. "I run a respectable place here."

"Aw, leave him be, Frank," one of the redhead's companions said. "Look at him. He's a pretty boy and he's scared."

Another laughed. "And he's too damned pretty to fight."

The redhead named Frank swaggered a little, but he sat again.

All three punchers continued to glance over at Shawn's table and talk among themselves, laughing.

Sedley smiled. "Now your brother Jake would have drawn down and killed all three of them," he said.

"Maybe. It would depend on his mood," Shawn said.

"Jake's mood is always bad," Sedley said.

"Some days badder than others," Shawn

said. Then, "This is none of my business, is it?"

"What? The redhead?"

"Yeah. I can't let him throw his life away and die a senseless death. In the past I've seen enough of those, my wife among them."

"Like you said, Shawn, it's none of your business. Hell, maybe he can shade Pete Caradas."

"He can't. The kid has never shaded anybody. He may be the big man with the iron around the Rafter-L because he can draw and hit an empty bean can. I guarantee you that he's never met a professional revolver fighter."

The question on his face was Sedley's only answer.

"I was raised by shootists," Shawn said. "Rightly or wrongly, my pa and his *segundo* Luther Ironside are man-killers and so is my brother Jacob."

He dabbed his great cavalry mustache with his napkin and tossed it onto the table. "Hamp, the cowboy hasn't killed a man in his life. Pete Caradas has gunned plenty."

Shawn rose to his feet and, his spurs ringing, stepped slowly toward the man called Frank's table. A sudden hush fell on the restaurant, but a woman made a little frightened sound in her throat.

Frank was elbowed by one of his friends who whispered, "Well, lookee here."

The redhead turned, saw Shawn, and grinned as though he welcomed this development. Rising to his feet he said, "Mister, you just don't get the message, do you?"

Shawn ignored that. He and Frank were just three feet apart.

"Shuck the iron, boy," Shawn said.

The young puncher was taken aback, his face surprised. "Are you calling me out?" he said.

"I sure am. Don't talk, boy. Skin the iron and get your work in," Shawn said.

The man called Frank tried to give himself more room and stepped back, but Shawn crowded him again.

"Do I have to shame you into drawing on me?" he asked.

The cowboy grinned like a wolf and said, "Well, all right then, rube. You just dug your own grave."

His hand streaked for his gun.

He didn't even clear leather.

Shawn drew with blinding speed, and in one violent, effortless motion slammed his Colt into the side of the young drover's head.

The buffalo was perfect and Frank

dropped like a felled ox.

Shawn would not have been an O'Brien had he missed an opportunity to make a grandstand play.

The flashing, nickel-plated Colt spun on his trigger finger a couple of times, then slapped into his palm.

"Can I accommodate either of you young gentlemen?" he said to the stunned drovers staring at their downed hero.

"No. Not us," one of the young men managed. "Hell, mister, we're just leaving for the ranch. I mean, right now. This very minute."

"Take Frank with you," Shawn said. "When he comes to, tell him he's not in Pete Caradas's class. Or mine. Tell him to stick to cow punching."

"We thought he was fast," the young cowboy said. "Everybody said Frank was chain lightning with a gun."

"He wasn't fast. He wasn't even close to fast. It's getting dark outside, so take him home and let him sleep it off in his bunk."

"I guess we all made a mistake," the young man said, his face ashen.

"Yup, and poor ol' Frank almost made another," Shawn said.

CHAPTER NINE

Shawn O'Brien sat at his table again, shifted his chair a little, and let the cowboys drag their unconscious friend past.

"Think that young feller has learned his lesson?" Hamp Sedley said.

"Well, now he knows what being fast with the iron means," Shawn said. "That's a valuable lesson."

"Will it sink in?"

"I certainly hope so."

"You sure played hob, mister." The plump proprietor stood by Shawn's chair table, his huge fists on his hips. But he was smiling.

Sedley said, "Kid had to learn."

"He learned all right," the big man said.

He stared at Shawn for a moment, then said, "His name is Frank Lester. His pa owns the Rafter-L, but young Frank gives him no end of trouble. You could have killed him."

Shawn nodded as he reached for the coffeepot. "I reckon."

"But you did not."

"No. I guess it just didn't occur to me."

"You're Shawn O'Brien, ain't you? The one they call the Town Tamer."

"The word gets around," Shawn said.

"Folks in Broken Bridle read the daily newspapers that come up from Rawlings on a deadheading cannonball. Your likeness was on all the front pages, but it didn't do you justice."

"I'm flattered," Shawn said.

"What needs tamed in this town, Mr. O'Brien? By the way my name is Dave Grambling. I own this place." The man stuck out his hand. "I was a range cook for good ol' Texas John Slaughter back in the day. You ever meet him?"

"Can't say as I have," Shawn said. He shook Grambling's hand, then said, "We're only passing through."

Grambling looked around him, reached into his back pocket, and removed a bill from the thin roll he carried. He held the bill up for Shawn's inspection. "Know what that is?" he said.

Sedley spoke. "It's a fifty-dollar bill. I haven't seen one of them in ages."

"Right first time, mister. Me, I pay one of these to Burt Becker every week for his protection. If you want to tame this town, tame Burt Becker first."

"What does Sheriff Purdy say about all this?" Shawn said.

"Nothing. He's in Becker's pocket, like a few others I could name."

"I'll talk to the sheriff," Shawn said.

"Yeah, talk, talk, talk. In the meantime while you're jawing I aim to form a vigilante committee to run Becker and his rabble out of town."

A loose arc of diners had formed behind Grambling, some of the men with napkins tucked into their collars, and there were a few mutters of agreement.

"A hemp noose cures all ills," a comely matron said. "My dear, late papa always told me that."

"A wise man," her companion said. He had a gravy stain on his chin.

"Are you willing to pay the butcher's bill, Grambling?" Shawn said.

"If I have to, yes."

"It will be high," Shawn said. He rose to his feet. "I'll talk with Burt Becker."

"When?"

"Now. Tonight."

"When your talking is done, come back and see me, O'Brien," Grambling said.

"I'll have no part of a vigilante action,"

Shawn said. "It always leaves too many widows, and towns die because of it."

"We'll take that chance," Grambling said.

But his face showed uncertainty, as though the reality of what he proposed had just dawned on him.

Shawn nodded. "You do what you have to. In the meantime I'll see Becker."

"You'll brace him?" Grambling said, a light in his eyes.

"No. We'll sit down to tea and cake and discuss matters like gentlemen," Shawn said.

CHAPTER TEN

The Streetcar was the grandest saloon in a not very grand town.

When Shawn O'Brien and Hamp Sedley stepped inside they were greeted by a vast amount of polished brass and red velvet and a huge mahogany bar. A large, elevated stage stood at the far end of the building where a nautical backdrop was still in place. At one end of the stage a placard on an easel proclaimed:

MR. GILBERT & MR. SULLIVAN'S
HMS PINAFORE
ONE PERFORMANCE ONLY
THURSDAY AT 7 SHARP
ALL LADIES MUST BE ATTENDED
NO FESTIVE REVOLVERS ALLOWED
BY ORDER OF SHERIFF J. PURDY

The remainder of the saloon consisted of tables and chairs and a dozen discreet booths set into dimly lit corners.

There were few patrons. Four miners played low stakes poker and a couple of broke cowboys nursed nickel beers. A female giggle chimed from one of the booths and a little calico bar cat paused to listen.

But Shawn's eye moved to the big man who sat, or rather sprawled, at a table to his right. He was huge, blond, and handsome with strong features and piercing blue eyes that looked as though they could reach across distance and pin a man in place. He wore a brace of ivory-handled revolvers and in front of him, stuck into the table by its point, was a huge bowie knife.

To his left sat a bored photographer in a checked wool suit and flat cap. A large wood and brass camera on a tripod leaned against the wall.

With wary eyes, Burt Becker had watched Shawn and Hamp Sedley step through the glass doors, assessing them.

He perceived no threat, grinned and boomed, "Come in, come in, gentlemen. Have your picture made with Burt Becker, the baddest, meanest outlaw on our Western frontier."

He pulled the bowie out of the table and

waved it around his head in an alarming fashion.

"I can out-punch Jem Mace, and out-shoot Wild Bill Hickok. My pa can lick any man in Texas and I can lick my pa. I've been shot, hung, and branded by the law, but I'm still here because I'm as tough as a ring-tailed bobcat and ten times as mean as a wounded grizzly."

Becker waved to a glass jar on the table.

"Two dollars in the jar, boys, and then set beside me and get your likeness made with fightin' Burt Becker, the most feared man in the West. Hell, it's something you'll show your grandkids and they'll show their own kids."

"Becker, I want to talk to you about —" Shawn began.

But Sedley brushed past him and said, "Where do I sit, Mr. Becker?"

"Right down there, young feller. Now put your two dollars in the jar."

The bored photographer busily set up his tripod and camera, and Sedley (Shawn thought he was grinning like a jackass) said, "I've never had my likeness made before, especially with a famous outlaw."

Becker beamed. "Well, you've come to the right place, gambling man."

He saw the question on Sedley's face and

said, "It takes one to know one, son, and we both wear the silver ring. What's your name?"

"Hamp Sedley, Mr. Becker. Hamp Sedley by name and Hamp Sedley by nature, my ma always said."

The photographer, who hitherto had been glum and silent, smiled with store-bought teeth and said, "You'll find that Mr. Becker is a remarkable man, Mr. Sedley. He is bright, intelligent, fearless, desperate, and there is nothing he can't do when it comes to the gambler's profession by way of shell games, dice, cards, and sure thing propositions."

The man glanced at Shawn as he added, "And he can play hob with a pistol."

Shawn O'Brien was irritated beyond measure. Caught flatfooted by Sedley's move he could only stand and fume as Hamp sat beside Becker and grinned as wide as a wave in a slop bucket.

"Where do you want the knife, Phil?" Becker said.

"Hold it across your chest, Mr. Becker, and look fierce."

"What about me?" Sedley said.

"Look scared. Right, here we go. Hold that pose for the count of three."

The photographer ducked under the black

cloth hood and removed the lens cap with his outstretched hand.

"One . . . two . . . three."

Phil's head reappeared like a turtle poking out of its shell. "Thank you, gentlemen."

Hamp Sedley stuck out his hand. "Thank you, Mr. Becker. This was a great honor."

But the big man waved the hand away and stuck the bowie knife in the table again. He'd already hooked and landed this sucker and now it was time to find another. His gaze fell on Shawn and he grinned.

"Now, there's a handsome young buck if ever I saw one. Put your two dollars in the jar and step right up."

Shawn smiled and walked to the camera. The man called Phil tried to stop him, but Shawn brushed him aside. He yanked out the plate holder and as he suspected, it was empty.

"My word," Becker said. "How did that happen?"

"My brother Patrick is a keen photographer," Shawn said. "Your man Phil here should have inserted a new plate before he made the picture."

Becker was shocked, or pretended to be. "Phil, how remiss of you," he said. "That just won't do."

"Cut the claptrap, Becker," Shawn said.

He took two dollars from the jar on the table and handed the money to Sedley. "Hamp, you should have known better than to get taken by a snake oil salesman," he said.

Sedley's anger flared. "Damn it, Shawn, who do I shoot first? Becker or the photographer?"

"Neither. Mr. Becker is a con artist and he and I are going to have a little talk."

The big man rose to his feet, splotches of red on his cheekbones. His hands were close to his guns. "Stranger, are you calling me a tinhorn?" he asked.

"I sure am," Shawn said.

"Who the hell are you?"

"Name's Shawn O'Brien."

"Any kin of big Jake O'Brien?"

"Yeah. He's my brother."

That last gave Becker pause. The handsome young man could be lying, but if he wasn't, Jake O'Brien made a bad enemy, especially if his kinfolk were involved. He decided to err on the side of caution.

"What do you want to talk to me about?" he said.

Shawn pulled a chair to him with his foot and sat. He indicated that Becker should do the same. When the big man was seated, he glared at Shawn for a moment, then said,

"Drink?"

"Beer if it's cold," Shawn said.

"It isn't."

"Then I'll have a rye."

After a waiter brought the drinks Becker said, "All right, get it off your chest, O'Brien."

"It's simple, Becker," Shawn said, smiling. "I want you the hell out of Broken Bridle."

CHAPTER ELEVEN

"Did I hear you correctly?" Burt Becker said.

"What did I say?" Shawn O'Brien said.

"That you want me to get out of town?"

"Then you heard me correctly." He tried his whiskey. "Ah, this is a good rye."

Becker waited until Shawn set his glass on the table again, then said, "What are you, O'Brien? Some kind of law?"

"Nope. Just call me an interested party."

"What's your beef?"

With his left hand, Shawn turned his glass around on the table and the whiskey caught the lamplight and glowed like liquid gold.

"Becker, at first I took you for a dangerous outlaw, but you're not. You're small-time, a two-bit con artist running a protection racket in a frightened town."

"Yeah, well listen to this: Pete Caradas, June Lacour, Little Face Denton, and half a dozen others. Does that sound small-time to you?"

"No, those boys don't come cheap, but that doesn't change my opinion about you, Becker. You're still a tinhorn."

The big man's eyes frosted, revealing the assassin behind the bluff facade. "I've killed men for less than that, O'Brien."

"No doubt you have," Shawn said. "And I'd guess apart from old men and farm boys, they all took a bullet in the back."

That was fighting talk, and Shawn knew it.

But it wasn't his intention to prod Becker into a draw. He didn't want to kill the man, just get rid of him.

The saloon was very quiet. The few other patrons that had wandered inside stood at the bar, muttered among themselves, and watched what they knew must surely end in a shooting scrape.

The smart money was on Burt Becker.

As the night had grown late the oil lamps began to smoke and burn dimmer. A saloon girl left a shadowed corner, pulled down her dress, and tucked away an errant coil of hair that had fallen across her forehead. She walked purposely toward the bar, her high heels clacking, but stopped suddenly as though the tension between Becker and Shawn had formed an impassible barrier.

But Becker backed up and then backed down.

"The people in this town need my protection," he said. "Do you know what's in those hills to the east of us?"

Shawn read Becker quickly. He could see that the big man wasn't intimidated by his Colt, but for some reason a gunfight was not convenient for him at that moment.

"I know what's in the Rattlesnake Hills. I was there."

"Then you met the devil himself," Becker said.

"No, not the devil, just a crazy man."

"That makes Tom Clouston even more dangerous."

Shawn was surprised. "You know him?"

Becker smiled. "No. But he sent me a message a few days back and that's how he signed it. The Devil. He told me to clear out of Broken Bridle or suffer the consequences." The big man grabbed the bowie and tap-tapped the blade on his shoulder. "As you can see, I'm still here. And O'Brien, you're not going to put the crawl on me, either."

"I can't figure you, Becker," Shawn said. "You've hired three of the fastest and most expensive guns in the country to nickel and dime a bunch of storekeepers and clerks. It doesn't make sense."

"It makes sense to me, O'Brien."

"Then so will this, Becker: The protection racket ends now. Tonight. If I hear otherwise I'll come looking for you, and next time I won't be so friendly."

"Why the hell do you care, O'Brien? This ain't your town."

"But it could be. Broken Bridle could be a fine town, and I won't stand by and let a lowlife like you destroy it and its young sheriff."

Becker went silent, as though he pondered what Shawn had said to him. But the big man was playing for time, only that and nothing more.

A few moments ticked past and the saloon went as quiet as a tomb.

Then Shawn saw Becker's flicker. Alarmed, his hand dropped to his gun. But he was way too late.

Strong arms grabbed him from behind and pinned his arms to his side. A moment later a powerful kidney punch dropped him to his knees.

Through a sea of pain, Shawn saw Becker step toward him, grinning. He was dimly aware that Hamp Sedley had drawn his gun, but then he, too, fell, downed by the bottle in the fist of a huge man wearing a black

Mexican sombrero.

"Get him to his feet," Becker said. He took a thick, metal-studded leather strap from his coat pocket and wrapped it around the knuckles of his massive right fist.

Two men dragged Shawn erect. But not for long. Becker's fist drove into his belly with the force of a pile driver. Shawn gasped with pain and his knees turned to jelly.

He was forced to his feet again and Becker's huge granite rock of a fist, made terrible by steel reinforced leather, slammed into his jaw. Shawn's head exploded with the light of a trillion stars, and again Shawn felt himself falling.

Becker hit him again, a vicious uppercut that snapped Shawn's head back in a scarlet fan of blood.

"All right, let him go!" the big man yelled.

Shawn dropped and Becker bent over, picked him up by the front of his shirt, and pounded blow after brutal blow into his face.

Finally Becker stood straight again and slammed a kick into Shawn's ribs.

"If you're still breathing, O'Brien, hear me," he said. "Get out of Broken Bridle or the next time I see you I'll finish the job."

Through swollen, split lips Shawn said, "Go to hell," and got another kick in the ribs for his pains.

A man laughed as Shawn got his hands under him and pushed up onto his knees. He stayed there on all fours for long moments as blood and saliva from his mouth formed long, scarlet strands and dropped onto the floor.

Finally Shawn found the strength to crawl out of the saloon and into the street. It was late, the town was quiet, and out in the darkness coyotes yipped at a waxing moon. He tried to get to his feet, but collapsed in a heap, blood welling from his split lips and broken face.

He heard footsteps, then suddenly Hamp Sedley kneeled beside him.

"Shawn," he said, "you took a brutal beating and you're sore hurt, maybe dead."

Every breath Shawn took was a gasp of pain, and his head clanged like a hammer on an anvil. "Seems like," he whispered.

"I'll get you to your feet," Sedley said.

Shawn was a big man, and it took a tremendous effort for Sedley to lift him. As it was, as soon as Shawn was standing they both staggered against the wall of the saloon and he heard the gambler's labored breath.

"Where?" Shawn said.

"The livery. We're getting out of town."

"No," Shawn said.

His hand dropped to his side. Good, his gun was still there.

"Help me back," he said. "To . . . to the saloon."

"You'll get killed," Sedley said. "Man, you can barely stand."

"There must be" — Shawn's head reeled and felt the sharp spike of broken ribs — "must be . . . a reckoning."

"That will come later," Sedley said. "Do you understand?"

But the sudden weight against him told him that Shawn O'Brien was no longer conscious.

CHAPTER TWELVE

Shawn O'Brien opened his eyes to darkness and the soft hiss of falling rain. He smelled damp earth and pines.

He tried to move, but the pain it caused discouraged any further attempts. His skull pounded, and he felt so weary his body seemed as though it was slowly sinking into the ground.

A voice, echoing from the far end of a long tunnel, penetrated his consciousness.

"Shawn, are you still alive?" Hamp Sedley's voice.

His voice a croak, Shawn said, "Yeah. I'm only half-dead."

"You're a sight," Sedley said.

"Thank you," Shawn said. Then, "Where are we?" It hurt to speak.

"I don't know."

Shawn tried to sit up, but the effort was too much and he sank back to the damp ground.

"I found us a hole to hide in," Sedley said. "That's all we can do until first light."

Slowly night sounds introduced themselves to Shawn one by one.

A long wind rustled in the trees, pushing the rattling rain before it, and somewhere close by a stream talked and a night bird fussed in the distance.

"You did all right, Hamp," Shawn said.

"Well, my brains are still scrambled. Somebody hit me with a bottle, empty of course, but it put me out for a spell."

"Who held my arms?" Shawn said.

"A ranny I never saw before. It wasn't June Lacour an' them. Hired guns don't do that kind of work. Might hurt their hands."

Shawn was barely holding on. "I'll meet . . . I'll . . ."

His eyes fluttered closed and he slept again.

When Shawn O'Brien opened his eyes again it was midafternoon. He lay quiet, listening. The summer rain had stopped and the only sounds were the chuckle of the stream and the wind in the tall pines.

He raised his aching head and looked around him. There was no sign of Hamp Sedley, and the gambler's horse was gone.

Shawn felt a spike of anger, but almost

immediately realized it was unjustified. Hamp Sedley owed him nothing, was beholden to him for nothing. If the gambler had decided to ride away and leave him to his fate, well, that was his prerogative. Hamp had no need to ask anybody's permission.

Still, it was a small betrayal, and it hurt.

Shawn listened into the day and pinpointed the whereabouts of the stream. It was somewhere off to his left, where a bare rock ledge lifted straight up from a green meadow. A few fat and lazy cattle grazed at its base, knee deep in grass and wildflowers, and close by so did a couple of whitetail deer.

Gingerly, Shawn placed his hands over his face. His lips were split in several places and both his eyes were hugely swollen. His jaw hurt and he found it difficult to breathe, and when he did catch a breath pain stabbed at his right side. A broken rib he guessed, or maybe two.

An attempt to get to his feet that set his head spinning and landed him flat on his back convinced Shawn that walking to the stream was out of the question.

He'd have to crawl.

A raging thirst driving him, he set out slowly, like a stricken animal. A pitiless sun hammered him, and pain was a constant companion that drained his strength and will. Still he kept going, teeth bared, each tortured breath hissing in and out of his bloody mouth like a steam engine.

Shawn crawled for an hour, the burning sun on his back, the fresh fragrance of green grass and wildflowers lost to his swollen, bloody nose. He'd covered a hundred yards, maybe less.

As far as he could tell, the stream ran along the base of the ridge where the pines gave way to cottonwoods, a few willows, and wild oak. By his reckoning, it was at least a quarter mile away.

Shawn groaned and sank to the ground. His thirst was a ferocious thing that gave him no peace.

He'd rest here for a few minutes in the warm grass, surrounded by the drone of insects and the faint sound of grazing cattle.

He closed his eyes and let the drowsy day lull him . . .

And fell instantly asleep.

The man's voice carried from far off. "Shawn! Shawn O'Brien! Where the hell are you?" It was Hamp Sedley's voice.

Shawn tried to call out, but the words clogged in his throat.

"His horse is still there," a woman called out, light and young.

"He's wandered off somewhere," Sedley said. "After the beating he took, he can't have gone far."

After unsuccessfully trying to yell a second time, Shawn raised his hand and waved it vigorously above the grass.

"There he is!" the woman said.

A sound of a horse swishing through greenery, then the face of an angel swam into Shawn's vision. Sky blue eyes met his and the girl said, "How do you feel?"

"Never better," Shawn croaked.

The girl smiled and cradled his head in her arm. She tilted a canteen to his lips, and Shawn drank greedily.

"That's enough for now," she said. "You can have more later."

Hamp Sedley took a knee beside Shawn and said, "You look even worse than you did last night, and that's saying something."

The water had washed down dried blood and lubricated Shawn's throat. He said, "Where the hell were you, Hamp?"

"I rode out to see if there was anywhere around I could find help. That's when I met Miss Campbell here."

The girl looked down at Shawn and smiled again.

"Judy Campbell. My father owns the Four Ace ranch down by Dry Creek."

"Right pleased to meet you," Shawn whispered.

"I can see he's taken a terrible beating," Judy said to Sedley. "We'll take him to the ranch."

"Shawn, can you ride?" Sedley said.

"No. But I think I can grab on to a horse."

"We'll help support you, Mr. O'Brien," the girl said.

"Call me Shawn, huh?"

Judy smiled.

"Then Shawn it is," she said.

CHAPTER THIRTEEN

Shawn O'Brien had little memory of his ride to the Four Ace.

Later Hamp Sedley said that he'd fallen off his horse three times. "Once into cactus and twice into cow shit." But he didn't know if that was true or not.

When he woke he slowly became aware that he lay in a soft feather bed. Around him the bedroom furniture was dark-stained and heavy in the Victorian style. The walls were covered in artichoke wallpaper, and a chandelier holding five small oil lamps hung from the ceiling. On the wall to Shawn's right, draped in somber crepe, hung a portrait of Robert E. Lee. The opposite wall bore a painting of old Queen Vic wearing a crown and the robes of empire and seemed to be an original.

Shawn made a mental effort and remembered what had happened.

There had been a girl, real pretty, who

had held his head in the long grass and she'd smelled sweet, of lavender water. And Hamp had been there.

Shawn became aware of a pain in his right side. He was tightly bandaged there, probably for broken ribs. He didn't touch his face, but it felt tight and rigid, like a wooden mask.

He'd never been one to lie in bed, unlike his brother Jacob who usually woke with the lunchtime gong when he visited Dromore. Looking around him, Shawn reckoned his duds were in the armoire. Now all he had to do was chart a course there and launch himself.

Easier said than done. When he tried to move, his side punished him so suddenly and so badly he sank back into the bed, sweat beading his forehead.

After a couple of minutes, he managed to sit up, propped on pillows.

"Right, Shawn," he said, fighting pain as he swung his legs over the bed. "Let's try that again."

But his plan was foiled when the door opened and Judy Campbell stepped inside. She carried a steaming bowl with a spoon sticking out of it and a folded napkin across one arm.

"What are you doing, Shawn O'Brien?"

the girl said.

"Getting up, or trying to."

"Get back into that bed instanter," Judy said. A frown gathered between her eyebrows. "You're not well enough to get up yet."

"I've got things to do," Shawn said. "People to have hard words with."

He tried to get to his feet but his weakness betrayed him. The room spun around him and he collapsed back on the bed.

"Oh dear," Judy said. "I knew this would happen."

She laid the bowl and napkin on the side table and lifted Shawn's legs into the bed and made a great show of covering them with the quilt.

"Don't do that again," she said. "If you do I'll be very cross."

"Damn it all, you're a hard, unfeeling woman," Shawn said, irritated.

"Please, no profanity," Judy said. The frown fled her face and she smiled. "Are you hungry?"

Shawn swallowed his wounded pride. Being bossed around by a slip of a girl was new to him. And he was hungry. Starving in fact.

"Yes, I am. Burn me a steak and smother it in half a dozen eggs with a bushel of fried potatoes on the side," he said.

"Good, I'm glad to hear that your appetite is returning," Judy said. She lifted the bowl and the napkin. "I have some nice beef broth for you."

"But I want a steak," Shawn said, aware that he sounded like a spoiled child.

"And later, if you can chew, you may have two lightly boiled eggs for lunch." Then, spoon poised. "Open wide."

"I can feed myself, thank you," Shawn said.

"Every drop now," Judy said, handing him the spoon. "It's good for you."

"It needs salt," Shawn said, making a face.

"I'll put salt on your eggs."

Shawn ate in silence for a few moments while the girl fussed with his pillows. Then he said, "I got in last night, I guess."

Judy shook her head. "Shawn, you've been here for three days."

"But that's impossible."

"Nevertheless, it's a fact."

The girl sat on the bed. She wore a pale blue gingham dress and a hair bow of the same color, and Shawn thought she looked as pretty and fresh as a spring morning.

"Burt Becker gave you a vicious beating," she said. "I don't think you know how close you came to dying."

"He had help," Shawn said, the girl touching the raw nerve of his male pride.

"Stay away from him, Shawn. The talk around Broken Bridle is that he plans to shoot you on sight."

"He'll get his chance. Depend on that."

Judy was silent for a while. Then she said, "Shawn, there's more involved. If Becker is killed, another person, an innocent person, will pay the price for his death."

"Maybe I recently took too many blows to the head, Judy, but I'm not catching your drift."

"There's a girl involved, a friend of mine, and . . . and she's Becker's life insurance policy." Judy saw the question still remained on Shawn's face and said, "It's too complicated to explain right now. I —"

A tap on the door, then, "May I come in?"

"Of course, Pa," Judy said.

"How is the patient?"

"Testy. He wants to be out of bed."

"A bit too early for that."

The tall, white-haired man stuck out his hand. "I'm Duncan Campbell. Judy's father."

Shawn took it and began, "I'm —"

"You're Shamus O'Brien's son, Shawn."

"You know my father?"

"For a time Colonel O'Brien and I served

in the same regiment during the war. He was a fine and gallant officer."

"Thank you," Shawn said. "I'm sure my father will say the same of you."

"That would be an honor indeed," Campbell said, giving a little bow.

His sweeping mustache was as white as his hair, but his skin was burned a deep mahogany brown, his eyes the same sky blue of his daughter's. The old rancher stood a couple of inches over six feet and was as lean as a rail, but he looked tough and enduring, a man who'd ridden many a hard trail.

"Your friend Mr. Sedley told me what happened," Campbell said. "I don't know the man personally, but from what I've been told Burt Becker is a harsh and dangerous man who cuts a wide path everywhere he goes."

"I plan to cut him down to size," Shawn said. His attempted smile was a pained grimace. "I know, big talk from a man who can barely stand."

"Maybe. But if I was Becker I think I'd be worried about now," Campbell said.

"Why is he in Broken Bridle, Mr. Campbell?"

"Please, call me Duncan. Mr. Sedley says he's running some kind of protection scheme, saving the town from its enemies."

"Becker is, but that's penny ante stuff. He's hired some named Texas draw fighters, and you don't need gunmen like those to scare a bunch of storekeepers, do you?" Shawn could tell by Campbell's expression that the rancher had drawn a blank and he said, "Tell me about the Rattlesnake Hills."

"What's to tell? It's an empty wilderness. You can't run cattle there, no decent graze."

"Gold?"

Campbell shook his head. "The hills have been prospected for years. Nobody has ever struck pay dirt, not even a quartz seam."

"Then what am I missing?" Shawn said. "There's got to be something."

"Maybe you're missing nothing. Becker will squeeze Broken Bridle until the money dries up, and then he'll move on."

"Duncan, have you ever heard of Thomas Clouston?"

The rancher shook his head. "Can't say as I have."

"He was a doctor once, but now he's camped out in the Rattlesnake Hills with a bunch of hired gunmen." Shawn laid his bowl on the table beside him, then said, "Why?"

"Well, it's pretty clear that Clouston is the reason the town is paying for protection,"

Campbell said. "A doctor you say?"

"Psychiatrist."

"And he's turned bandit?"

"Seems like."

"Then he plans to raid Broken Bridle but right now he's afraid of Burt Becker and his Texicans."

"I guess that could be the case," Shawn said. "There isn't another major settlement within fifty miles in any direction."

"And that brings up an obvious question," Campbell said. "Why did Becker choose Broken Bridle in the first place?"

"Because of the Rattlesnake Hills," Shawn said, surprised by his own answer.

"All right, that's enough, you two," Judy said. "Shawn, you must rest now."

Duncan Campbell smiled. "My daughter is always right, Shawn. Rest and get your strength back."

"Scoot, Pa," Judy said, as though she was shooing a chicken. "Scoot, scoot."

"I'll see you later, Shawn," Campbell said.

After her father left, Judy's face turned grave. "Shawn, my father fought Cheyenne and Sioux, then Yankees and then Cheyenne and Sioux all over again. He's a brave man and by times foolhardy; that's why I don't want him involved in Broken Bridle's troubles, or yours."

"I fight my own battles, Judy," Shawn said. "You think me cold and unfeeling."

"Not in the least. You're looking out for your father. In your shoes I'd do the same."

"Then we understand each other?"

"Perfectly."

"You'll be well enough to ride in a few more days, Shawn. Leave this place. I mean leave the Wyoming Territory and never return. The only thing for you here is a pine box."

CHAPTER FOURTEEN

Old Ephraim was hurting and he'd holed up somewhere in the hills.

Nathan Hansberry was pretty dang sure of that. He needed that grizz for him and his Shoshone woman because come the winter snows a bearskin rug would be mighty cozy.

Hansberry drew rein on his mule, and his wife, who'd been walking behind, looked up at him and said, "Do you see him?"

"Nope. But I got a ball into him so he's there all right."

"Nathan, a wounded grizzly is dangerous and has great power."

Only half listening, Hansberry said, "Hell, even an unwounded grizz is dangerous."

He kneed his mule forward and the Shoshone woman grabbed the animal's tail and followed.

Nathan Hansberry was seventy-seven years old that summer, a skinny old mountain man in buckskins and fur hat. He carried an old Hawken rifle, and, a sign of his great prosperity, his shirt was decorated with silver pesos and fine beadwork. His white beard was long, his shoulder-length hair braided with black and red ribbons.

Ahead of him the barren Rattlesnake Hills looked like the carcass of some terrible beast picked clean by buzzards. In all that vast wilderness of earth and sky nothing moved, and there was no sound.

The hills seemed empty and Hansberry listened into the silences.

"Ephraim!" he yelled. "I'm coming fer you, ol' Ephraim."

The old mountain man climbed out of the saddle. Leading the mule, he scouted the ground and found what he was looking for, a blood trail that pointed directly to a niche in the rock.

"Take the mule, woman," Hansberry said. "I'll go the rest of the way on foot."

"Nathan, be careful," the Shoshone said. "I feel danger all around us."

"Don't fuss, woman," the old man said.

An instant later his wife fell dead at his feet.

The flat echo of the rifle shot rang around the hills, and Hansberry saw a drift of powder smoke on a ridge to his left.

He triggered a shot into the smoke, but heard the bullet *spaaang!* harmlessly off rock. The old man quickly recharged the Hawken with powder and ball and looked around for a target. He saw nothing.

A glance at the red rose that blossomed between his plump wife's large breasts told him that she'd been dead when she hit the ground.

Hansberry had no time for grief, but took a moment to allow to himself that the Shoshone had been a good woman, fat enough to keep him warm in winter and shade him in summer, well worth the paint pony and Blackfoot scalp he'd paid for her.

And now someone had murdered her.

The old man rose to his feet, killing on his mind. He turned and looked toward the hills, the Hawken ready across his chest. Somewhere in those badlands was the man who'd killed his wife, and Hansberry aimed to find him.

Old Ephraim forgotten, his hand strayed to the Green River knife in his belt. His face grim he took a solemn vow: It would take the murderer a long time to die.

Nathan Hansberry was halfway to the niche in the rock where he would begin his hunt, when he stopped in his tracks. Horsemen poured from the cleft, then spread out in a skirmish line.

The old man counted a dozen, then thirteen when another man joined them. He rode a massive horse and his hand rested on some kind of tomahawk.

The riders stayed in line, unmoving, and Hansberry felt their eyes on him. He felt a sudden surge of fear, then fought it off. One of those thirteen could be the killer of his wife. This was not the time to be afraid.

About thirty yards separated Hansberry from the horsemen.

"Did one of you rannies shoot my wife?" he called out. "If he did, let him step forward, confess his crime, and take his medicine."

Silence. None of the riders moved.

The sun was hot and sweat trickled from under the old man's fur hat. Above him a buzzard quartered the sky, then another. The air was still, as though the winds had all died in their caves, and he heard his labored breath rattle in his chest.

"Speak up now," Hansberry yelled. "If the murderer is among you let him identify himself, for I aim to kill him straight off."

Again no sound. No movement. But the atmosphere was as menacing as the cocked hammer of a .45.

"All right then, if that's the way you boys want it, I'm comin' over there," the old man said. He was no longer afraid. "And I intend to play hob."

But Hansberry had taken only a few steps when the man on the big horse left the others and advanced toward him at a walk.

When he was within talking distance of Hansberry he reined up his mount.

"Are you insane?" the man said, resting the ax on his shoulder. "Come now, answer the question."

"No more'n other folks," the old mountain man said.

"All right, let me put it this way, my good man: Do you believe you're sane?"

"Yeah, I reckon I do. As sane as you, mister. Now, unless you're the one as killed my Shoshone woman, give me the road."

"You're not sane!" the horseman shrieked. "You're insane. Only a mentally ill man would trespass here where none are allowed. Ergo, my diagnosis is that you're criminally insane. In other words, my dear fellow, you're stark, raving mad."

"Who shot my woman?" the old man said.

The horseman's eyes were odd, full of strange blue fire, and they made Hansberry uneasy.

"Why, I don't really know. One of my followers I suspect. They're ordered to shoot interlopers on sight."

"Well, mister, if it was one of your'n, then you're the ranny who takes the blame," Hansberry said. He raised the Hawken. "He's comin' right at ya."

But he never got the chance to bring the rifle to bear.

The horseman's battle-ax, thrown with terrifying, malevolent force, spun through the clean air and embedded itself in Hansberry's forehead, crashing into bone and brain.

Death took the old mountain man so quickly he had no time to cry out. He dropped to the ground, his crossed eyes staring at the blade, and lay still.

Dr. Thomas Clouston waved his men forward, then said, "One of you retrieve my war ax." He looked distressed. "I do hope that fool hasn't damaged the edge."

A rider swung out of the saddle and levered the ax out of the old man's skull. "Looks fine, boss," he said.

"Clean it on his person. I don't want an insane man's diseased brains all over it." Clouston raised his voice, now talking to the men around him.

"Observe, gentlemen, that sometimes the

99

only way to deal with the criminally insane is to destroy them before they become a danger to others." He patted the neck of his restive horse. "Do we agree on that?"

Clouston was rewarded by confused mutters, the violent thugs who rode for him having little interest in the niceties of mental health.

"Ah," he said, "and here is my ax as good as new."

Before he swung his horse away, he said, "Bury that trash and then one of you kill and skin the wounded bear in the arroyo. Its pelt will make me a warm cloak come the winter snows."

CHAPTER FIFTEEN

"I thought there was a handsome face under all that bruising and swelling," Judy Campbell said. "And I was right."

She and Shawn O'Brien sat on a bench under the huge oak that stood close to the ranch house. Sunshine filtered through the leaves and dappled the grass around them. Dim in the distance the steady *thunk, thunk* of Hamp Sedley's ax was the only sound.

"At least I can shave again," Shawn said. "Well, barely. I've cut myself a dozen times."

He idly watched Hamp Sedley chop wood near the barn, swinging the broad-bladed ax with more enthusiasm than skill.

"There's a sight you don't see every day, a riverboat gambler at honest labor," Shawn said.

"Father convinced him that he would go to seed without exercise," Judy said. Sunlight tangled in her hair and added turquoise to her eyes. "Hamp seems to have taken him at his word."

"Hamp worries about his health," Shawn said. "He read a medical book one time and convinced himself that he was on a path to getting every ailment known to man, including his favorite, Pelizaeus-Merzbacher disease."

"What's that?" Judy said.

"Hamp has no idea, nor does anyone else, myself included. But he says a misery with a fancy name like that has to be lying in wait for him somewhere."

The girl laughed, a charming sound that pleased Shawn greatly.

After a while she said, "Tell me about her, Shawn."

Shawn smiled. "Now, that's a woman's question."

"Hamp told me you still grieve for her."

"Hamp talks too much."

Shawn took his time to light up one of Duncan Campbell's cigars. When it was drawing well, he said, "I had Judith for only a little while and then I lost her."

"You loved her?"

"With all my heart and soul."

"She died young."

"Judith was murdered. It happened in England, at a place called Dartmoor. She was kidnapped by escaped convicts and they killed her."

Judy touched the back of Shawn's hand with her slender fingers. "I'm so sorry," she said.

"You would have liked her," Shawn said. "Judith was a wonderful woman. She loved life and the living of it." Then, "Hamp swings that ax like a maiden aunt. He's going to do himself an injury."

Judy accepted Shawn's cue and smiled. "It's almost time for lunch, so we can save Hamp from himself."

But the gambler had already decided that enough was enough. He drove the ax into the stump, picked up his coat, and strode toward them, his gunbelt slung over his shoulder.

"How much wood is a cord?" he said.

"A lot," Shawn said.

"Well, I must have chopped ten cords into kindling," Hamp said. He held up his hands. "Look at the blisters. An ax handle does terrible things to a man's hands, especially a gambling man's."

"Hard work isn't easy," Shawn said. "Or so they tell me."

"Yeah, well I'm done with that. From now on I'm saving my mitts for Antony, Cleopatra, and one-eyed Jack."

"A wise decision, Hamp," Shawn said.

"And I couldn't agree with you more."

Sedley was suspicious. "What do you mean by that?" he asked.

"Oh, nothing," Shawn said, his face empty. "I was just saying to Judy that you swing an ax like a professional."

"Damn right," the gambler said. "But now I'm done with it."

"A great loss to the entire wood-cutting industry," Shawn said.

For a second time suspicion clouded Sedley's face, but Judy, suppressing a grin, said, "I think it's time for lunch."

"The offer is tempting, Duncan, but I have to be moving on," Shawn O'Brien said.

"But Shawn, if you take Pa's offer you can put down roots here," Judy said. "Maybe even start your own ranch."

"I already have roots, Judy," Shawn said. "They're back at Dromore in the New Mexico Territory."

"I do need a foreman," Duncan Campbell said.

"I know that, and I appreciate the thought, but I'm just not your man. I have other things to do."

"You mean like go up against Burt Becker?" Judy said.

"That, and to stand by a promise I made

to help a certain young lawman."

Judy was suddenly alarmed. "You mean Jeremiah Purdy? No! That's the very worst thing you could do."

A silence fell over the table and Campbell stared sternly at his daughter. "Judy, do you know something you're not telling us?" he said.

"Pa, I —"

The girl's beautiful eyes were wild, as though she felt trapped. "Pa, there's someone's life at stake. I . . . I can't tell you."

"Judy, has this something to do with Sheriff Purdy?" Shawn said.

"It has everything to do with Sheriff Purdy," Judy said. "Don't ask me to tell you any more because I can't."

Shawn's and Duncan Campbell's eyes met. The old man seemed both puzzled and worried.

Judy rose from the table, a small handkerchief to her eyes, and then Shawn heard her bedroom door close.

"It's not like my daughter to keep a secret from me," Campbell said.

"She's frightened," Sedley said. He pulled his napkin out of his collar and tossed it on the table. "Not for herself but for somebody else."

"But who?" the old man said.

"I think Jeremiah Purdy knows the answer to that question," Shawn said. "And I plan to ask him today."

CHAPTER SIXTEEN

"Go looking for trouble, Pete," Burt Becker said. "I want you, Little Face, and June to do some serious killing."

"How many are up there in the hills, boss?" June Lacour said.

"Last I heard a dozen and the crazy doc makes thirteen, an unlucky number."

"For them or for us?" Pete Caradas said, admiring his morning bourbon in the glass.

"You three are the fastest guns that ever came out of Texas," Becker said. "So I say unlucky for Tom Clouston."

He stood and stared out the window of his hotel room, and his back still turned, he said, "Kill as many as you can and the rest we'll leave. But Clouston himself will be your main target."

"You ever seen him, boss?" Little Face Denton said.

Now Becker turned, the black cigar in his hand wreathing smoke. "No one's seen him since he was drummed out of the medical profession," he said. "But he'll be the ranny in charge so you'll recognize him."

Becker stepped to the table and splashed more whiskey into his glass.

"Gentlemen, I want this done quickly and I want it done well. There's millions, maybe tens of millions, of dollars at stake here. Don't get into a prolonged gunfight, just get among them, kill as many as you can, and then get the hell out of there. Don't be heroes. We'll mop up later."

"What about the Chinese?" Caradas said.

"They'll play ball. I can hire as many as I need for fifty cents a day per man. Leave the business side of our enterprise to me."

June Lacour looked at the others, then said, "We got the whole day ahead of us, let's go get it done."

"I'll give a three-hundred-dollar bonus to each of you when the job is done. Kill them all and I'll double it."

"We'll do our best, boss," Caradas said. "I'll kill the crazy doc for you personally."

Pete Caradas and the others rode out of Broken Bridle under a blue morning sky that was still lightly tinged with pink. The morning promised heat to come, and a breeze blowing from the south would do little to cool the day.

Unseen by the three riders, Sheriff Jeremiah Purdy watched from the shadows. His face was deeply troubled.

After an hour, the three gunmen were within earshot of throbbing drums that warned them their coming had been noticed and any chance of a surprise attack was gone.

Little Face Denton drew rein. He seemed concerned.

"Hold up, boys," he said. "This just don't feel right."

"You mean it doesn't sound right," June Lacour said. "Drums in the morning never bode well. Well, as far as I know they don't."

Pete Caradas stood in the stirrups and his eyes reached into distance. He saw no sign of movement. Ahead of them lay a narrow draw, and something heavy crashed around on its brushy floor.

A bear probably, Caradas decided. The men they hunted were unlikely to make a racket like that.

"What do we do now, Pete?" Denton said. He was unsure of himself and his mouth was dry. "We can't ride in, shoot 'em up, and then ride out again. They know we're here for God's sake."

"Drums scaring you, Little Face?" Caradas said. But his unease showed in his eyes and his right hand never strayed far from his gun.

Before Denton could answer, Lacour said, "He's got a right to be scared, Pete. Those damned drums can get into a man's head, and right now they're saying, 'Come right on in, fellers. We're waiting for you.' "

"Maybe that's the idea," Pete Caradas said. "The crazy doc trying to keep us off balance."

"He's succeeding," Lacour said.

Little Face, neither as smart nor as brave as his companions, said, "I say we go back."

"And I say we go ahead and do what we came here to do," Caradas said. "Clouston and his boys are running scared. That's why they're banging on drums to drive us away."

Lacour said, "Pete, they know we're coming so they'll be laying for us."

"I reckon I know that. We'll scout a little ways ahead, and if it even smells like we're riding into an ambush we get the hell out of there and try it again some other day."

"Or night," Lacour said.

Caradas nodded. "You got an idea there, June. All right, we move slowly and see to your guns."

"I don't like this," Denton said. "I don't

like this one bit. It just don't set right with me."

Lacour looked at him but said nothing, his mouth tight under his mustache.

A ribbon of game trail led through the draw, then wound through some thick brush and timber country toward a V-shaped gap in the hills. A long-ago lightning fire had blackened about ten acres of ground to the south, and the charred trunk of a wild oak still stood, a single skeletal branch pointing the way to the break.

The rangeland on both sides of the trail was dominated by sagebrush, but here and there sego lily, prickly pear, larkspur, and bitterroot added flowering splashes of red, yellow, pink, and orange.

The straw man was fixed to a stand of cactus.

Pete Caradas drew rein next to the prickly pear and took down the effigy. It was crudely made but was unmistakably a male figure.

"What the hell is that?" June Lacour said.

"A child's toy maybe?" Little Face Denton said. "But what's it doing all the way out here?"

"It's not a toy," Caradas said. "It's a warning."

"Strange kind of warning," Lacour said.

"It must mean something to somebody," Caradas said. "But I'm damned if I know what it is."

"It's one of us," Denton said. "It's a straw man, made to look like me or one of you."

"It doesn't look like anybody," Caradas said.

The straw man was about a foot tall and hurriedly made. It had small black hairpins for eyes.

"How do we play this, Pete?" Lacour said. "I say we get the hell out of here."

Caradas stared at the straw man for a few moments, then said, "I still think they're trying to scare us away. They don't want to fight."

The drums suddenly stopped, leaving a strange, ominous silence.

"Pete, today is not our day," Lacour said. "Like the drums, that straw man can talk. He's telling us to light a shuck."

Caradas tossed the effigy away, then said, "I reckon he's saying just that, June." His eyes searched the hills. "I don't see anything."

Denton said, "You two can do whatever you want, but I'm heading back to town." He swung his horse around and kicked the animal into motion.

The horse trotted forward, but Little Face didn't.

A loop snaked out of the brush and yanked him, yelling, from the saddle.

"What the hell?" Lacour said, drawing his Colt.

But a second loop pinned his arms to his sides, and a moment later Lacour left the saddle and crashed to the ground in an ungainly heap.

Taken completely by surprise, Caradas didn't immediately react. A rope reached for him, but he turned his horse quickly, slipped the noose, and palmed his gun. He shot a man running at him with a rope in his hand, shot him again as he dropped the rope and reached for his revolver. His prancing horse kicking up clouds of dust, Caradas held his gun high and looked around for another target.

He found none. Both Denton and Lacour had disappeared, dragged into the brush. Dust slowly sifting back to the ground marked their last desperate struggles.

Heat hammered from the sun that burned like a red-hot coin in the denim-blue sky. A heat haze stretched to the horizons, and the Rattlesnake Hills shimmered and looked as though they floated on a lake. It was hot, stifling, and sweat trickled down Caradas's back and his gun hand felt slick on the ivory handle of his Colt.

He stood in the stirrups and yelled, "June! Little Face!"

Echoes mocked him. Then the drums started again.

Pete Caradas had sand, but there's a limit to every man's courage and even to his foolhardiness. He kicked his horse into a gallop and took to the trail. After a couple of moments a rifle bullet buzzed past his left ear like an angry hornet. Then another stung his right, drawing blood.

Pete Caradas knew then that the marksman could easily have killed him. The shots were meant only to scare.

For the first time in his life the Texas draw fighter felt fear. No, much worse than that, he experienced a few moments of terror so bad that the gorge rose in his throat. He gagged, then leaned over the side of his running horse and threw up strings of green bile.

CHAPTER SEVENTEEN

It was an hour before noon when Shawn O'Brien and Hamp Sedley rode into Broken Bridle. Sedley's face was solemn, a man nursing a grievance. And before leaving the Four Ace ranch he'd made it known to Shawn.

"Some men," he said, "are worth saving. But the college boy sheriff isn't one of them."

"Don't fold on him just yet, Hamp," Shawn said. "I think Jeremiah Purdy is worth one last try."

The upshot was that Sedley was determined to ignore Purdy and spend whatever time he had left in town in the saloon, fleecing the rubes. Or so he hoped. He'd been trying to outrun a losing streak for two years now, but a gambler is a man who makes his living out of hope, and Sedley figured Lady Luck, his fickle lover, was due to return to his side.

"Let the cards fall where they may," he said as he and Shawn rode onto Main Street.

"Huh?" Shawn said.

"Nothing. I was just thinking out loud," Sedley said. He turned his head to say something more, but the words died on his lips.

Beside him Shawn had stiffened in the saddle, his eyes fixed on the street ahead of him. He looked like a hawk about to swoop.

Sedley followed the younger man's gaze. A couple of delivery drays passed each other and a woman shaded by a parasol crossed from one boardwalk to the other.

But then Sedley saw what Shawn had seen.

Burt Becker, his back to them, had just left the hotel and was crossing the street in the direction of the saloon, waving to people on the boardwalk as he went. Very few returned his salute.

Without a word, Shawn kicked his startled horse into a gallop.

"No!" Sedley yelled. He was too late.

Shawn drove his big sorrel directly at Becker.

The man heard the pound of hooves behind him and began to turn.

But the right flank of the horse slammed

116

into Becker and knocked him sprawling on his back.

Shawn drew rein and swung off his rearing, wild-eyed stud. His ribs hurting, the bed weakness still on him, he knew he had to end this quickly or Becker would kill him.

Cursing, Becker scrambled to his feet and Shawn met him with a hard straight right to the chin. The big man staggered back but Shawn crowded him, jabbing with his left before landing another haymaker right to Becker's jaw. The punch shook Becker, but he didn't fall.

Suddenly Shawn was worried.

He'd not fully realized how huge Burt Becker was. The man was massive in the chest and shoulders and his hands and wrists enormous. He looked as formidable as an enraged grizzly.

And Becker was enraged, mad clean through and ready to kill.

"O'Brien," he said through a bloody split lip, "I'm going to cripple you."

Becker came in with both fists swinging, and Shawn took a wicked left to the chin. His head exploded with stars, and he was surprised to find himself on his back in the street.

Far off, he heard men roar and a woman cried out for the sheriff.

Becker stood with his legs spread, a triumphant grin on his face and a terrible, raging hatred in his eyes.

"On your feet, O'Brien," he said. "You got a lot more coming. I'm gonna take you apart."

Shawn forced himself to stand upright, his broken ribs paining him mercilessly. Becker stepped in on him, and Shawn threw a feeble right that the big man effortlessly parried. A sadistic light in his eyes, Becker pounded Shawn back to the ground and then stepped in quickly for the kill.

But Shawn rolled into Becker's legs, and, unable to stop, the big man tripped and fell on top of him. Shawn, lean as a lobo wolf and flexible as an eel, wriggled out from under Becker and scrambled to his feet.

He had to end this thing. Now. Before it was too late.

As Becker pushed himself to his feet he dropped his head for a moment, and Shawn smashed a powerful kick into the man's face. Blood sprayed in a scarlet arc as Becker's head jerked back, and Shawn stood wide-legged as the man staggered to his feet. Shawn measured the distance and then landed a roundhouse punch to the big man's chin.

Becker fell on his side and Shawn waited

for him to rise.

Groggy now, when he got up off the street Becker lowered his head and charged like a maddened bull. But he held his enormous fists low. It was a bad mistake and it cost him.

As the big man got within range, Shawn drove his hard, horseman's knee upward into Becker's face. He felt the man's nose shatter.

Becker might have fallen, but Shawn stepped inside, held Becker upright by the lapels of his frockcoat, and head-butted him hard, smashing bone between the big man's eyes.

Becker groaned and dropped. But there was much anger and no mercy in Shawn now. This was skull and boot fighting as it had been taught to the brothers O'Brien by wicked old Luther Ironside. The beaten man was not expected to walk away from such an encounter.

But there was no quit in Burt Becker that day.

He staggered up again with stony determination, his face a nightmare of blood and bone, both swollen eyes almost closed. For a moment Becker just stood there, swaying, and shook blood from his face.

Drawing on the last of his fading strength,

Shawn hit him with a right that sounded like an ax hitting a tree trunk.

Becker staggered, then fell flat on his face, and Shawn knew the big man had no fight left in him.

Hamp Sedley handed Shawn his hat.

He glanced at Becker's huge frame sprawled in the dust and shook his head. "Not one to hold a grudge, are you, Shawn?" he said.

"This was of his own making," Shawn said. "He called it."

A tall, middle-aged man detached himself from the crowd of gawkers and said, "I'm Doctor John Walsh." He studied Shawn's face and said, "I think you'd better come with me, young man."

"I'll be just fine, Doc," Shawn said.

"The cut above your left eye needs a couple of sutures," Walsh said. "And I can treat those swollen hands. Any jaw pain?"

Shawn shook his head and then nodded to Becker, who was now groggily sitting up.

"What about him?"

"A couple of strong men will carry him to my office. It's at the end of the boardwalk with the hanging sign outside. Follow me, please."

"Go ahead, Shawn," Sedley said. "I'll put

up the horses."

Dr. Walsh, a thin, austere man with a shock of gray hair, split his time between Shawn and Becker, after both men left their guns at the door.

He finished with Shawn first.

"No broken bones, but the fractured ribs you already have are still several weeks away from healing. I suggest no more fistfights for at least a month."

Shawn smiled. "I've no great desire to try one of those again anytime soon, Doc."

"Good. And the salve I gave you will work to reduce your swollen hands and eye."

"How is Becker?"

"He took a bad beating," the physician said, a slightly accusing note in his voice. "He has three fractured ribs, a broken nose, and, worst of all for a great trencherman like Mr. Becker, his jaw is broken." Walsh shook his head and said, "The jaw will be bound up for at least six weeks, I'm afraid. He'll need to eat soft foods and he'll find it very difficult to talk."

Shawn O'Brien flexed the fingers of his right hand. The knuckles were swollen and painful. "Becker brought this on himself," he said. "You heard what happened in the saloon?"

"Yes, I did. Violence begets violence, I suppose."

The doctor lifted his head and listened into the day. "The drums have started again," he said.

Shawn nodded. "I think the violence you speak of is yet to begin," he said.

CHAPTER EIGHTEEN

Pete Caradas left his horse at the livery and went looking for Burt Becker. The big man was not at his usual table in the Streetcar, and all of a sudden Caradas was troubled.

"Where is he?" he asked the bartender.

The man nodded in the direction of the street. "At his room in the hotel. Mr. Becker ain't feeling too good."

Caradas ordered a whiskey, drank it down, and ordered another. As his nerves settled, he said, "What ails him?"

"A feller by the name of Shawn O'Brien is what ails him," the barman said.

Again anxiety spiked at Caradas. "He isn't shot, is he?"

"Who?"

"Damn it, Becker, of course."

"No. But O'Brien beat him up real bad." The bartender made a motion of tying a bandage at the top of his head. "His jaw is broke and so is his nose. Ribs, too, I heard."

The barman laid down the glass he'd been polishing. "Sunny Swanson is with him. Taking care of him, like."

"That's what he needs, I guess, a whore with a heart of gold."

The bartender snorted. "Yeah, that's what you think. Becker is paying Sunny to be there in his hour of need."

Caradas drained his glass. "I better go see him." Then, "Is Shawn O'Brien still alive?"

"Sure he is. He won the fight, didn't he?"

Caradas shook his head. My God, that was hard to believe.

He'd been told Shawn O'Brien was good with a gun, but also that he was a rich man's son and something of a drawing room ornament. He'd heard nothing about him being a knockdown, drag-out, bareknuckle fist fighter. Who the hell had taught him that?

"I'll go talk to Becker," Caradas said. It seemed that this was a day to share bad news.

"He can't talk back," the bartender said, grinning slyly as he again made that tying movement above his head.

The barman's name was Ferguson and Pete Caradas wanted to shoot him real bad.

Pete Caradas tapped on the door of Becker's room.

A slender brunette in a plain gingham dress, her hair pulled back and held in place by a tortoiseshell comb, answered.

Sunny Swanson didn't look like a whore. But she was. She let Caradas inside, then said, "He's sleeping or unconscious, take your choice."

"Can I see him?"

"Sure, why not."

Burt Becker lay in bed, and it looked as if a stampeding buffalo herd had trampled him. His face looked like a strawberry pie dropped onto a bakery floor, and a tight bandage was wound around his jaw and tied off at the top of his head. His breathing was labored, as though his throat was thick with blood.

"Did O'Brien have help?" Caradas asked.

"No," Sunny said. She had a wide, expressive mouth that now showed the hint of a wry smile. "He did it all by his little self."

Like most elite shootists, fist fighting was an anathema to Pete Caradas. As John Wesley Hardin once summed it up, "If God wanted me to fight with my fists he would have given me claws." Caradas considered pugilists lowdown trash and knife fighters not far behind. At one time or another, he'd killed both and it did not trouble his conscience one bit.

Yet O'Brien was fast on the draw and shoot. Beating Becker with his bare hands meant that he was capable of using any means to win a fight, and that made him a more dangerous man than Caradas had originally believed.

Then a thought troubled Pete Caradas. Was Shawn O'Brien in Broken Bridle because he was somehow linked to the crazy doctor Thomas Clouston? Was there something in the Rattlesnake Hills they both wanted and would kill to keep?

He had questions without answers, and Caradas was a worried man when he left the hotel and made his way to Sheriff Purdy's office.

The young lawman was not glad to see him. "What do you want now?" Jeremiah Purdy asked.

"You heard about Becker?" Caradas said.

"Yes."

"He's still unconscious and his jaw is broken."

"Yes. I know."

Caradas took a chair, then said, "I lost Little Face Denton and June Lacour in the Rattlesnake Hills."

"I'm sure they'll find their own way home," Purdy said.

"I mean they were taken, roped, and

dragged into the brush. I killed one of the attackers and barely made it out of there alive."

"A white man?"

"Yeah, he was." Then, "Is Shawn O'Brien in cahoots with the crazy doc?"

"I don't know what you're talking about," Purdy said.

"Why does Thomas Clouston want those hills, Purdy?" Caradas said.

"I imagine for the same reason your boss wants them."

"And why is that?"

"He hasn't told me. But he says the Rattlesnake Hills are worth a pile of money. That might be why O'Brien is interested."

"There's nothing of value in those hills. I told O'Brien that already," Caradas said.

"So he is interested?" Purdy sat back in his chair and sighed. "Caradas, I'll wire the United States Marshal and see if he's willing to investigate the disappearance of your friends."

"Why not take a posse up there yourself?"

"It's way out of my jurisdiction."

Caradas rose to his feet. "We'll see what Burt Becker has to say about that." The gunman stepped toward the door, but Purdy's voice stopped him.

"Where is Jane?" he asked.

Caradas turned, surprised. "I don't know," he said. Then, reading the expression on the young lawman's face, he said, "She's well. That's all I know."

"Where is she?"

"I told you, I don't know. But the agreement stays the same, Purdy. Do as you're told and your woman will stay well. Step out of line and Becker will kill her."

"Caradas, how can you have a hand in this and still live with yourself?" Purdy said.

"For money, Sheriff. The best reason of all."

CHAPTER NINETEEN

"You two shall know the truth and the truth will make you madder still," said Dr. Thomas Clouston. "It will drive you even more insane."

"What is the truth?" June Lacour said.

"That there is no truth, only falsehoods and deceit. Our entire lives are a lie, a wheel within a wheel of fabrication. Ha, now you understand, straw man. Is that not so?"

"Mister," Lacour said, "I don't know what the hell you're talking about. Where is Pete Caradas?"

"Is that who he was? He killed one of my followers and escaped. He is mad, like you. Mad as a hatter."

"What are you going to do with us?" Little Face Denton said.

Clouston shrugged. "As madmen you are both worthless, but I will use you to carry a message to Burt Becker, that vile cretin, that criminal lunatic."

A rising prairie wind flapped the canvas roof of the ruined cabin that lay between two hogback bluffs, well hidden from anyone entering the Rattlesnake Hills or riding the few thin trails that lay to the east.

The tents of Clouston's men were scattered around the cabin, earth-colored and almost invisible to the naked eye at a distance.

The doctor had chosen his hiding place well. This was wild, desolate country, some of it still known only to God. If the Cheyenne had once hunted here they had left no scars on the land.

The abandoned cabin retained three walls, and canvas substituted for the fourth. But somehow after his disgrace and his demented flight west, Clouston had managed to hold on to some of his furniture. A huge oak bed stood against one wall, a dresser against another, and a fine Persian rug covered the flagstone floor. A crystal chandelier hung from one of the few roof beams, and in the evenings its oil lamps would cast a splendid light for a reader sitting in the overstuffed leather chair by the still intact fireplace.

"You're letting us go?" Denton said. Bound hand and foot and badly beaten, he was scared.

"In a manner of speaking, yes," Clouston said. "But you'll save your worthless skin, don't worry."

One of the two stocky gunmen standing guard sniggered.

Clouston looked at him and smiled slightly, as though at a private joke.

June Lacour, in terrible pain from a smashed cheekbone, had sand enough to ask, "What's in all this for you, Clouston?"

The doctor, sitting in the leather chair, reached inside his coat and took time to light a large, elaborate pipe before answering.

"*Doctor* Clouston, if you please." He grinned at Lacour. "Here is a riddle: Why is a raven like a writing desk?"

The gunman's face was blank, his eyes puzzled.

"Ha, I made a jest," Clouston said. "That is not the riddle at all. But you may answer this one: Why are the Chinese the key that unlocks the riches that make weak men mad?"

"I don't know," Lacour said, shaking his head.

"Come now, fellow. Think. Use what little brain you possess."

Lacour wanted to get out of this alive and he humored the crazy man.

"They build the railroads?"

"Fool. Madman. Straw man. That is not the correct answer. Mr. Stockman, punish him for being such an imbecile."

One of the guards backhanded Lacour across the face, drawing blood from the gunman's mouth.

"Enough, Mr. Stockman," Clouston said. Then to Lacour, "Do you wish to know the answer?"

Lacour, bleeding from broken lips, said nothing.

"Well, I'm not going to tell you the answer, so there," Clouston said. "If I liked you I'd tell you, but I don't, so I won't. Yah!"

He waved his pipe and blue smoke spiraled from the glowing bowl.

"Mr. Stockman, behold, if you will, the obstinacy of the insane," he said. "When I was in practice, I'd beat such stubbornness out of my patients with a dog whip." He looked into the guard's grinning face. "Alas, for every five patients I treated I'd cure one and kill four. Still, many mental institutions envied my twenty percent cure rate and that's why they took a set against me."

Little Face Denton had been in seven gunfights, killed three men and shared another. He was not a coward, but he was up against something he'd never encountered before . . . something so evil that, being a man of limited intelligence, he could not comprehend.

He glanced at Lacour's battered face, then said, "Will you release us now . . . Doctor?"

"Yes, if you solve the riddle: Why are the Chinese the key?"

"I don't know," Denton said. He hoped his honesty would prevail.

"Numbskull! Straw man!" Clouston yelled. "You don't know the answer because you're psychotic. The mad lose all powers of reason. Mr. Stockman!"

"Yeah, Doc?" the guard said.

"Take them away. I've diagnosed both and they are clinically insane, and it's beyond my power to cure them."

"What do I do with them, Doc?" Stockman said.

Clouston smiled and motioned with his pipe. "Why, turn them into straw men, of course."

Chapter Twenty

Judy Campbell knew why Jane Collins was missing. But she had no idea where the girl was being held captive.

Sheriff Jeremiah Purdy had been of little help. "Leave well enough alone, Judy," he'd warned her. "I don't want to put Jane's life in more danger than it already is."

She believed him when he said that he had no idea where Jane was, and Burt Becker might intimidate Purdy by claiming he had a gun to Jane's head, but that threat didn't cut any ice with Judy Campbell.

If her best friend wasn't in Broken Bridle, then she must be somewhere close to town. The question was, where?

Now, as she'd done several times in the past month, Judy scouted the rugged country around Broken Bridle. Riding a mountain-bred cow pony, a Winchester in the boot under her knee, she was a dozen miles due north of the old Oregon Trail when she swung toward Saddle Rock, riding across rocky, broken country.

After fetching through a shallow canyon Judy picked up a wisp of a game trail and followed it past Sagehen Hill. A mile to her west lay the eastern slopes of the Rattlesnake Hills, ahead of her Eagles Canyon, where she planned to stop and eat the lunch the ranch cook had packed for her.

She'd left the Four Ace just after sunup and now the sun was almost directly overhead, but she'd seen nothing, no cave, arroyo, or abandoned cabin that could be used to hide a captive.

Judy pulled into the shade of the timber, removed her hat, and with the back of her hand wiped beads of perspiration from her forehead. She decided to ride as far as Eagles Canyon and then call it a day.

The sun was already almost unbearable and would only get hotter.

In the meantime . . .

She untied the lunch sack hanging from the saddle horn, chose an egg salad sandwich, and held it to her nose. Good. It was still fresh. She was chewing on the first bite when she saw a rider come through a rippling heat haze to the north.

At first man and horse seemed elongated, like the tall, angular image of Don Quixote

135

in the yellowed page of an ancient book, but as they emerged from the haze the rider shrank to normal size.

The man came on steadily at a walk, and Judy had no doubt that he'd seen her. Her first instinct was to turn around and head back to the ranch. But Judy Campbell had a streak of Scottish stubbornness that would not allow her to turn tail and run from a stranger who probably meant her no harm.

A few moments later she regretted that decision.

The man who approached her rode a mouse-colored mustang, and despite the stifling heat he wore a bearskin coat that Judy fancied she smelled when the rider was still yards away.

The man drew rein, lifted his sweat-stained plug hat, and grinned. "Howdy, little lady. All by yourself?" He carried a Henry rifle across his saddle.

"No," Judy said. "My father and brothers are just behind me."

The man's mud-colored eyes flicked to the girl's back trail and his grin widened. "Now what's a pretty little filly like you doing in this wilderness, and riding a five-hunnerd-dollar cuttin' hoss to boot?"

"I told you, I'm riding with my father and brothers," Judy said. "Now please be on your way."

"An' that's a damned lie," the man said. He swung up the muzzle of his rifle, then, "Git off that pony. Go on now, or I'll blow you off'n it."

"I have money," Judy said. Her brain busily calculated how fast she could shuck her rifle. Not fast enough. "You can have it."

"What I want from you ain't money, little gal," the man said. "After you get a taste of me you'll beg to become my woman, lay to that."

"I swear, my father will hang you," Judy said.

"I'll take my chances."

The man's lips peeled back from a few black teeth. He had the eyes of a reptile. "Now git off that hoss, girlie. Do it!"

Judy had a Barlow folding knife in the pocket of her canvas riding skirt.

She pinned her hope on its carbon steel blade . . . if she could get to it.

After Judy stepped out of the saddle the bearded rider motioned to a grassy narrow bank wedged between two huge boulders.

"Git over there and lie down," he said. He grinned. "Smell the flowers."

Blue and white wildflowers peeped shyly through the grass. It was a shady, peaceful spot where something unspeakable was about to take place.

Judy lay on her back and reached into her pocket. She retrieved the knife but had no way of opening the blade without being seen.

Her heart thumped in her breast and her mouth was dry with fear as the man, massive in the bear fur, swung from the saddle and stepped toward her.

"Git them duds off, little lady," he said. "And I mean all of them."

Playing for time, Judy fumbled with the top buttons of her shirt. She smelled the man's rank stench, the animal stink of him.

He shrugged out of the fur coat and let it fall to his feet. "Now it's fun time," he said. He started to unbutton his pants.

At exactly the same moment Judy Campbell lost all hope, the rapist and murderer named Sam Ball lost a large chunk of his head.

The heavy caliber bullet hit the back of Ball's skull and exited an inch above his right eye, taking with it a great mass of bone and brain. When he dropped at Judy Campbell's feet her would-be rapist was still unbuttoning his pants in hell.

The girl sat up as a handsome, white-haired man on a great dappled gray rode at a walk toward her. He held an elegant English hunting rifle upright on his thigh, and a black cloak hung from his shoulders and draped over the hindquarters of his horse. A steel ax hung from his saddle.

Dr. Thomas Clouston drew rein, a look of concern on his face.

"Are you all right, my dear?" he asked.

Judy nodded. Then, "He was going to —"

"Yes, I know. He was obviously criminally insane and that's why I destroyed him. It is all you can do in cases like his."

Clouston stared at the girl. She thought his burning eyes strange and intrusive.

"Why are you here?" he said. He nodded in the direction of the dead man. "Step away from that, please. I'll deal with it later."

"My friend is . . . missing and I'm trying to find her," Judy said, walking to her horse.

"You won't find her here."

Judy looked up at the man. A tall man on a tall horse was an impressive combination. "No. I think not," she said.

"There are many ways a person can disappear in this country, and it has a thousand ways to kill a man, or a woman."

"I want to thank you for saving my —"

"Think nothing of it, child. I was only doing my duty as a gentleman."

"I'm so glad you were near."

"And so am I."

Clouston pointed behind him. "Stay away from the Rattlesnake Hills," he said. "There are many perils there to beset the unwary."

"I doubt my friend is there," Judy said.

"I know she is not there. It's time for you to go home. Where is your home?"

"My father owns the Four Ace ranch southwest of here." Judy stepped into the saddle, and then said, "Jane Collins, my friend, was kidnapped by Burt Becker. Do you know him?"

Clouston rubbed his temples with the thumb and fingers of his left hand.

"That name . . . that awful name. It makes my head reel," he said, his eyes squeezed tight shut. "He wants to take what's rightfully mine."

Alarmed by the man's evident agitation, Judy said, "Because he has Jane, Becker rules Broken Bridle. I don't think he has anything else in mind."

"Oh, but he does," Clouston said. "And it will be his undoing. Unfortunately, the town will also suffer for Becker's ambition, except for the Chinese. They are the key to everything."

He pointed at Judy. "You are not psychotic. Now there is good news."

"I'm glad to hear it," the girl said. She

had no idea what psychotic meant.

"Your father owns the Four Ace ranch you said."

"Yes, he does."

"Perhaps at a later date I can call on you."

Without a moment's hesitation the girl said, "You would be most welcome." She didn't mean a word of it.

"My name is Dr. Thomas Clouston," the tall rider said. "Have you heard of me?"

"I'm afraid I haven't."

"No matter, you soon will. Leave now."

Judy needed no second invitation. She swung her horse around and rode away at a smart trot.

When the girl glanced behind her she saw Clouston staring at her, and she was relieved when she was veiled by dust and distance.

CHAPTER TWENTY-ONE

Folks on the street smiled at Shawn O'Brien as he and Hamp Sedley walked along the boardwalk toward Sheriff Purdy's office.

"Seems like Broken Bridle approves of what you done to Becker," the gambler said. "You're a local hero."

"I guess he was strong-arming a lot of people," Shawn said.

"I got a feeling he won't do it again," Sedley said, smiling.

Shawn nodded, his battered face grim. "Next time, if there is a next time, my gun will do the talking," he said. "Becker's the kind of man who takes a hell of convincing."

"Hey, look at that," Sedley said.

A little calico kitten rushed out of a general store and hid between Shawn's feet. The angry proprietor suddenly loomed in the doorway.

"Damned cat was into my butter again,"

he said. "Is she yours?"

"No," Shawn said.

"Well, looks like she is now," the man said. He stepped back inside, muttering.

Shawn picked up the kitten. "She's purring," he said.

"Maybe it's a he," Sedley said.

"No, calicoes are nearly always female. We always had a few of them at Dromore. Good mousers."

Shawn made cooing noises that Sedley thought him incapable of producing, tipped back his hat, and rubbed foreheads with the kitten.

"Pretty kittlin' that," Sedley said.

"Do you want her?" Shawn said.

"Hell no. Cats make me sneeze."

"Ow!" Shawn said. "She scratched me."

Suddenly the purring bundle of fur was transformed into a roll of barbed wire, and he looked for a way to put her down without being mauled.

"What are you doing to my Annabelle?"

Sunny Swanson, in a pink silk dress and large, shady hat, snapped shut her parasol and used it to thwack Shawn across the shoulder.

"Give me my kitten!" she yelled, her face furious. "You . . . you animal abuser."

"Take her!" Shawn said. "She's scratching

the hell out of me."

"Come here, Annabelle," Sunny said. She took the calico and cradled her in her arm. "What did the bad man do to you, snookums?" she cooed. "Did he hurt you?"

The cat snuggled into the woman's arm and purred.

Shawn was outraged at Sunny's accusation. "Madam, I assure you —"

"Don't sorry me, Shawn O'Brien," the woman said. "Maybe you can bully poor Burt Becker, but you can't bully me or my cat."

Sunny swung her parasol like a club.

"And don't" — *thwack* — "try" — *thwack* — "to" — *thwack* — "kidnap" — *thwack* — "my" — *thwack* — "kitty cat" — *thwack* — "again!"

The woman lifted her head, sniffed, and stalked away in a snowy flurry of laced petticoats and the drum of high-heeled ankle boots.

Shawn looked after Sunny as he rubbed his tormented left arm and shoulder. "I bullied poor Burt Becker?" he asked.

"I told you not to touch the lady's cat," Sedley said, looking smug.

Irritated, Shawn said, "You didn't tell me that."

"But if I'd known it was hers, I would have."

Before Shawn could utter the sharp retort at the tip of his tongue, a plump matron bustled between him and Sedley.

"I saw what happened, Mr. O'Brien," the woman said. She had a large head, a plump body, and the alabaster fingers she laid on Shawn's shoulder were adorned with marcasite rings. "I have a good mind to slap that hussy's face."

"It's quite all right, dear lady," Shawn said. "It was all an unfortunate misunderstanding. I'm really quite fond of kittens."

"To be assaulted like that and after what you've done for this town," the matron said as though she hadn't heard. She leaned closer to Shawn and dropped her voice to a whisper. "Now see what you can do about those infernal drums."

"I certainly will," Shawn said. "I'll study on it right away."

"And the Chinese over at the rail depot. Born troublemakers the lot of them."

"I'll talk to them, too," Shawn said.

"Give them harsh words, Mr. O'Brien, harsh words. Show them heathens what it means to be a Christian white man around here."

"Depend on it, ma'am," Shawn said.

"You got a laundry list of stuff to do, huh, Shawn?" Sedley said.

And Shawn angled him a look.

"Well, it's been nice talking with you, Mr. O'Brien," the woman said. "And don't forget, harsh words, a white man's words."

Shawn touched his hat. "I'll heed your advice, ma'am," he said.

After the woman was gone, Shawn glared at Sedley and snorted, "Laundry list!"

"Well, you can bully Burt Becker all you want, but lay off the Chinese folks who do my shirts," Sedley said.

CHAPTER TWENTY-TWO

"You look like you've just been hit by a runaway freight train," Sheriff Jeremiah Purdy said.

"You should see the other guy," Shawn O'Brien said.

"I did. He's in bad shape."

"Becker called it, Sheriff," Shawn said.

"Yes, I know."

"I've got a question to ask," Shawn said.

"Ask it," Purdy said. He looked uncomfortable.

"Who is Jane Collins?"

"If you ask that question, you know who she is."

"You and she were walking out together."

"We were . . . are . . . engaged to be married."

"Where is she?"

Purdy tried to find a way out, but found none. "I don't know," the young sheriff said.

"Burt Becker has her. Isn't that right?"

147

"No," Purdy said. Then, after a moment he hung his head and said, "Yes. Becker has her . . . somewhere."

"And that's how he keeps you in line?" Shawn said.

"If anything happens to Becker, anything at all, my fault, somebody else's fault, Jane dies."

"Where is she?"

"I don't know. If I knew where she was I'd go after her."

"Would you?"

"Of course I would. I'm a man, not a boy."

"Purdy, in my opinion you don't stack up to being any kind of a man. I reckon all you do is sit in that chair and plan your future political career. Well I have news for you. Our country doesn't need leaders like you. We have enough of your kind already."

That last struck a nerve. The young man slammed to his feet, anger staining his cheekbones. "Damn you, O'Brien, Jane is my fiancée and the woman I love," he said. He shoved his glasses higher on his nose. "I'd die for her if that's what it took to free her."

"Where is she?" This from Hamp Sedley who was eyeing the sheriff with little enthusiasm.

"I told you, I don't know."

"Then get up off your ass and go look for her," Sedley said. He glanced at the .32 on Purdy's desk. "And take along a bigger gun."

Purdy sat again. He was no longer mad.

"I have looked for her, all over the country and around town. Jane is nowhere to be found."

"Did you search the Chinese encampment?" Shawn said.

"Yes, I did. She wasn't there, either."

Sedley was not a man to mince words. "Maybe she's dead already," he said.

Purdy nodded, his face bleak. "I've faced that possibility. If Jane is dead, Burt Becker won't leave Broken Bridle alive."

"You'll need a bigger gun," Sedley said.

"It's not the caliber of the gun that counts, Mr. Sedley, it's the caliber of the man using it," Purdy said.

Shawn and Sedley exchanged glances but left their thoughts unspoken.

"I promised to give you the help you needed, Purdy, and I'll live up to that promise," Shawn said. "Hamp and I will scout around town and hunt for your girl."

"If we find her we'll tell you and you can rescue her," Sedley said. "Be her knight in shining armor, like."

"Hamp, let him be," Shawn said. "He's

149

got things to think about."

Sedley raised his voice. "Think about! Why —"

The door slammed open and a man poked his head inside. "Sheriff, it just happened! A man rode through the Chinese camp and killed two men and wounded a woman."

"A white man?" Purdy said, rising from his chair.

"As you and me," the messenger said.

"Mind if we tag along, Purdy?" Shawn said.

"Suit yourself," the sheriff said.

He grabbed his pouched revolver and shoved it into his pocket.

The railroad companies, constantly losing skilled men to the gold camps, had in 1866 desperately recruited Chinese laborers to lay their tracks. To everybody's surprise the Chinese turned out to be excellent workers, swinging picks and shovels with a strength that belied their slender frames. The Fremont, Elkhorn & Missouri Valley Railroad had recruited their Chinese labor from San Francisco and Sacramento, then directly from China.

Now, fueled by alcohol and opium, the Orientals felt that the company had abandoned them, and the tent city was a volatile mix of resentment, poverty, restlessness, and suppressed rage.

All this had gone mostly unnoticed by the white community of Broken Bridle, but as sheriff, Jeremiah Purdy was better informed and more aware of the seething cauldron that was Chinatown.

When Purdy arrived he was met by an angry mob that formed a wall of men, women, and children around the small bodies of the murdered men. There was no sign of the wounded woman.

A mob is a many-headed, savage beast, and when the yelled threats and hoarse cries for revenge die away to a low threatening growl a peace officer knows he's in big trouble.

And Jeremiah Purdy knew it now.

The young sheriff then did something that surprised Shawn O'Brien.

He pulled the .32 from his pocket and fired a shot into the air.

It was a calculated risk, but it paid off. The crowd quieted, seemingly stunned.

Purdy knew no Chinese but in English he yelled, "Somebody talk to me!"

A tiny, wrinkled old woman stepped forward. She wore an oversized coolie hat that made her look like an overripe mushroom. "What do you wish us to say?" she asked. Her voice was fragile, her accent decidedly English, the result of a missionary school.

"Can anyone describe the men who did this?" Purdy said.

The old woman turned to the crowd, a sea of angry faces.

She spoke in rapid Chinese that to the Western ears of Shawn and the others sounded like the discordant twanging of an out-of-tune banjo.

A man replied, drawing pictures in the air with his hands.

When the man finished — and spit at Purdy's feet the period at the end of his last sentence — the old woman said, "There was only one murderer, a big man on a brown horse. He was a white man."

"Taimu," Shawn said, using the Chinese honorific for *Grandmother,* "where did the white man go?"

"That I saw myself," the woman said. She pointed northeast, in the direction of the Rattlesnake Hills.

Purdy shoved his revolver back into his pocket and said, "Tell your people I will find the murderer and bring him to justice."

A man, tall and broad for a Chinese, stepped forward. He carried a heavy spike maul, a knife in his waistband, and a chip on his shoulder.

"You will bring him here to face our justice," the man said. He wore a battered plug hat and his English was perfect.

"No. Whoever this murderer is, he'll be treated according to the law of the United States," Purdy said.

The big man grasped the twelve-pound maul tighter and took a step forward. Then another.

Shawn O'Brien tensed. The Chinese had gotten himself within swinging distance, and the spike maul could crush Purdy's skull like an eggshell.

"You will bring him to us," the man said. He pointed to the two dead men. "Chinese blood is on his hands and the right of vengeance is ours, not yours."

Behind him, the mob growled its approval.

Things were getting out of hand fast, but Purdy seemed oblivious.

"If he is found guilty, you will see him hang," he said. "I promise you."

Sedley, looking uneasy, whispered to the back of Purdy's head, "Hell, boy, you ain't one for backing up, are you?"

The big Chinese man's face was a mask of fury. Using a very fast motion he readied the hammer for a swing.

Shawn didn't think. He reacted. He drew

and fired . . .

Not at the man, but at the steel head of the spike maul.

Bullets are mighty capricious, but the big .45 behaved better than Shawn had dared to hope. The lead *spaaanged!* off the maul, turned almost at a right angle, and hit the brim of the big Chinese man's plug hat. The hat, spinning, was blown off his head, spiraled a couple of feet into the air, and then, like a stricken bird, fell to the dirt.

"The next one goes right between your eyes, Chinaman," Shawn said.

It was an empty threat, a desperate, box seat play when he could think of no other. Shawn knew if he killed the Chinese, in its present mood the mob would tear him apart.

But it had been an incredibly lucky shot and it took the fight out of the big Oriental. He stepped back and examined the head of the maul with wide eyes, a thin trickle of blood running from his hairline.

Purdy seized the moment.

He told the old woman to translate for him, then said, "I promise that after I bring in the murderer, we will talk again."

It was a risky throw of the dice and for a moment the situation hung in the balance, the crowd drawn tight. But it was a bad time for Dave Grambling, the restaurant owner, to show up with half a dozen of his heavily armed vigilantes.

Beside him, Shawn heard Sedley whisper, "Get ready. The ball is about to open."

"We're right behind you, Sheriff," Grambling said. "Just say the word."

Then, an instant later, he heard the flat statement of Grambling's shotgun hammers clicking to full cock, a sound that stirred the nervous crowd as though a rattlesnake had been cast among them.

"No! I don't want that!" Purdy yelled, swinging around to confront the man. But he was a split second too late.

CHAPTER TWENTY-THREE

Dave Grambling was a man of volatile temperament and deep prejudices, and he had a tendency to violence. He triggered his shotgun at random into the crowd. Two Chinese men fell.

Cursing, Grambling threw his Greener aside and pulled his Colt.

"Pour it into them, boys!" he yelled.

The vigilantes opened up with rifles and revolvers, and two more men and the old woman who'd translated for Purdy went down.

Then the Chinese closed, wielding axes, cleavers, clubs, and knives, screaming war cries that no one understood but them.

Shawn O'Brien watched the group of vigilantes, half of them veterans of the war, stand like a rock until a wave of humanity crashed over them.

Halos of blood erupted above the vigilantes as meat cleavers and axes thudded into bone and flesh.

Above the shrieks of men dying in pain amid clouds of kicked-up dust, Shawn shouted at Hamp Sedley to fall back before they were overwhelmed. Guns in their hands, Shawn and Sedley gave ground. So far neither had fired a shot since the attack began. But soon that had to change.

A section of the mob had noticed the retreat of the two white men.

Screaming, brandishing their bloody weapons, at least two dozen men and a few young women descended on Shawn and Sedley.

"Oh my God," Shawn yelled. "Not this!"

But suddenly he was in a fight for his life and rational thought gave way to the instinct for survival.

The Colt in Shawn's fist hammered dry. Beside him Sedley fired steadily, his face grim as he beheld the slaughter he and Shawn were inflicting on the Chinese.

Unable to stand against such sustained fire, the survivors broke and ran. Seven bodies lay sprawled on the ground, one of them a young woman.

"What have we done?" Sedley said, his face anguished.

Shawn made no answer. He watched Dave Grambling. Instead of making a run for it, the big man stood firm and tried to reload his revolver. He never made it.

Grambling was engulfed by Chinese and, kicking and screaming, dragged away.

Then suddenly it was all over. The mob, out for blood, followed after Grambling. His end would not be quick or painless.

Shawn reloaded his Colt and shoved it back in the holster.

White and Chinese bodies littered the ground, and two of the dead vigilantes had been beheaded. Close by, Jeremiah Purdy, on his hands and knees, spat blood into the dirt.

Somewhere in town a frightened dog barked endlessly.

Shawn O'Brien stepped to Purdy and took a knee beside him.

He put his hand on the young man's back and said, "How badly are you hurt?"

Purdy turned his head, revealing a bloody mouth.

"Took an elbow from somebody," he said. "That's all I remember." Then, "Help me to my feet, O'Brien."

After the sheriff stood, he looked around him. He'd managed to keep his glasses, and behind the thick lenses his eyes were wide, unbelieving, shocked by the carnage that had taken place.

Now it was a time for widows.

Wailing, sobbing women, both white and Oriental, moved among the dead or lay prostrate in grief beside the bodies of husbands and sons.

One new widow, young, blond, and barely out of childhood, cradled her husband's decapitated head in her lap. She made no sound, already in a midnight place from where she would never return.

Worse, or some might say better, was to come.

Dim drums in the distant Rattlesnake Hills pounded into the dying day, adding to the tension and fear in Broken Bridle. But the drumming took the knife-edge off Dave Grambling's agonized shrieks, though his cries were still raw and primal, the screams of a man dying a hundred small deaths.

Hamp Sedley, a man not easily shaken, looked at Shawn with frantic eyes. "We can't let that happen to a white man," he said. "Let's go get him."

"No," Shawn said. "We'd have to go in with guns and there's been enough killing in this town already."

"What about you, sonny?" Sedley said to Purdy. The gambler's anger and frustration showed.

"Grambling brought this down on himself," the sheriff said. "There's nothing we can do for him now except pray that he dies soon."

"Well, be damned to both of you for cowards," Sedley said. "I'm going after him."

Purdy's little revolver came out of his pocket with admirable speed.

"Mr. Sedley, if I have to I'll put a bullet in your brainpan right here and now," he said. "I will have no more Chinese killed or white men, either."

A crowd gathered around the three men, watching.

Sedley stared hard at Purdy. "Damn you, you mean it," he said.

"Don't try me, Mr. Sedley," the sheriff said. The Smith & Wesson was rock steady in his hand.

And for the first time Shawn O'Brien realized that a fighting man with bark on him lurked under the callow boy.

Distant drums . . . screams . . . a barking dog . . . the widow wails of women . . .

These sounds seemed to penetrate Sedley's fevered brain.

He blinked and his hand dropped from his holstered Colt. "I need a drink," he said.

"I need a lot of drinks."

Then he turned and walked away.

CHAPTER TWENTY-FOUR

Dr. Thomas Clouston was livid, in a killing rage. His plan to goad the Chinese into revolt and destroy Broken Bridle had failed miserably.

The town still stood, a thorn in his side, and no doubt the lowlife Burt Becker was well and plotting more mischief.

But then, he hadn't met his straw men yet. Despite his anger, a smile touched Clouston's lips. Lord, how he'd like to be there and see Becker's reaction. It would be exquisite.

He turned his attention back to business.

"Tell me again," he said. "I want all the details. Don't go crazy on me."

The man he addressed was a malodorous, scar-faced brute who went by the name of Nate Tryon. He had a reputation as a killer and that was why Clouston had chosen him for the task of inciting the Orientals.

But the man had bungled, the damned fool.

"I done what you asked," Tryon said. "Damn it all, I done everything you asked."

"You're surly, Nate," Clouston said. "I can't abide surly. I saw enough of surly among the stinking, insane paupers who hung around the gates of my clinic."

"Sorry, boss," Tryon said.

"Tell me again."

"I rode through them like you tole me, guns a-blazing an' a whooping an' a hollering like a demon. You recollect that you tole me to make like a demon."

"How many did you kill?"

"Oh, five, six, maybe." Tryon grinned. "One of them was a woman."

"The gender of the dead is unimportant," Clouston said. "The woman you killed was probably insane, led astray by all that Confucian nonsense. After the raid you promptly rode out of town. Am I correct?"

"I sure did. And then I took up a position on a hill like you tole me. I could see the whole damn burg through that there spyglass you gave me."

"And you saw, exactly what?"

"I seen the Chinese charge at a bunch of white men who came to see what had happened. Then all kinds of shootin' started, and by and by the Chinese all ran away, leaving their dead on the ground."

"How many white men went down?"

"I don't rightly know, boss. Things was real confused down there in town, folks shootin' an' runnin' an' raisin' dust an' all."

Clouston was silent for a while. He sat in what he called, with bourgeois primness, his parlor. He smoked his S-shaped pipe and his battle-ax lay at his feet, hidden by the blanket that covered his knees.

"You made no effort to return and infiltrate the Chinese mob and tell them that they must take terrible vengeance on the town?"

"Boss, you're joking, right?" Tryon said. "They would have recognized me straight off an' pulled me off my hoss and done fer me right there and then."

"I never joke. I never speak in jest."

"But you know they would have recognized me. Hell, I'd just rode through them, killing."

"You could have changed your appearance, taken off your coat and hat perhaps. The Chinese would have been too agitated to notice."

"But they'd have sure recognized that snowcap Palouse hoss of mine and this" — he traced a forefinger down the terrible scar that ran from the corner of his left eye to his mouth — "is a dead giveaway."

Clouston sighed. "Yes, perhaps you're right, Nate. I blame myself for asking too much of you."

"I'll get it right the next time, boss. Kill a dozen, maybe, an' get them Chinamen riled up real good."

"Is that ever so, Nate? Then we are perfect friends again."

Clouston indicated to the floor in front of him. "Come, kneel before me and I will impart my blessing and pray that we mend fences."

If Tryon thought that strange, he didn't let it show. He kneeled in front of Clouston, removed his hat, and lowered his head.

He died so quickly it's doubtful he felt the ax blow that split his skull open. Nor did he have time to realize that Dr. Thomas Clouston did not tolerate failure.

As Tryon toppled over onto his side, the doctor yelled, "Somebody!"

A few moments later a couple of his men stepped into the parlor.

"Remove that," Clouston said. "It's leaking brains all over my floor."

He puffed his pipe into life and without visible emotion watched his men drag the corpse outside.

"Oh, Hansen," he called out. "Has Wilson arrived with the new men yet?"

The man called Hansen dropped his part of the deadweight burden and said, "Not yet, boss."

"Then let me know when they do," Clouston said. "I want to welcome them to our merry outlaw band."

The doctor's anger had somewhat abated now the guilty party had been punished, but he vowed he'd no longer put trust in the Chinese.

With the new men he'd recruited — hopefully Dan Wilson had done his job — a direct assault on Broken Bridle was the obvious course.

The only real opposition he'd face was Burt Becker and his gunmen, but they could be overwhelmed, especially if his straw men idea went as planned.

Clouston sighed. The burden of command was indeed a heavy one.

Then he sat upright with a jolt, remembering something he'd almost forgotten . . . his reason for journeying to Wyoming in the first place.

Suppose he hadn't cured Hugo Harcourt, one of his last patients before he was booted from the medical profession? Suppose, even after his best efforts, the man had remained stark, raving mad? Could he have imagined the stuff about the Rattlesnake Hills and sent him on a wild goose chase?

Clouston sat back in his chair and thought the problem through.

No, it was impossible of course. When Dr. Thomas Clouston said a madman was cured, then he was cured, especially when his family had paid a small fortune for his treatment.

Hugo's millionaire father had his finger on the pulse of the New York business scene, where rumors were rampant about the hills and the millions that could be made. And old Sanderson Harcourt himself had provided that information, not his idiot son.

Clouston smiled to himself.

No, all was well. But the Chinese still remained the key.

Chapter Twenty-Five

The Chinese riot had the town of Broken Bridle on high alert as Burt Becker struggled out of bed, fighting back the pain of his broken ribs and fractured jaw.

For a moment he held on to the headboard as the room spun around him and the floor rocked under his feet. But Becker's pain and weakness filled him with a mighty resolve.

For every moment of agony he suffered, Shawn O'Brien would be paid back a hundredfold. In the end the pretty boy would beg for death and Becker would laugh in his face, then kick his damned teeth in.

Unsteadily, the big man made his way to his hotel room window and pulled wide the curtains. Immediately he was bathed in morning light; yet there were already armed men in the street, on guard and ready.

What the hell had happened?

Becker had no time to ponder that question, because the door opened and Sunny Swanson stepped inside. She looked more school ma'am than saloon whore. Her morning dress was gray with white at the collars and cuffs as befitted a respectable young lady, and her hair was pulled back in a severe chignon.

"You shouldn't be out of bed," she said.

Becker tried to speak but the tight bandage wrapped around his jaw stifled his words.

"Hnn . . . hnn . . . hnn . . ." he said, his head jerking back and forth from the effort. He didn't try to speak again.

Sunny put down the bowl of thin beef broth she carried. "Back to bed and eat this, Mr. Becker," she said, waggling a forefinger. "You're a very naughty boy."

Becker ignored that and the broth and slowly, laboriously, and painfully he began to climb into his clothes. As he pulled on his boots Sunny chided him unmercifully, but he ignored her, his mind fixed on what had happened in the town.

He didn't ask himself any more questions. He'd discover all the answers he needed very soon. But now her nursemaid job was apparently over, Sunny decided to fill Becker in on what had happened while he lay unconscious.

"The Chinese rioted yesterday," she said. "They tortured Dave Grambling to death, turned his body inside out the newspaper says."

The girl read the question on Becker's surprised face. "Seven white men dead and twice that number of Chinese," she said. "That's what the paper says."

The big man's expression changed from amazement to concern.

"Pete Caradas wasn't among them," she said.

Relief flooded through Becker. He buckled on his revolvers, then shrugged, wincing, into his frockcoat. He got his wallet from the inside pocket and threw some bills onto the bedside table.

"Sssanks," he said through teeth as tight as a bear trap.

Sunny picked up the money, gave it a onceover, smiled, then said, "You're welcome. You can call on me anytime, Mr. Becker."

Becker nodded and picked up the soup bowl. He tilted back his head and let the broth trickle into his mouth until it was gone. The bandage under his chin was stained brown.

The beef broth helped, but Becker felt weak and light-headed. He was in no shape for a fight of any kind, not today and probably not tomorrow, or even next week.

For the first time in his life he felt powerless and vulnerable.

He walked to the door, opened it for Sunny . . . and took his first step into hell.

The early morning sun hung in the blue sky like a gold coin as Burt Becker stood on the porch of the hotel and lit a cigar. To his joy a man could still smoke, even with a broken jaw.

Men with rifles lounged on boardwalks and stared at the pretty women who passed, then exchanged grins and whispers.

But most of the riflemen, at least a dozen in number, were concentrated at the western edge of town where they could meet any attack from the Chinese.

Usually at this time of day, the tent city would be noisy, clamoring with Oriental voices, but that morning it was eerily silent, as though holding its breath, waiting for something to happen.

A locomotive, two cars and a boxcar attached, hissed and steamed on the track like a snoozing dragon. The engineer leaned out his window and talked to Sheriff Purdy, who looked small and insignificant beside the massive bulk of the 4-4-0.

There were no passengers in sight, and no Chinese, either.

Worrisome that, Becker thought, kind of eerie. But no matter, his fight must be with crazy Tom Clouston, not with a bunch of rioting Orientals.

Becker's battered face and hogtied jaw drew the attention of what he called the local yokels. Some of the men on guard stared in his direction and sniggered.

In no shape to fight, he decided it was high time he was off the street and into the dark, cool confines of the Streetcar Saloon.

And that led to another thought.

Had that mouthy little slut Jane Collins been fed in his absence? If not she must be mighty hungry about now. Ah well, serve her right for being so damned uppity. Becker's grin hurt his jaw.

"Riders coming in," one of the guards yelled.

Becker's eyes probed the wagon road that led into town. Two men were coming on at a walk, sitting their horses straight, like cavalrymen on parade. Army officers, maybe, he thought.

Becker was about to dismiss the men, but as they drew closer the black and white cowhide vest one of them wore caught his eye.

June Lacour wore a vest like that.

So he and Little Face Denton hadn't been killed! Somehow two of his top gun hands had survived and this was going to be a cause for celebration. A man with a broken jaw could still drink whiskey.

Smiling tight, Becker walked forward to greet his men. But after ten paces he stopped.

And learned that a man with a broken jaw could also scream.

Chapter Twenty-Six

"I never heard a man make a sound like that," Sheriff Jeremiah Purdy said. "And I never saw a man fall apart the way Burt Becker did."

"Straw men, you say?" Hamp Sedley said.

"They was skun," said Utah Beadles, a mean old former range cook Purdy had sworn in as a deputy after the Chinese troubles.

The young sheriff answered the question on Shawn O'Brien's face.

"Both men had been skinned by an expert," he said. "The skins were stuffed with straw, even the faces and most of the hands."

"June Lacour and Little Face Denton," Shawn said. "You're sure it was them?"

"Damn sure," Beadles said.

The new deputy had a huge head, and a few strands of lank gray hair dripped from under his hat and fell on his shoulders. His left eye was as white as a seashell, but his shooting eye was blue and keen. Beadles was a thin old man, but he was significant.

"It was them all right," Purdy said. "Becker called out their names over and over."

"Where is Becker?" Shawn said.

"He was carried into the Streetcar."

"His eyes rolling in his head, raving like a lunatic," Beadles said. "I guess ol' Burt never seen fellers skun afore."

"Have you?" Sedley asked. He'd decided to dislike the old-timer.

Beadles was nonplussed. "Down to the Strawberry River way I seen a puncher after the Utes got through with him. His name was Bob Hughes and he got hisself skun from big toes to scalp. A rum one was ol' Bob, an' no mistake. He was too fond of squaws and in the end that done for him."

"Some Ute women are said to be real pretty," Sedley said, warming to the deputy a little.

"I reckon they are," Beadles said. "But I always was keen on Cheyenne gals myself, the younger the better. Sun dries them out early."

"Where are the" — Shawn hesitated a heartbeat — "the bodies?"

"At the livery," Purdy said. "Utah and me got them off the street in a hurry. The folks in this town are scared enough, and those two boys don't need a doctor."

The four men stood on the boardwalk and now the young sheriff looked in the direction of the Rattlesnake Hills. "Damn those drums," he said. Then, "O'Brien, do you want to take a look at the —" He waved a despairing hand.

"Yeah," Shawn said. "I doubt if we'll learn anything, but it's worth a try."

"Learn anything?" Beadles said. "Hell, sonny, we all know who done it."

"The crazy doc you mean?" Sedley said.

"None other," Beadles said. "Listen to the damned drums, sonny. You think they ain't on the brag, telling us he done it?"

It did seem to Shawn that the drums were louder, more insistent and menacing.

Purdy turned bleak, hopeless eyes to him. "This town has five new widows and a grieving mother," he said. "God knows, the Chinese may have three times that number."

"You're telling me you won't ride against Clouston?" Shawn said.

"I'm telling you Broken Bridle won't accept more dead men, O'Brien. The women sure as hell won't."

"What about Becker's hired guns?" Sedley said.

"What hired guns? Now he's only got Pete

Caradas and a couple more."

"Except ol' Burt ain't fit to do anything, not after he saw them straw men," Beadles said.

"Shawn, you got friends in Washington," Sedley said. "Call in some favors and get the army here. Hell, a troop of cavalry will be enough to take care of Doc Clouston and his guns."

"This is a civilian matter and the army is already stretched thin with the Indian problem," Purdy said. "You can wire Washington, O'Brien, but I don't think you'll get anywhere."

"I don't think so, either," Shawn said. "Besides, it's my father who has the ear of the government bigwigs. I reckon we have it to do by ourselves."

"Tell me how," Purdy said. He looked incredible young and vulnerable, like a timid twelve-year-old surrounded by bullies.

"I don't know how," Shawn said. "Not yet I don't. But I think this town is worth saving. Make what you will of that, Sheriff."

The men shuffled to one side of the boardwalk to let a pretty woman in a poke bonnet pass. She had a couple of young 'uns clinging to her skirt.

But the woman stopped and said to Purdy,

"Sheriff, is it true that the Chinese have threatened to murder us all in our beds?"

Purdy managed a smile. "Who told you that, Mrs. Wright?" he said.

"Mrs. McGivney told me. She heard it from Mrs. Scott who heard it from —"

"Madam, I assure you that you're quite safe," Purdy said. "The Chinese harbor no ill will toward Broken Bridle and its citizens."

"Well, I hope not," the woman said. "Mr. Wright is talking about pulling up stakes and heading for Cheyenne where it's safe for a young family like ours." She put her hands to her ears. "Away from those awful drums."

"No need to leave, Mrs. Wright," Purdy said. "You and your husband and children will be perfectly safe and sound, I assure you."

"I do hope so, Sheriff," the woman said. "Mr. Wright has been unwell of late and is under the doctor's care. I do worry about him so."

Shawn O'Brien touched his hat and smiled.

"Give Mr. Wright our regards, ma'am, and tell him we wish him a speedy recovery."

The woman dropped a little curtsy and said, "Thank you, kind sir."

Shawn bowed. "Your obedient servant, ma'am."

After Mrs. Wright left with her brood, Sedley grinned and said, "Shawn, you're still very much the Southern gentleman, aren't you?"

"Is there any other kind of gentleman?" Shawn said.

The straw men had been removed from their horses and were propped in a corner of the livery and partially covered with hay.

Shawn O'Brien pulled the straw away and his breath caught in his throat. Beside him he heard Hamp Sedley's sharp intake of breath.

The skins were grotesque, stuffed with prairie grass and straw and then held upright with a T-shaped frame before they were tied onto the horses.

There was no longer anything human about them.

The eyes, nose cavities, and mouths looked like holes burned in canvas with a cigar. Shawn couldn't tell June Lacour or Little Face Denton apart.

"This is an obscene thing to do to men," Sedley said.

"From all I've heard about Clouston, the man himself is an obscenity," Shawn said.

"In the name of medical science he's taken more innocent lives than the West's worst outlaws combined." He stood and stared at the vile things that once had been men. "Judging by the amount of blood on their hides, Lacour and Denton were not dead when this happened to them," he said.

"Skinned alive, by God," Sedley said.

"I reckon that's how it was," Shawn said. "Nothing they ever did in life deserved such a death."

He covered up the remains again and said, "Later, I guess this is what we bury and call them bodies."

"It will be kinda like burying a well-dressed gent's duds instead of him," Sedley said.

"Yeah. Kinda like that," Shawn said. He stepped to the barn door. "Let's go talk with Burt Becker."

"Is that wise, Shawn?" Sedley asked. "He's liable to take one look at you and start shooting."

"From what I hear, Becker is in no shape to shoot anybody," Shawn said.

"Unless he's faking it," Sedley said. "He's a sneaky one is ol' Burt."

CHAPTER TWENTY-SEVEN

The two D'eth brothers rode across the grass and sagebrush country west of Savage Peak. Ahead of them lay uplifted, craggy mountains of red granite rock, here and there stands of limber pine, aspen, and juniper.

It was wild, untamed country, hard and unforgiving, but no wilder or harder than the two young men who rode among its shadows.

Both were tall, lean as hungry wolves, their eyes, mustaches, and hair black as ink, a mark of their French Roma heritage. Each carried an ivory-handled Colt shoved into his waistband and a boot knife with a three-inch steel blade.

Petsha and Milos D'eth were twins, two separate bodies conjoined in spirit — heartless, pitiless, vicious assassins for hire who came at a bargain rate, two for the price of one.

But lawmen from Texas to Montana would swear that one D'eth twin was plenty more than enough.

When the brothers spotted the sagging clapboard cabin ahead of them they drew rein. A trickle of smoke rose from the chimney and a pregnant sow rooted in the front yard.

At the same time both men kneed their horses forward, and when they were within a few feet of the door they again halted.

After a few moments a dour, bearded man stepped outside. He held a Sharps rifle across his chest.

"Go away. I have nothing for you," he said.

Now, a man with even a lick of sense should have known that strangers who rode blood horses and dressed in the broadcloth and white linen finery of gentlemen don't seek handouts.

But John Layton, tinpan miner and former farm laborer, was far from being a smart man. Not that it made any difference, since the D'eth brothers planned on killing him anyway, stupid or clever.

Unnerved by the brothers' silence, Layton, who had a reputation as a mean, nasty son-of-a-bitch, said, "On your way. There's no grub or money for you here."

The D'eth brothers drew at the same moment, and Layton fell with two bullets in his chest. The chickens in a coop at the side of the cabin flapped and clucked in alarm.

A small spotted pup, malnourished and dragging its left hind leg, scrambled out of the cabin and sniffed around the fallen man.

Then, displaying a dog's infinite capacity to forgive and forget, the pup looked up at the twins, whined a little, then sat awkwardly, its injured leg paining the animal.

The brother called Petsha swung out of the saddle as Layton groaned and tried to push up on his arms. Petsha's face expressionless, he casually shot the miner in the back of the head. Layton jerked, then lay still.

Petsha holstered his revolver and picked up the frightened puppy. With gentle hands he soothed the little creature, then checked its leg. The dog yelped a little, and looking concerned, he carried it to his brother.

Milos's hands were as careful as those of his brother. He examined the leg and after a while he kissed the puppy on the top of his head and tucked him into his coat.

He dismounted and both men entered the cabin.

Despite the brightness of the day, it was dark inside and one of the twins lit the oil lamp. The light spread into the cabin, revealing an untidy room but one that was fairly clean.

A coffeepot smoked on the stove. The brother who carried the puppy hefted the pot, then lifted the lid and sniffed.

Satisfied, he found a couple of clean tin cups and poured.

Petsha stepped across the room to a timber pole that was hammered into the wall. The pole served as a clothes hanger for underwear, much worn and stained, a couple of bib overalls, and several patched shirts.

The man grunted and threw the overalls and a couple of shirts on the floor. After some searching he tossed a ragged newsboy cap and a straw boater onto the pile.

Like his brother, he built a cigarette and smoked in silence as he drank coffee.

Later, another search uncovered a can of meat that the D'eth brothers fed to the hungry pup. The little dog had been kicked and his leg might be broken, but only a mule doctor would be able to treat it.

They hoped to find one of those in Broken Bridle.

Quickly the brothers stripped off their fine clothes and carefully laid them over the clothes pole. They each changed into a pair of overalls and Layton's shirts that proved to be too small for them. But they would have to do.

Finally they discarded their flat-brimmed, low-crowned black hats and grinned when they saw each other in the newsboy cap and straw boater.

But they looked like a couple of rubes, and that was exactly the impression they wanted to give.

There was nothing they could do about their tooled Texas boots. It seemed the dead man had only one pair of shoes and he was wearing them. They were too small anyway.

But then, how closely do folks look at a couple of hayseeds in town to see the bright lights and fancy women?

Their big American horses they could stake out on grass a fair ways from town. The man they'd killed had a rawboned yellow mustang in the corral and riding it two-up without a saddle would complete their disguise.

The brothers used string to cinch the waists of their overalls tight, and each shoved his short-barreled Colt into the bib where it would be hidden.

They smoked and drank more coffee, then scooped up the spotted pup and stepped outside.

Once the mustang was bridled the D'eth

brothers mounted up and left the dead man where he lay.

The spotted pup wriggled his way upward and licked the face of the brother who held him. Milos grinned and gently patted the little mutt's head.

Like his brother Petsha he hated people . . . but he loved dogs.

CHAPTER TWENTY-EIGHT

"Burt is in no state to see anyone," Sunny Swanson said. "He is very ill."

"He'll see me," Shawn O'Brien said.

"No, I'm afraid he won't."

This from Pete Caradas who sprawled tall and elegant at a table, a crystal decanter of brandy in front of him.

"No offense, O'Brien," he said. "I'm sure you understand."

"Why are you so damned sure he won't see me?" Shawn said.

"He has a brain fever," Caradas said. Then, "You saw what happened to June and Little Face. Well, so did Burt and he hasn't been right in the head since."

"Where do you stand, Pete?" Shawn said.

"Right now I'm sitting." Caradas smiled. "Stand on what? As of today I believe I'm still on Burt Becker's payroll, and I haven't thought it through any further than that."

"Now on to a more pleasant topic." He

flicked the decanter with a forefinger and after the *ting!* said, "I'm assured, if I can believe the Streetcar mixologist, that this cognac is from a new winery, the Chateau de Triac in France. Oddly enough I find it quite pleasant if a trifle pretentious. May I pour you a snifter? I'd like your opinion."

Shawn glanced at the decanter. "Judging by the mature color I believe it's a Bonaparte," he said. "But I've never tried that particular chateau before."

"Then there's a first time for everything."

Shawn nodded. "Then you may pour."

Caradas tipped cognac into a clean glass.

Shawn sniffed, then sampled the alcohol. He rolled the cognac around in his mouth for a while to allow the aromas and flavors to fully develop, *La Minute Mystique,* as the French connoisseurs called it, then swallowed.

"Well?" Caradas said, smiling slightly.

"A tad rustic for my taste, earthy overtones of dried apricot, mushroom, and a hint of cigar leaves, but nonetheless, as you said, a pleasant enough cognac."

"Another?" Caradas said.

"Not when I'm on business," Shawn said.

Caradas was silent for a few moments, then he tensed and said, "Not on revolver-fighting business, I trust."

Shawn smiled. "No, Pete. But when I am, you'll be the first to know."

"Thank you kindly for the courtesy," Caradas said.

"Where's Becker?" Shawn said.

Caradas nodded to the balcony that stretched on both sides of the saloon. "In a crib up there. You won't get a lick of sense out of him."

"He needs to recover quickly," Shawn said. "Becker is all that stands between Thomas Clouston and this town."

Suddenly Caradas's gray eyes shrouded, a fleeting moment like the shadow of a scudding cloud on prairie grass. "They made me puke," he said. "Or, in cruder terms, they made me throw my guts up."

"Huh?" Shawn said. "I'm not catching your drift."

"Clouston's men. They scared me so bad I got sick from fright," Caradas said. "I thought I'd stopped being scared around the time I bought my first Colt. The mad doctor showed me otherwise."

"Seeing what happened to June Lacour and Little Face, you'd a right to be scared," Sedley said, speaking for the first time.

"Imagine getting scared and having to hurl in the middle of a gunfight," Caradas said. "That should never happen to a man who makes his living with a revolver."

"Tell me about the fight," Shawn said.

"There isn't much to tell. After Lacour and Denton were caught, Clouston's boys took pots at me with rifles. They weren't trying to hit me, just put the fear of God into me. I guess they figured I was a man who scared real easy."

"A yellow belly today can be a hero tomorrow," Sedley said.

"Hamp," Shawn said, "that really didn't help."

Caradas smiled. "Look on the bright side, O'Brien," he said. "If you ever come calling on revolver business I may be so scared I'll cut and run."

"I don't think I'll put my faith in that happening," Shawn said.

"Damn right, Pete," Sedley said. "You're the fastest man with a gun around these parts."

"That didn't help, either, Hamp," Shawn said, angling the gambler an irritated glance.

Caradas grinned and slowly rose to his feet, unwinding like a watch spring. "I'll take you to Becker," he said.

But Sunny Swanson would have none of it. "I told you, Burt is ailing. He's not in a fit state to see anyone," she said.

More than ever she looked like a scolding

school ma'am.

"Sunny, if Burt is that sick, I don't think he's paying our wages any longer," Caradas said.

"We owe him," the woman said. "Well, I owe him."

"I want to talk with him," Shawn said.

"He can't talk. He raves, but that's not talk," Sunny said.

"I'd like to find that out for myself," Shawn said.

Sunny reached into the pocket of her dress and came up with a Remington derringer that she pointed at Shawn's face.

"And I say you won't, Mr. O'Brien."

"Sunny, put the stinger away," Caradas said.

"I'll be damned if I will," the woman said.

"You'll be damned if you don't," Shawn said.

He moved as fast as a striking rattler. His head darted to one side as his left arm came up and grabbed Sunny by the wrist.

The woman yelled and triggered a shot into the ceiling.

Shawn used his right, battered and painful as it was, to wrench the derringer from Sunny's hand.

The woman rubbed her wrist. "You brute, you hurt me," she said. "Pete, did you see that? He attacked a woman."

"What do you want me to do about it, Sunny?" Caradas said, smiling.

"Shoot him! Shoot him now! He's . . . he's a savage."

Shawn unloaded the Remington and passed it back to the angry woman. "Don't drop it," he said. "You could break a toe."

Sunny took a step back from Shawn and her tone bitter she said, "Haven't you done enough to Burt already, O'Brien? You beat him to within an inch of his life and now you want to piss on him when he's down? What kind of man are you?"

"The kind that tells you to get your facts straight, lady," Shawn said.

He stepped around Sunny and walked to the stairs, feeling his anger on a slow burn.

Pete Caradas was right behind him. "Don't be too hard on Sunny," he said. "I think she actually loves Becker."

Shawn turned and smiled slightly. "Wildcat, isn't she?" he said.

Caradas nodded. "She's all of that."

"My kind of woman," Shawn said. "In some ways her bravery and loyalty reminds me of my wife." He shook his head, his face stiff. "Oh hell, why did I say that and open an old wound."

CHAPTER TWENTY-NINE

Burt Becker lay in a narrow cot in a crib only a little larger than a steamer trunk. Both cot and crib were not designed for comfort but for quick business deals.

The big man lay on his back, his tied-up jaw giving him the appearance of a corpse laid out for display. His wide-open eyes stared at the bright red ceiling. The tiny room smelled of women and of Becker himself, a heady mix of sweet and sour.

"Becker," Shawn said. Then, aware that he whispered, he said in a normal voice, "I want to talk with you."

He got no response.

Shawn moved closer and stared into Becker's face.

The man's features were blank, eyes flat, as though someone had placed silver coins in the sockets to pay the ferryman.

"Becker," Shawn said. "Can you hear me?"

After a few moments, Pete Caradas said, "He's been like that for hours, not moving, saying nothing. He just stares at the ceiling."

"Ol' Burt gets the same view as the girls, huh?" Hamp Sedley said, grinning.

"Hamp, is it just me or does anyone else think you're particularly irritating today?" Shawn said.

"He's irritating," Caradas said.

"See if I talk again," Sedley said.

"Becker isn't going to talk again, that's for certain," Caradas said.

"Well, you've seen all you want, and now I want you all out of here," Sunny said. "I don't know where Burt has gone, but I'm the only one who can bring him back and that will take time and patience."

She glared at Shawn. "Why are you so all fired determined to talk to him?"

"Ma'am, this town is in grave danger," Shawn said. "We need his help."

"From the Chinese? We already know that."

"No, from Thomas Clouston, the little drummer boy. He wants the Rattlesnake Hills, and Broken Bridle stands in his way."

"What's that got to do with Burt?" Sunny said. "This town has already rejected him."

"Perhaps if he tells where he's holding

Jane Collins the folks will welcome him back to the fold," Sedley said, a man who couldn't remain silent for long.

By the shocked look on the woman's face Sedley had hit a nerve. But she quickly shrugged it off.

"I don't know what you're talking about," Sunny said. "The little slut has probably lit a shuck with a whiskey drummer. Now all of you get out of here."

Shawn remained where he was. "Listen, Miss Swanson, as far as I'm concerned, Burt Becker is a sorry piece of trash but he's a skilled revolver fighter, and so is Caradas. Who else is in town, Pete?"

The tall hired gun gave a languid shrug. "Coop Hunter and Uriah Spade. They're a pair of onetime lawmen up from the Arizona Territory."

"Are they good?" Shawn said.

"They'll do."

"Including myself and Hamp we can count on maybe half a dozen professional guns and the rest will be storekeepers," Shawn said. "When Clouston attacks, Becker needs to be on his feet."

"Let the sheriff handle it," Sunny said. "That's what he's being paid for."

"He can't handle it," Caradas said. "That's the problem."

"And that's why I'm willing to make a deal with the devil," Shawn said.

"As soon as Burt is able to ride, him and me are getting out of here," Sunny said. "Let this town fend for itself, I say. It isn't worth dying for."

Sedley glanced around him. "What's that damned scratching sound I've been hearing since I came in here?"

"Rats," Sunny said quickly. "They come in from the cattle pens and Chinatown."

"Big rats," Sedley said.

"Now, out, all of you," Sunny said. The look she gave Shawn was less than friendly. "When Burt recovers I'll tell him your proposition." She smiled. "Hell, what is your proposition exactly?"

"If Becker helps defend this town against Clouston, when it's done he can ride on out of here. I'll do nothing to stop him."

"And what about Jane Collins?" Sunny said.

"I'll expect him to tell me where she's being held."

"Dream big, mister," Sunny said. "Burt will leave Broken Bridle when he feels like it. And he doesn't know where that little Collins baggage is."

Shawn nodded. "You're lying. I think you know where the girl is."

"Get out of here," Sunny said.

On the cot Burt Becker groaned and twitched, his mind haunted by dreadful visions.

CHAPTER THIRTY

There was fortune to be made in the Rattlesnake Hills for men who were good with a gun and not overly squeamish about whom they shot with it.

Rank Mason was such a man. During an outlaw career that spanned two decades he'd killed both men and women for profit, and none of those murders troubled his conscience even a smidgen.

Mason was tailor-made for Thomas Clouston's enterprise as were the three hardcases that rode with him.

The oldest was Jim Mulholland, a bank robber, hired gun, sometimes lawman, and a vicious, unfeeling killer. He was fifty that year. Ten years younger, Dave King was an all-around bad man with rotten teeth and a worse attitude. He'd killed three men and considered himself an elite shootist. The youngest was William Anderson, an eighteen-year-old draw fighter and killer who liked to call himself Billy the Kid. The real Billy would have dismissed him as a coward and a braggart.

Following orders from Clouston, Mason led a routine patrol of the rugged hill country east of Fales Rocks. He planned to head southeast, pick up the middle fork of Casper Creek, and follow it back into the Rattlesnakes.

Mason had ridden that patrol seventeen times and was yet to come across a human being. Bears were scarce in the brush country and wolves generally kept to the high timber, so the land seemed empty, shimmering in the heat, the silence funereal as a fallen warrior's tomb.

But Clouston insisted that the patrols were necessary to keep interlopers at bay, and Mason had orders to shoot any such trespassers on sight.

Imagine the gunman's joy then when Billy the Kid Anderson's sharp young eyes spotted a couple of riders in the distance.

He cried out to Mason and pointed. "Rank, lookee there!"

The older man's gaze followed Anderson's pointing finger. He looked for a while, grunted, and raised the field glasses that hung around his neck — yet another Clouston precaution.

Mason studied the riders through the glasses for long moments, and Anderson, with the impatience of youth, said, "Hell, Rank, what do you see? Lawmen?"

Mason lowered the field glass and shook his head, a bemused look on his hard-planed, bearded face.

"Well?" Anderson said.

"Rubes. A couple of rubes riding two-up on a yeller hoss."

Dave King spat a stream of chewing tobacco over the side of his mount and said, "What the hell are rubes doing out here?"

"Damned if I know," Mason said. He passed the glasses to King. "Here, take a look for yourself. By the dead wild oak yonder."

After a while King turned to the others and said, "Rank called it right. Two farm boys in overalls riding a mustang. Hell, now I've seen everything."

"Must be on their way to Broken Bridle to see the bright lights and fancy women," Anderson said.

"I reckon so," Mason said. He sighed deeply. "Well, let's ride on down there and kill them."

"I'll kill them," Anderson said, grinning. "I've never shot me a couple of farm boys before."

"Shut your trap!" Jim Mulholland said. "Dave, give me them glasses."

"You don't speak to me like that, you old coot," Anderson said, his face pale with anger. "You want to climb off that bay and we'll have it out?"

Suddenly Mulholland's Colt was in his hand, the muzzle shoved into the bridge of Anderson's nose.

"Don't say another word, boy," he said. "Not one more word."

"Billy," Mason said, his voice so low it was almost a whisper. His eyes flickered to Mulholland's face and he saw death. "Don't move and don't say a word."

In that moment Billy the Kid Anderson realized he was a callow boy in the company of close-lipped, dangerous men. His eyes wide and frightened, he kept his mouth shut.

Mulholland shoved his revolver back into its cross draw holster and lifted the glasses to his eyes. A few seconds later he lowered and said, "Let those boys be, Rank."

Suddenly Mulholland looked much older than his fifty years. His brown eyes were haunted.

"They're rubes, Jim, for God's sake," Mason said. "We ride down there and shoot them off the pony and we're done."

"Not me, Rank. Not now, not ever."

Now Mulholland's gun had been taken out of his face, Anderson found his courage and his sneer again. His hand was on his Colt. "You scared?"

The older man sat his saddle in silence for long moments, gazing at the oncoming riders. A hawk glided overhead and for a moment cast an angular shadow that looked as though it had been razored from black paper. The kid had talked again and Mason expected a shooting, but Mulholland surprised him.

"Yeah, I'm scared, and so should you be," he said. He looked at Mason. "Ride away, Rank. Give them boys the road."

Mason read something in Mulholland's face that deeply disturbed him. Nonetheless he said, "I can't do that, Jim." He made a lame attempt at humor. "Just following doctor's orders."

Mulholland nodded. He reached into his shirt and pulled out a small wooden crucifix on a silver chain. "Rank, are you a Roman Catholic?" he asked.

The gunman shook his head. "Got no time for popery, Jim."

"Maybe that's so, but this I can do for you. For old time's sake, you understand?"

Mulholland raised the crucifix and made

the sign of the cross over Mason. *"Requiescat in pace,* Rank," he said. Then, to the others, "Maybe I'll see you boys around one day, but I doubt it."

Mulholland swung his horse away and rode south at a fast gallop. He didn't even glance in the direction of the D'eth brothers, nor did he look back.

When all that remained of Mulholland's frantic flight was a drifting cloud of dust, Billy Anderson grinned and said, "What the hell was that all about?"

"Maybe he's scared of rubes," Dave King said.

Rank Mason stared at the two men on the yellow mustang, then said, "All right boys, let's go get them."

Mason's first mistake was to ignore Mulholland's warning. Now he made a series of others.

He should have stayed at a distance and cut down the D'eth brothers with rifle fire. But maybe Anderson's exultant yell of, "This is gonna be fun!" influenced Mason's thinking and gave him false confidence.

The rubes had no weapons showing, and the big gunman assumed they were unarmed. That was his second error.

His third and most fatal miscalculation

was his belief that he, Dave King, and Billy the Kid Anderson were the top guns in the Wyoming Territory.

The D'eth brothers would soon show him otherwise.

CHAPTER THIRTY-ONE

Billy the Kid Anderson, thinking this was going to be easy, opened the ball. He had his Colt in his hand.

"Get off that pony, farm boys," he said, grinning. "And start running" — he pointed back along the trail — "that away."

The D'eth brothers sat the mustang, their black Gypsy eyes unblinking, staring silently at Anderson.

"I'll make it sporting," Anderson said. "If you make it to the dead wild oak without getting hit, I'll let you go."

Dave King grinned. "Seems like they don't understand plain American, Billy."

"Look like Greasers to me," Anderson said. He spat. "Or breeds."

The sun had reached its highest point, and men and horse cast no shadow. The parched day was quieter than the quietest night, and oppressive heat lay on the land heavy as a Hudson's Bay trade blanket.

Rank Mason was about to spoil Anderson's fun. He decided to end the game right then and he reached for his gun.

The D'eth brothers rolled off the mustang, landed on their feet, and began firing, a sound of rolling thunder.

Anderson went down, a cry of surprise and shock shrieking from his lips. Dave King died on his horse's back but stayed in the saddle, wide-jawed in a silent scream.

Rank Mason, the best of them, got off a shot that went high into the pine canopy. Bullets then tore great holes in his chest and hammered him into the ground.

Milos stepped through a fog of gun smoke and shot Anderson, who'd been up on one elbow, whimpering, his left arm extended in a plea for mercy. Clemency of any kind for the fallen never entered into the D'eth brothers' thinking, and Billy the Kid Anderson's death was no nobler than that of the man he'd tried so desperately to emulate.

The D'eth brothers reloaded their Colts and shoved them back into the bibs of their overalls. They had not exchanged a word, had not speculated on the identities of their attackers or their possible motives, because all that was of no interest to them. They had been threatened and had taken care of it. That was all that mattered.

The dead men had nothing the brothers wanted, so they let the bodies lay where they fell. That is, except for Dave King who still sat his horse, his eyes wide open but blinded by death. That last mildly amused Milos, but brother Petsha didn't spare the equestrian corpse a second glance. He climbed onto the bony back of the mustang and waited.

The spotted pup, scared by the gunfire, lay in the middle of a grass clearing with his huge front paws over his eyes. Milos gently picked up the little dog, kissed the top of his warm head, and carried him to the horse.

Petsha broke the silence. "How is he?"

"Just fine. Trembling a little bit."

"Hold him close and he'll calm down."

"What will we call him, Petsha?"

"Otto. We will call him Otto," Petsha said.

"Why?"

"It's a German name, a good name for a dog."

Milos held the puppy up to his face and said, "Hello, Otto."

The little dog licked Milos's face with his pink tongue, and the man smiled and said, "He likes that name."

"Then Otto it is," Petsha said. "Now let us ride on, brother."

The livery stable man cackled like a scrawny old rooster.

"You boys here to see the sights an' spark the pretty gals, huh?" he said. "Maybe taste some real whiskey instead o' that there moonshine y'all guzzle back home?"

The D'eth brothers were born actors, very much a necessity in the hired assassins line of work. And from the New York ganglands to San Francisco's Barbary Coast they were the best available. They worked quietly, efficiently, and offered a no-kill-no-fee guarantee. Not once had they been obliged to honor it.

Milos D'eth let out a guffaw that sounded like the bray of a Tennessee mule. "Purty gals is what we want afore whiskey," he said. "How much do they charge around these parts?"

"Oh, about two dollars. You got two dollars?" the liveryman asked.

Milos nodded an idiotic grin. "Me an' my brother got fifty dollars in Yankee money. Ain't that so, Petsha?"

"Sure do. Pa gave it us afore he kicked us out of the cabin down on Muddy Gap and tole us to find our own way in the world.

He called that fifty dollars a legacy an' that's what it is."

"Take us a long time to spend fifty dollars," Milos said.

The old stable man was about to say, "Not in this town it won't," but he changed his mind and said, "You boys will have a time with all that money. See you save two bits a night for the hoss."

"We sure will," Milos said. He brayed like a mule again. "Lead the way, brother Petsha."

Playing the country bumpkin tore up Milos D'eth, as though he was being dragged through a buckthorn wire fence, but he and Petsha had to get close to make the kill and sometimes playing the fool was necessary. Just a month before they'd disguised themselves as a pair of lacy maiden aunts to assassinate the whiskey-nosed, gouty old railroad magnate L. Justin Bennett, stabbing him to death with the sharped spikes of their parasols. He and Petsha were both six feet tall, and playing bent, elderly ladies had been a chore. But it was necessary, as was their current role of green hayseeds come to the big city to see the sights.

The reflector lamps were lit along the street and the Streetcar Saloon was ablaze with light. The respectable element was at home in the bosom of their families, but the sporting crowd jostled on the boardwalks and the champagne whores were already practicing their profession. As they did every night, drums droned from the Rattlesnake Hills and men joked about the ghosts of Apaches and the lost Spanish army that had come this far looking for gold.

It was a balmy evening, one made for men to roister among the whiskey and whores. That it would end in tragedy none knew, except the already drunk and perhaps the few Chinese who glided in the shadows and said nothing but saw everything.

Keeping up their charade, the D'eth brothers stepped into the Streetcar and stood just inside the door and gaped at the splendor around them, jaws hanging open. Men in gold watch chains and broadcloth mingled with dusty cowboys, drifters, miners, gamblers, and professional drinkers. Saloon girls in candy cane dresses circulated among the crowd, and a cunning-eyed brunette spotted the brothers and said, "Howdy boys. You just standin' or are you drinkin'?"

"Drinkin'," Milos said. Then, after a donkey bray, "I never seen nothing like you afore."

"How come that doesn't surprise me?"

the girl said. She petted the spotted pup and then said her name was Suzette and she was working to support her widowed mother. "Buy me a drink, boys?"

Milos stepped to the bar and ordered whiskey. Suzette said she wanted champagne. The bartender nodded and gave the girl a wink. He was about to take a whiskey bottle from the shelf behind him but changed his mind and retrieved one from the floor where the cockroaches lived. He poured the rotgut into two glasses and said, "And champagne for the lady."

The champagne was fizzy water from an opened bottle, but what did rubes know?

"That will be five dollars," the bartender said.

"Huh?" Milos said. He knew he was being taken but remained in character.

"Big city, big prices," the bartender said. "Comes as a shock to a country boy, don't it?"

Milos made a mental note to kill the man before he left Broken Bridle, but he paid the five dollars without too much fuss and Suzette said, "Let's get a table, boys, and we'll talk." She smiled, promising much. "Unless you want to do something else." She elbowed the silent Petsha. "Something real nice, huh, big boy?"

"I guess we'll have this whiskey first," Milos said. "Me and my brother ain't never tasted drinkin' whiskey that came so dear."

Suzette laid her glass on the bar. "Well, I'll be around when you boys get worked up enough to need me," she said. She patted the pup's head. "That doesn't include you."

The serious drinkers were all upstanding men, and the D'eth brothers found a table without much difficulty. They sat straight in the cane-backed chairs like worshippers in church.

Pete Caradas, a man with restless eyes, spotted the rubes before they sat down. One carried a slat-ribbed pup with a wet, inquisitive nose, and both wore denim overalls that were a size too small for them. They were both very dark, ink black hair and eyes that gave them the look of Gypsies, and their hayseed exterior was belied by their erect carriage and the slightly arrogant tilt of their heads. When the men sat, their pants legs rode up and exposed their boots, not the coarse brogans of country boys, but finely stitched riding boots that would cost a working cowboy three months' wages.

Caradas recognized the yellow and scarlet butterfly overlays that decorated the boot shafts and the radically under-slung, two-

212

inch heels as the work of Sol and Abe Rosenberg of Abilene. A man wearing Rosenberg boots couldn't hobble very far, but he surely cut a dash on horseback.

A couple of ragged rubes wearing fancy boots set off an alarm bell in Caradas's head. He pegged them as the D'eth brothers, Milos and Petsha, killers for hire who didn't come cheap.

But why were they in Broken Bridle?

Burt Becker had left plenty of enemies on his back trail, and he was the obvious target. Could one of those foes be well heeled enough to buy the costly but lethal services of the terrible twins?

It was possible. In fact Caradas considered it more than possible — it was damned likely.

And now was the time to consider his next move.

CHAPTER THIRTY-TWO

Shawn O'Brien was worn out and Hamp Sedley was in no better shape, but they decided to give Burt Becker one more try before they called it a night.

Cigar smoke hung in the Streetcar like a fog, and the wall-to-wall crowd was getting animated. Gambling was going on at three tables, and over by the piano player a saloon girl warbled, "The Quaker Lass Fallen in Shame," but nobody listened. Shawn was hit by the familiar saloon smells of packed bodies, stale beer, cigars, and cheap perfume. White moths fluttered around the oil lamps like snowflakes, and a drunken rooster wearing a high celluloid collar balanced a glass of whiskey on the crown of his plug hat as he tiptoed along a chalk line drawn on the floor. When he tripped over his own feet and fell, the crowd laughed and one of his companions gave him a playful boot or two in the ribs.

Shawn was big and significant, and he made his way through the crowd like a frontier Moses parting the Red Sea.

Pete Caradas sat at his usual table, and he smiled and motioned Shawn and Sedley over. "Sorry for the dishes," he said. "I guess they can't find the time to clear them."

"Hey, Pete, you going to eat that last lamb chop on your plate?" Sedley asked.

"Help yourself," Caradas said.

"Obliged," Sedley said. He sat and with surprising daintiness picked up the chop and began to eat. "Good," he said, chewing out the word.

"You see them, O'Brien?" Caradas said. His elegantly booted foot pushed a chair closer. "Take a load off."

"Yes, I saw them," Shawn said. "Pumpkin rollers wearing hundred-dollar boots catch a man's eye."

"They're not pumpkin rollers," Caradas said. "Each of them has a gun stuffed into his bib overalls, and their hands have never been near a plow. They're in disguise, and that's how they work. Dredging up some old around-the-stove talk, I'd bet the farm those are the D'eth brothers, come to Broken Bridle to do somebody harm. I've heard about them, but this is the first time I ever saw them in the flesh."

"Those boys are looking at you, Shawn," Sedley said. He had an odd, knowing expression on his face. "My guess is they don't like what they see."

"Yeah, and they've been giving me the mean eye since they sat down as well," Caradas said. "I've never met them, but they have me pegged. And now you, O'Brien."

"Pegged you fellers as what?" Sedley said.

"Guns, just like themselves," Caradas said. "I reckon they don't harbor any animosity against us, but men in their kind of work hate complications." The man smiled. "Kinda like me finding you in Broken Bridle, O'Brien."

"Do I need to guess who they're after?" Shawn said, ignoring that last.

"No, you don't need to guess. It has to be Becker."

"Then you have a hand to play, Pete," Shawn said.

"Seems like," Caradas said. He smiled at Shawn. "The good news is I'm not scared."

"Why should you be, Pete?" Sedley said, amazed. "You shuck that Colt on your hips faster than anyone around."

"Let's just say I had a bad experience recently and let it go at that," Caradas said.

Sedley opened his mouth to speak, but

Shawn said, "And let it go at that, Hamp." Ignoring Sedley's disgruntled scowl, he said to Caradas, "Maybe the target is Thomas Clouston. Listen to those drums. Does he know they're here?"

For most residents of Broken Bridle the constant drumming had faded into background noise, like the hum of Chinatown or the constant rumble of freight wagons in the street. But since sundown the relentless racket of the drums had increased in intensity and was now more ominous, threatening, and aggressive.

"Clouston did all his killing back East where it was legal," Caradas said. "I doubt that back in Philadelphia a relative grieving for a deceased loved one would know how to hire the D'eth brothers, or if it even would enter his thinking. In the big cities you hire lawyers, not guns."

"Well, there's one way to find out," Sedley said. "I'll go ask them."

The protest died on Shawn's lips as Sedley rose and strode purposely in the direction of the D'eth brothers.

Shawn's hand dropped to the Colt on his hip, and beside him Caradas stiffened, watching. But the moment passed. As though of one mind the brothers rose, turned their backs on Sedley, and walked out of the saloon, closing the door quietly behind them.

Sedley stood in the middle of the floor, baffled, as merrymakers milled around him. He turned on his heel and walked back to Shawn and Caradas.

"I guess they didn't want to talk to me," Sedley said.

Suddenly Caradas was angry. "Sedley, I warn you, don't ever do that again. If they'd drawn down on me you'd have been between me and them, obscuring my targets. That's the only edge the D'eth brothers need."

Sedley was apologetic and shrugged his shoulders high, hands spread. "Hell, Pete, they don't even know you work for Burt Becker."

"Maybe they don't, but I can't count on that." Caradas forced himself to simmer down. "Just don't pull a grandstand play like that again."

"Shawn?" Sedley said.

"Man's right, Hamp. If they'd had a mind to, the D'eth boys could have used you for cover." Shawn smiled. "You'd have been a great loss to the gambling profession."

Caradas nodded. "I usually just shoot people who get in my way, Hamp." But he said it grinning and Sedley took no offense.

Sedley's rash move had been a minor irritation, nothing more.

But much worse was to come, and soon the death knell would toll in Broken Bridle.

CHAPTER THIRTY-THREE

At first Shawn O'Brien thought a fistfight had broken out on the dance floor, but he quickly realized that was not the case . . . it was more serious than that.

Above the noise of the crowd he heard a man yell, "I say we kill every man jack of them and hang the crazy doc!"

"Shut up them damned drums forever!" another man shouted.

That last drew the excited approval of men who'd drunk too much whiskey. They considered themselves as individuals no longer but part of a mob, and that was much more exciting.

A portly man in a broadcloth coat and collarless shirt waved his arms for quiet. "Listen, everybody. Listen to me! Quiet down."

After the babble of conversation died away, a saloon girl yelled, "Talk to us, Oskar!"

Oskar Janacek, the brewer, puffed up a little with self-importance.

"Every man who can carry a rifle follow me to the brewery," he said. "I have a wagon big enough to carry all of us and a pair of Percherons to haul it." When the cheering passed, Janacek yelled, "By God it's high time we rousted out those black-hearted villains in the Rattlesnake Hills!"

Like a conquering general with an army at his back, the big brewer stomped to the door and others followed him.

Whiskey and smoldering resentment is a combustible mix, and Shawn reckoned Janacek had been rabble-rousing for some time before the crowd got worked up and the shouting started.

Beside him, Pete Caradas said, "Oh dear, I have a feeling this isn't going to end well."

One of the relief bartenders hollered, "Wait for me, boys!" He untied his apron, threw it on the floor, and hurried from behind the bar.

"Here, Joe, you'll need this," a gray-haired man said. He pulled a four-barreled pepperpot revolver from his pants pocket and passed it to the bartender, a tall, sallow man with a prominent Adam's apple.

"Give 'em hell, Joe," the gray-haired man said.

Joe grinned and ran to the door, waving the pepperpot above his head to cheers from the thinning crowd.

"I'd better stop this," Shawn said.

"It's none of your concern, O'Brien," Caradas said.

"I promised to save this town, not sit back and watch it destroy itself."

"Then it's a job for the sheriff, not you."

Shawn rose to his feet and adjusted his gun belt. "I could use your help, Pete," he said.

The gunman shook his handsome head. "Count me out. My job is to protect Burt Becker and I'll do it right here."

"A wise move, Pete. Especially now them D'eth brothers are in town," Sedley said.

"Hamp, you're always such a big help to me," Shawn said, frowning.

He walked to the door and Sedley followed. Behind them, Pete Caradas shook his head and smiled.

A glowing moon rode high over Broken Bridle and spread a silver light, but Shawn O'Brien was struck by how dark and gloomy the town seemed, the stores and businesses lining the boardwalks as dreary as a row of slave quarters. North to the Rattlesnake Hills drums pounded a warning into the night, and alarmed coyotes yipped and howled among the shadowed hollows. There was no wind and the air smelled of dust and horse dung.

Their spurs ringing, Shawn and Hamp Sedley walked along the boardwalk toward the brewery where male voices were raised, playfully loud and chiding.

A team of big gray Percherons was already hitched to the brewery dray, a flatbed wagon with two rows of retaining chains on each side. A dozen men had already clambered aboard, carrying an assortment of long guns. Bottles passed around and laughter bellowed with whiskey courage.

When Shawn reached the open ground where the dray stood, he realized he was stepping into a powder keg that was about to blow.

Sheriff Jeremiah Purdy, his arms waving, was exhorting Oskar Janacek to go home to bed. Two men holding rifles and lanterns flanked the big brewer, and he was obviously on the prod.

"No, Sheriff, you go home to bed," Janacek said. "You're damned useless and that's why we're taking the law into our own hands."

"Wait until tomorrow and we'll talk then," Purdy said.

"Talk! That's all you ever do is talk!" the brewer said. He poked Purdy in the chest with a forefinger as thick and stiff as a hickory wheel spoke. "Where are the Chinese who murdered Dave Grambling? Why haven't you hung them? Because you're yellow, Sheriff, and you're weak. Now get the hell out of my way."

Janacek pushed Purdy aside and stepped to the wagon. "Are we ready to quiet those drums forever, boys?" This drew a ragged cheer, and a man in the dray yelled, "Let's go get 'em, Oskar."

"Oskar Janacek!"

The brewer turned. Purdy had his .38 at eye level, aimed directly at the big man's head. "You're leading those men nowhere," the sheriff said. "Go home, and that goes for the rest of you."

Janacek was a big man who weighed two hundred and fifty pounds, all of it solid, and in all his fifty years he'd stepped aside for no one. He was one of the few merchants in town who'd refused to pay tribute to Burt Becker, and now he did what Shawn O'Brien feared he'd do.

Moving with surprising speed and agility, Janacek stepped in on Purdy, wrenched the revolver from his fist, and backhanded him, a powerful blow that sent the young sheriff to his knees.

Beside him, Shawn heard Sedley groan. But when the brewer steadied himself to get the boot in, Shawn yelled, "No! That's enough!" His Colt was in his hand.

Immediately long guns rattled, and a dozen and more rifles and shotguns were trained on Shawn.

"You dealing yourself a hand, O'Brien?" Janacek said.

"I told you he's had enough," Shawn said. "If I take cards in this game, you'll be the first to know it, Janacek."

The big man had sand, but now was not the time to prove it. If the ball opened, O'Brien would not survive, but then neither would he. Janacek let it go.

"Come on, boys," he said. "We've wasted enough time here."

He tossed Purdy's revolver into the dirt in front of him, and amid cheers and some jeers directed at Shawn, Janacek clambered into the driver's seat of the dray and slapped the reins.

The Percherons took the strain and the wagon trundled into the street, lanterns bobbing with its every movement. Someone took up a song and the others joined in, singing lustily, the whiskey bottles making their rounds.

Tramp, tramp, tramp, the boys are
    marching,
Cheer up comrades they will come,
And beneath the starry flag
We shall breathe the air again,
Of the free land of our own beloved home.

"Sing now," Shawn said, watching the
dray leave. "As my father says, you'll soon
be supping sorrow with the spoon of grief."

Jeremiah Purdy struggled to get to his feet.
"I have to stop them," he said.

"You can't stop them," Shawn said.
"Nothing can stop them, not now."

"Those damned drums . . ." the sheriff
said.

"Where those boys are headed there will
be plenty of drums and a warm welcoming
committee, depend on it," Shawn said.

"I'm going after them," Purdy said. "I
have to turn them, bring them back. Let me
up, O'Brien."

"You haven't done very well so far, Sheriff," Sedley said. "What do you plan to do
different?"

"I don't know. I'll play it as I see it when I
get there."

"How come that doesn't inspire me with
confidence?" Sedley said.

"Hamp, leave him alone. He's had a bad

night," Shawn said. He helped Purdy to get to his feet, gave him his .32, and said, "You're the town sheriff and you've got a job to do. I won't stand in your way."

Sedley bent and picked up something from the ground. He handed Purdy his round, wire-rimmed glasses and said, "Here, you might need these, help you see better when you set off that little pistol."

After the young sheriff put on the spectacles he looked like a fourteen-year-old boy. "Don't like me much, do you, Hamp?" he said.

"Nope, I sure don't. I think you should go back East and be a professor or something. You ain't doing much good in this town."

"Maybe I will go back East, but only when my work here in Broken Bridle is done."

Sedley shook his head. "You may be a college boy, but I think you're as dumb as a snubbin' post."

To Shawn's surprise, Purdy smiled. "You know, you could be right," he said.

Ragged volleys of gunfire scarred across the dark face of the quiet night.

"Oh God no, not that," Shawn said. He read the question on Purdy's face. "They're shooting up Chinatown as they drive past."

Purdy looked stricken. "We have to stop

them!" he said.

Without another word he turned on his heel and ran into the street. Shawn and Sedley followed, but they walked. The shooting had stopped and the culprits were well gone. There was no need for hurry. Now the only question was: How many Chinese had been killed?

CHAPTER THIRTY-FOUR

The total casualties from the attack on Chinatown were three: A chicken trampled in the stampede away from the firing, a mule grazed by a flying bullet, and an iron cooking pot holed by a .44-40 rifle slug.

Sheriff Jeremiah Purdy was relieved, but the tent city at the end of the tracks was now a dangerous place for a white man to be. The town was angry, like a wounded, fanged, and clawed beast ready to lash out at its tormentors, and now its rage found a focus, the man who represented the law in Broken Bridle.

"Those who did this will be found and punished," Purdy said as a hostile crowd gathered around him. "I give you my word the guilty parties will be brought to justice."

Silence is a terrible weapon.

A sea of faces, their eyes hollowed by darkness, stared at the lawman. No one uttered a sound, but the basilisk breath of the crowd was an ominous hiss in the quiet.

Shawn O'Brien had it figured out. If the crowd broke violent he had five shots to turn it. But if the Chinese took their hits and kept on coming, then he was a dead man. Beside him, Hamp Sedley looked unwell.

Then something incredible happened. The crowd shut down, turned their backs, and silently filed away into the gloom, now and then light from colored paper lanterns gleaming on bent heads and stooped shoulders.

The three white men found themselves alone, surrounded only by darkness.

"Well, don't that beat all," Sedley said. He sounded relieved.

Purdy turned to Shawn. "What do you make of it?" he asked.

Shawn shook his head. "I don't know what to make of it. They had me scared for a while there."

"Well, they're quiet now," Purdy said. "I guess that's the main thing."

"I reckon it's the lull before the storm," Sedley said, exactly echoing Shawn's own thought.

"You men should go back to the hotel," Purdy said. "I'm going after those idiots and bringing them back here."

As the drums pounded from the Rattle-snake Hills, Shawn said, "Better be quick, Sheriff. Or there will be none left to bring back."

"There's always a chance Janacek and the others will prevail and drive Clouston and his gang away," Purdy said.

"And there's always a chance pigs will fly," Sedley said.

"Look on the bright side, O'Brien," Pete Caradas said. "Maybe Clouston will ignore them, let Janacek and his boys bumble around in the dark for a while before they come back to town with hangovers and their tails between their legs."

"You think that's likely?" Shawn said.

"As likely as you being the best man at my wedding," Caradas said.

"I'm very hurt," Shawn said.

Caradas's smile fleeted, then his face grew grim. "Those boys are headed into serious trouble. Clouston will lay for them and cut them to pieces. He has fighting men. Do you know what professional guns can do to a drunken rabble?"

"Put them through a meat grinder, especially in the dark," Sedley said.

"You got that right, gambling man," Caradas said.

"That's why I'm here," Shawn said. "We have to get Becker on his feet and put a gun in his hand. After routing Janacek, Clouston could counterattack and drive right into Broken Bridle."

Caradas looked around at the thinning saloon crowd, then turned back to Shawn and smiled. "O'Brien, I'm not going to fight for this one-horse town and neither is Becker. Is that clear or do I have to put it in writing?"

"If Clouston gets here, you'll have to fight," Shawn said.

"Why? He's got nothing against me."

"You killed one of his men," Shawn said. "Clouston will nail you to a cross or flay your hide for that."

"He let me go, remember?" Caradas said.

"Only because he knew he'd catch up with you later," Shawn said. "You haven't tried to leave town recently, have you? I don't think you'd make it a mile before Clouston caught you."

Uncertainty flickered in Caradas's strange, lifeless eyes. He looked over the saloon patrons again. "Most of them went home after the Chinese were attacked," he said. "They're scared."

"And so they should be. They should be scared of both the Chinese and Clouston.

Of the two, I'd say Clouston is the worst."

"What do you say, gambling man?" Caradas said.

"I say this, Pete. You see the clock on the wall over the bar, what is it telling us?" Sedley said.

"That it's thirty minutes after midnight," Caradas said.

"No, it's telling us that time is running out fast," Sedley said. "I say at first light we get the hell out of this town." He turned his attention to Shawn. "You made a promise to a man you barely know to save his son. Well, you discovered that the son isn't worth saving, so cut your losses and move on now, before it's too late."

"No, Hamp, I'm no longer in the business of saving Connall Purdy's son, I'm trying to save this town. Broken Bridle isn't much, a mean little outpost of civilization on the edge of nowhere, but as a civilized man I recognize its right to exist. Men like Thomas Clouston would take us back to barbarity by destroying the very fabric of our civilization for his own ends. He seeks to end the basic right of freedom, free speech, and the right to live without fear of oppression. Damn it, I'm an American and I won't lick the boots of any tin pot dictator. To me this town represents freedom, ideals, the ability of Americans to strive for something better for our children than we knew, and I won't let madmen like the Thomas Cloustons of this world destroy it."

Shawn smiled. "And if I ever talk that much again you have my permission to shoot me."

"Willingly," Pete Caradas said.

"Well, Abraham Lincoln, does that mean we stay?" Sedley asked.

"It means I stay, Hamp," Shawn said. "You have to make your own decision."

"Then I guess I'll stick," Sedley said. "Right at the moment I've nothing better to do."

Caradas roused himself from thought. "Here's what I'll do, O'Brien: If Clouston raids into Broken Bridle and fires shots at my valuable person, I'll shoot back. Can I say fairer than that?"

"You obviously didn't take my speech to heart," Shawn said. "But, yes, I'll accept that for now."

"Good, now have a glass of this wine and we'll drink on it," Caradas said. "Afterward, I'll see if I can rouse the sleeping beauty upstairs."

"What kind of wine is that, Pete?" Sedley said.

"Monkey piss," Caradas said. "It's what

234

passes for claret in this outpost of American civilization."

CHAPTER THIRTY-FIVE

The marching songs had ended, ground away by the jolting misery of the brewer's dray. The whiskey bottles were empty and men yawned and thought of soft beds and warm, drowsy wives. Moonlight lay on the ground like hoar frost, and now that the drums were silenced, there was no sound but the steady creak of the wagon and the soft footfalls of the massive hooves of the Percherons.

Oskar Janacek drew rein when the towering bulk of a Rattlesnake Hills blacked out the stars. His voice loud in the quiet, he said, "Scouts forward."

The two men designated for the job remained where they were, huddled in the back of the dray. Near them a man coughed up phlegm and spit over the side. A cloud obscured the jolly face of the moon, like a fat man using a handkerchief.

Janacek's voice took on an edge. "McPhee,

Baker, forward."

"Go to hell, Janacek," the man called Baker said. "There's nothing here but cactus."

"I say we turn around," Lou McPhee said. He was a tall, stringy, sour man, and his passion for the expedition had waned an hour before. "What do you say, boys? We can go back and kill some more of them heathen Chinese."

That last was greeted with little enthusiasm. What in town had seemed a splendid adventure had rapidly become an ordeal. The dray was designed to transport beer barrels, not men, and it was an uncomfortable perch. Add to that burgeoning hangovers and the open hostility of the land around them, and the expedition had started to fall apart. Men whispered to one another that the drums had stopped and wasn't that the whole point of the exercise in the first place?

Janacek was aware that his command was in jeopardy, and he said, "Hell, I'll scout myself. One of you men come up here and take the reins."

The dray creaked as the brewer stepped to the ground and a man took his place in the driver's seat. Janacek grabbed a lantern and said, "When I yell to come on, bring the wagon forward. And be alert, all of you."

This was met with no response. Janacek shook his head and stepped into the darkness, the lantern raised in his left hand, a Winchester in his right. Soon he was swallowed by gloom, and the Percherons stirred in their traces, uneasy with the night and the malevolent, hidden things that prowled its vastness.

Several minutes passed. The moon spread a silvery light made for lovers, and the air was sweet and cool on the tongue, like mint.

There was as yet no beckoning call from Oskar Janacek.

The steel battle-ax is a cleaving weapon. Its honed edge splits bone apart to the marrow and therefore doesn't crush like a club. When used on the human skull the ax doesn't scatter brain but bites deep into the gray matter and inflicts a horrific wound that kills — or so Janacek's loved ones later hoped — instantly.

The lone survivor of what would be called "The Rattlesnake Hills Expedition" by the local newspaper would later testify that Janacek cried out only once and then fell silent.

What is known is that after Dr. Thomas Clouston levered his battle-ax out of Janacek's skull, he pointed his bloody weapon at the brewery dray and ordered his horsemen forward.

Lit fore and aft by lanterns, the wagon was a blazing target in the darkness, its fourteen occupants packed so closely together they had little room to deploy their weapons, and Clouston's riders fell on the men of Broken Bridle like the wrath of God.

Madman though he was, the doctor had chosen his gunmen with care. Raised and trained in the Texan tradition, to a man they understood the ways of revolver fighting on horseback, and when they attacked the wagon they were as hawks descending on doves.

Clouston's riders attacked both flanks of the dray, raking it with a withering crossfire. They opened up as they rode past, then wheeled around and struck again.

Cramming themselves together as untrained men do under fire, the men in the wagon lost half their number in the first two volleys, and suddenly the wood floor of the dray was awash in blood and scarlet beads ticked through the slats onto the ground.

The man in the driver's seat, a normally meek accountant named Lawson, was a dreadful sight. His lower jaw had been shot away, yet driven by some incredible force of will he managed to turn the wagon around before he was blasted into the dirt.

Another man took Lawson's place and urged the terrified team into a lumbering trot. Behind him, a rifleman cheered as he scored a hit, but his triumphant cry went unanswered by the living, the dying, and the dead. The driver had handled a team before, and he rammed the lurching dray into a narrow break between the trees, praying that he didn't shatter an axle. For a few moments there was a respite from the constant, heavy fire as Clouston's men slowed before funneling two abreast into the narrow clearing.

"Can we hold them off?" the man at the reins yelled over his shoulder.

"Hell no!" a voice answered. It sounded like McPhee. "We got mostly dead men back here!"

The driver hoorawed the team, fear sweat trickling down his spine. Moonlight tangled in clouds of billowing dust, and the dray was momentarily lost in amber darkness, the lanterns long since thrown over the side. A couple of men fired into the murk, scored no hits, but a returning volley fire killed a man kneeling next to McPhee. Splattered by the dead man's blood and brains, McPhee shrieked in horror, then mindless panic.

"Damn you, slow down!" McPhee yelled. "We must surrender!"

"Not this wagon!" the driver answered. He slapped the reins and the Percherons stretched into a gallop.

Bullets splitting the air around him, fired by men who had not made a sound since the attack began, McPhee tossed his rifle away and drew a Colt from his waistband. Standing upright on the wagon bed was like balancing on the storm deck of a schooner in a force ten gale, but he held on to the back of the seat and shoved the muzzle of his revolver into the back of the driver's neck.

"Stop this rig now or I'll kill you!" he yelled into the man's ear. McPhee was hysterical with terror and his voice was shrill.

"You go to hell!" the driver said.

McPhee pulled the trigger. The driver fell forward in the seat, and McPhee snatched the reins from his lifeless hands and hauled the team to a shuddering halt.

It was then, as the Percherons steamed in the morning chill and tossed their heads, that a sixteen-year-old orphan who went by the name Bobby Miller made his bid for freedom.

The following dust cloud caught up with

the wagon, and shrouded for a moment, the boy dropped over the side and crawled into the brush. Small and skinny for his age, he was soon hidden under a thick cover of sage and wheatgrass.

The youngster looked back in time to see McPhee die.

The riders had harried the dray and kept up a steady fire. They'd lost two of their number and that added fury to their blood-lust. After the lanterns had been thrown away, in the crimson-seared darkness three surviving Broken Bridle riflemen, two of them former soldiers, had calmly gotten in some plucky work with Winchesters, but now all three lay dead. Before they were gunned down, one of the veterans had hit a third Clouston rider . . . moments before a horn sounded from the hills and the attackers drew rein and ceased firing.

Lou McPhee threw his Colt away and raised his arms. Because of the dust and darkness he saw nothing and heard only the groans of the dying in the bed of the dray.

Long moments passed, then McPhee called out, "I surrender! I'm unarmed."

His voice sounded hollow in the terrible quiet. Insects chirped, a breeze moved in the trees, and a harness jangled as a Percheron snorted and shook its massive head.

Bobby Miller tried to make himself even smaller, flattening himself against the ground. Scared, he kept his eyes on McPhee. If the man's surrender was accepted, he planned to give himself up.

Time ticked slowly, then a man with long gray hair astride a great horse appeared through the murk. He wore a cloak and Bobby thought he carried himself nobly, like King Arthur in the picture books. Surely such a chivalrous figure would be merciful to his captured enemies? But then Bobby saw the man's bloody battle-ax and he became very afraid.

The statuesque rider drew rein at the wagon, and McPhee swallowed hard and said, "I surrender."

"Are you sane?" Dr. Thomas Clouston said.

"I just want out of the fight," McPhee said. "I'm done. There are wounded men here."

"The fight is over, yet you don't realize that it is," Clouston said. "Ergo, you are completely insane and a danger to all of us."

"No . . . no, I'm not. I just want to go home to my wife and kids," McPhee said.

Clouston took a breath, then roared, "That won't do! I will not release the mentally deranged back into the community. Lord God Almighty, how the souls of your victims would cry out to me for vengeance!"

"I'm a laborer," McPhee said in a small, timid voice.

"Liar!" Clouston yelled, so loudly the normally placid Percherons jumped and McPhee grabbed the driver's seat for support. "Who but an insane man would admit to being a common laborer?"

The doctor indicated with his ax. "Come, stand before me in tribunal and I will render judgment, both on your sanity and your wanton, spiteful attack on my person."

"Don't . . . don't hurt me," McPhee said.

Huddled in the brush, Bobby Miller pressed his face into the dirt, ashamed for Lou McPhee and his cowardice.

"Stand before me, cretin," Clouston said.

McPhee, sobbing, climbed from the wagon and walked to his fate.

Bobby saw the ax rise and fall, heard the thin sound of its whispering death, then McPhee's shriek as he fell.

Tears welling in his eyes, the boy heard Clouston call out, "Unhitch the great horses, then kill all in the wagon. Let none survive."

A few minutes later, after the team was

unhitched, Clouston's riders systematically and coldly shot both the dying and the dead.

"Search around, make sure none escaped," Clouston said.

Bobby Miller lay still, hardly daring to breathe. He heard the footfalls of a booted man come close . . . closer . . . then a thick stream of warm water cascaded onto the back of his head. The boy stayed where he was. Better to be pissed on than have his skull split open with an ax.

Finally he heard the man button up and step away.

Then the man on the big horse said, "Let the dogs lie where they fell. Now back to the hills where we will mourn our dead."

Fifteen minutes later, amid silence, Bobby Miller got to his feet and ran.

And ten minutes after that he met Sheriff Jeremiah Purdy leading a lame horse.

CHAPTER THIRTY-SIX

"They're all dead, Sheriff," Bobby Miller said. "They shot every one of them."

"Who, Bobby, who shot them?" Purdy said.

"Didn't you hear it?" the boy said, a frantic light in his pale eyes.

"I heard the shooting, but I saw nothing," Purdy said. He felt sick to his stomach.

"Riders came out of the hills and bushwhacked us. Everybody's dead. Lou McPhee was killed with an ax and I reckon so was Mr. Janacek. They slaughtered us, Sheriff. They shot into the wagon and . . . and Lou tried to surrender and a man on a tall horse came and split his head open with an ax."

Purdy was in shock, beyond thinking logically. Now he tried to get it together. "Bobby, how do you know this?" he said.

"I escaped and hid in the brush. I saw it all. Then a man pissed on my head. I need your canteen, Sheriff. I smell real bad."

"But how did —"

"He didn't know I was there."

Young as he was, Bobby saw that the sheriff was numb from the impact of what he'd told him. He stepped around Purdy and removed the canteen from his horse. The bay favored its right foreleg, holding the hoof off the ground.

The boy lifted the canteen over his head and let the water tumble over his hair and face. Purdy watched him, a detached expression on his ashen face.

"I'm not going back there, Sheriff," Bobby said, strands of wet hair falling over his forehead. "Nothing on earth could make me go back."

"But what about the town?" Purdy said. "What's to become of Broken Bridle? So many men . . ."

Bobby realized the young sheriff was talking to himself, not to him, and he didn't answer.

Purdy stared into the darkness, at the moon-silvered peaks of the Rattlesnake Hills. Now the racketing roars of the guns were silent, the land was hushed, and the whispering wind sounded like the voices of the dead.

Bobby drank from the canteen, wiped off

his mouth, then said, "We'd better go back to town and get help, Sheriff."

Purdy roused like a man awaking from a deep sleep. "Help? There is no help. All the men are dead." He gathered the reins of his horse and handed them to the boy. "Take him back to town."

"Where are you headed, Sheriff?" Bobby said.

Purdy nodded in the direction of the hills. "There."

"Why?"

"To make some arrests."

"You're crazy," the boy said. He grabbed Purdy's arm. "You'll get your head split open like the others."

"I plan to arrest Thomas Clouston and see him hang for murder," the sheriff said, wrenching himself away from Bobby's grasp.

Bobby Miller had been raised hard in a succession of vile foster homes where he'd been beaten and worked like a slave. He'd run away from such a home six months before and now worked odd jobs around town, bedding down where he could and eating when someone felt inclined to pay him. As a result of years of hardscrabble survival he was wise beyond his age, and he revealed that now.

"After you're dead, Sheriff, and you will

be, what about the people left in Broken Bridle?" he asked. "What about the women and children with no menfolk to protect them?"

Purdy stared at the small, thin teenager as if seeing him for the first time. Bobby Miller's eyes stared back at him, as big and round as silver dollars. Whatever he'd seen had thrust him into adulthood in the course of a single night. He'd been forced to grow up too fast too soon, just another casualty of Thomas Clouston's mad ambition.

The sheriff made up his mind, the reality of his situation hitting him like a bucket of cold water.

"You're right, we'll go back," he said. Purdy struggled for words to justify his action but couldn't find any. Finally he settled on, "We'll . . . regroup."

Bobby could have said, "Regroup what?" but he bit his tongue and said nothing.

The haloed moon had dropped, leaving room for the stars, and the breeze rustled from the south, scented with sage and pine.

Purdy let his hobbling horse set the pace, Bobby Miller walking close beside him, as though for protection.

The sheriff walked with his head lowered, deep in thought, but he had lost his way and could think only of problems that had no solutions.

CHAPTER THIRTY-SEVEN

At dawn Shawn O'Brien stood at his open hotel room window and watched women gather in the street. There were no wails, not yet, just worry and concern for husbands and sons.

During his time in England, Shawn remembered seeing an illustration in the *London Review* of grim, shawled women standing vigil at a Welsh coal mine as they waited for news of the two hundred and fifty men and boys trapped below after an explosion. All the miners died and their once-thriving village, unable to sustain such a loss, died with them.

Oskar Janacek and his men had not yet returned. Had they suffered a similar fate?

Shawn dressed hurriedly and pounded on Hamp Sedley's door. "Get up!" he yelled. "Meet me in the street!"

Without waiting for an answer, Shawn ran downstairs and onto the hotel porch. Pete

Caradas already lounged against a post on the opposite boardwalk outside the Streetcar Saloon. He wore a red robe with a velveteen black collar, Turkish carpet slippers, and smoked a cigar. A cautious man, his gun belt was slung over his left shoulder.

Shawn was halfway across the street when Caradas answered the question he had not yet asked. "Dead or alive, they're still out there," he said.

Shawn glanced at the score of women gathered in the street. Most stared fixedly in the direction of the Rattlesnake Hills, but a few pale faces turned to him and Caradas, anguished wives and mothers looking for someone, anyone, to blame for what they sensed was now an impending disaster.

Hamp Sedley stepped out of the hotel and crossed the street, an irritated scowl on his face, a nocturnal creature forced to face the searing light of dawn.

"What the hell?" was his surly greeting.

"The wagon hasn't come back yet," Shawn said.

Hamp looked at the women. "Seems like the ladies have buried them already," he said. He opened his mouth to say further, then snapped it shut.

The drums started again. The beat was the same, slow, monotonous, intimidating, designed by the warped genius of a malevolent psychiatrist to drive people mad.

Judging by the reaction of the women of Broken Bridle, he'd succeeded. They held to each other, sobbing. Older women who could find no comfort of their own desperately tried to bring it to the young and the vulnerable. But hope hadn't yet died. There was always a possibility their men had triumphed and had lingered in the hills to bury the dead and deal with prisoners.

Shawn decided it was time to end the uncertainty.

"Hamp, I'm riding out to take a look," he said. "You want to come?"

"You don't need to ask me that," Sedley said. He seemed offended.

"Pete, will you join us?" Shawn said. "We could use your gun."

Caradas shook his head. "Like I said before, my job is to stick right here."

"How is Becker this morning?" Shawn said.

"Still the same. If he improves you'll be the first to know."

Shawn nodded. "I'd appreciate it."

Caradas's voice dropped to a whisper. "They're all dead, you know."

"Maybe. But I reckon I'll settle it one way or the other."

"O'Brien, don't ride into those hills. Not today," Caradas said.

"I'll study on that, Pete," Shawn said.

Caradas tossed his cigar butt into the street. "Then you ride careful," he said. He turned and walked into the saloon.

"Hell, does ol' Pete know something we don't?" Sedley said.

"I reckon not. He just doesn't like the odds."

"That makes two of us," Sedley said.

Shawn smiled. "No it doesn't. It makes all three of us."

Petsha and Milos D'eth stood outside the livery and watched the women gather in the street. They'd been very aware of the presence of Pete Caradas and Shawn O'Brien, guns to step around until their work here was done.

Milos broke his morning silence. "He will come to us," he said.

"Perhaps," Petsha said.

"We should be ready."

Petsha nodded. "The clock will soon strike midnight."

The promise of a bright morning was stillborn as purple thunderheads piled high above the Granite Mountains to the south and threatened to drive north on the prevailing wind. The air was thick with the scent of sage and the breeze was cool, but the growing gloom of the day boded ill, like a black-cloaked figure stalking a dark alley.

"Ahead of us," Shawn said.

"I see them," Sedley said.

Shawn slid the Winchester from the boot under his knee. His eyes searched into distance. "Two of them, leading a horse."

"Clouston's men?" Sedley said.

"Could be, but I don't think so. One of them looks like a half-grown boy."

The drums were silent and the brushy slopes of the Rattlesnake Hills seemed deserted. Apart from a few white clouds, the sky above the peaks was still a flawless blue, like an upturned Wedgewood bowl. But thunder to the south growled threats and the wind picked up.

Shawn drew rein and Sedley put a couple of yards of separation between them, then did the same. They waited.

When the man leading the horse drew closer, Sedley said, "Hell, it's the college boy and he's got some kid protecting him."

Shawn said nothing. By the slump of Purdy's shoulders and his lame horse, Shawn figured Purdy had met with little success. But where had the boy come from?

When the young sheriff was within talking distance, Sedley said, "Howdy, Sheriff, out for a morning stroll?"

Purdy ignored that. His gray features were hollow and shadowed, like the face of a dead man, and his eyes behind his glasses peered, blinking, at Shawn O'Brien without really seeing him.

"We took you for the mad doctor's men," the boy said. "I thought we were done for."

Shawn swung out of the saddle, fetched his canteen, and handed it to the boy. "Take a drink," he said. He waited until the kid drank about a pint of water, then said, "What's your name, son?"

"Bobby Miller. I —"

"They're all dead, O'Brien," Purdy said. He looked like a sleepwalker.

"Did you see them, Sheriff?" Shawn said.

Purdy didn't hear. "Thirteen men of the town, a banker, lawyer, brewer, merchants . . . husbands, fathers, sons . . . all dead."

"I escaped," Bobby Miller said. "That's how come I'm here."

"Tell me how it happened," Shawn said.

The boy told the same story as Purdy had heard. He used words sparingly, but his expressive brown eyes revealed by turns horror, disbelief, wonder, and primitive terror.

When Bobby stopped talking there were tears on his sallow cheeks. Shawn patted the boy on his shoulder and told him he'd done good.

"I don't feel so good," Bobby said.

Suddenly Jeremiah Purdy woke from his lethargy.

"O'Brien, I'm commandeering your horse," he said. "I have arrests to make. I have people to bring to justice. I have murderers to hang. I have . . ." The young sheriff stopped, blinked a few times, then buried his face in his hands and sobbed.

Hamp Sedley, much embarrassed by this emotional display, turned away and suddenly saw something of great interest on the far horizon. For his part, Shawn, born to the volatile Irish temperament and its heart-scalding moments of grief, understood what Purdy was going through. The sheriff wasn't much more than a boy himself and ill-suited to handle the monumental tragedy that had befallen him.

"Bobby, escort Sheriff Purdy home," he said. "Let the horse set the pace. He's real sore-footed."

"What will you do, mister?" Bobby said.

"I don't rightly know. See if there's anybody left alive, I guess, and hope I run into Thomas Clouston."

"I hope you don't," the boy said. He turned away and took Purdy by the arm. "You ready to go, Sheriff?" he said.

The young lawman nodded, never lifting his eyes from the ground. Every man has a limit on what he can endure and still function, and Purdy had reached his.

Shawn thought it sad. Sedley thought it weak. And Jeremiah Purdy didn't think about it at all.

The evidence of the massacre remained, though the bloody-beaked crows had been busy and elegant buzzards glided against an iron-gray sky. Thunder rolled and lightning flickered over the landscape like limelight illuminating a darkened stage.

The horse team was gone and the sprawled, ashen dead had been stripped of their weapons. Two of the men, Oskar Janacek and one other whom Shawn didn't know, had massive head wounds.

Like a nervous tic, Hamp Sedley's gun hand kept dropping to the butt of his holstered Colt. "I don't see anything, do you?" he said.

"Not a damn thing," Shawn said.

"Rain's coming," Sedley said.

"Seems like," Shawn said. Then, "We'll ride into the hills, see if there's any sign of Clouston and his men."

"And if there is?" Sedley said. "What do we do then?"

"Hightail it," Shawn said. "Maybe we'll get a chance to count numbers before they spot us." He shrugged into his slicker. "I'm not too confident about what I just said."

"I'm not too confident about what you just said, either," Sedley said.

He proceeded to button into a gigantic black oilskin with SS SPINDRIFT painted on the back. Answering Shawn's unanswered question, Sedley said, "Won it from a sailor-man and I've been lugging it around ever since."

"It becomes you," Shawn said.

"No it doesn't, but it keeps me dry, well, mostly dry."

Shawn smiled. "Let's ride, thou apparition."

"Nothing," Hamp Sedley said, rain dripping off the brim of his hat. "Miles and miles of nothing."

Shawn O'Brien scanned barren hills misted by the downpour and low cloud. "They must have a camp nearby," he said. A flash of lightning illuminated the clean-

259

cut planes of his face and added electric blue to his eyes. "Damn it all, Hamp, they must be close."

"We could search if we had a regiment of cavalry," Sedley said. "But since we don't have one of them, I say we head back to town and arrange for the bodies to be collected."

"Yes, I guess so," Shawn said. "But who would want to be in Broken Bridle tonight?"

"Nobody. But we got it to do," Sedley said.

Shawn nodded. "All right, then let's get it done."

Rain drummed on Sedley's oilskin. His face was drawn, dark, without humor. "How long do you give the town?" he asked.

"Who knows?" Then, "Not long."

"And us?"

Shawn reached into his slicker and brought out a black and silver rosary. He removed his hat and slid the beads over his head and let the cross hang on his chest.

"Bury me with it, Hamp," he said.

CHAPTER THIRTY-EIGHT

Dr. Thomas Clouston was going a-courtin'.

The thunderstorm that caught up with him shortly after he left camp had cramped his style somewhat, but under his cloak he wore a suit of gray broadcloth, a celluloid collar, and a red-and-white-striped tie. Deeming it unsuitable for a gentleman caller, he'd left his battle-ax at home, but a pearl-handled Colt rode in a shoulder holster under his coat. He held a bouquet of wildflowers tied with a black ribbon.

That Judy Campbell might reject his advances didn't enter Clouston's thinking. He was sophisticated and charming, a man of the world, and what young woman in her right mind could resist him? The icing on the cake was that soon he'd be obscenely rich.

Clouston smiled to himself. Why, pretty Judy would leap headfirst into his bed.

The hilly scrub country gave way to grassy

flats, and here and there stood stands of timber and hardwoods. Fat cattle sheltered from the storm under the trees, and once Clouston watched a grizzly drag something dead and bloody into the brush.

He followed the course of Dry Creek south, then swung west in the direction of the Four Ace ranch. There was no letup from the rain, and lightning scrawled across the ashen sky like the signature of a demented god. But Clouston rode on, confident that a man of his stature would come to no harm.

In that he was correct.

A racketing rain falling around him, he drew rein outside the Campbell house. The day was dark; lamps glowed inside with orange light, and a ribbon of smoke rose from the chimney.

A tall puncher wearing a slicker stepped from the barn and saw Clouston. He stepped to the man and said, "They're probably in the kitchen. Better knock on the door."

Clouston nodded and swung out of the saddle. He turned and peered closely at the puncher, a middle-aged man with a lot of gray in his hair.

"Take my horse to the barn," he said.

"Take it your ownself," the puncher said.

"Listen, when I tell a man to do a thing he does it," Clouston said.

"And when you see me do this" — the puncher shook his head — "it means I ain't doing it."

"Then you're insane," Clouston said.

"And you're the one standing out in the rain," the puncher said.

He turned on his heel and walked toward the bunkhouse.

Clouston watched the man go and was wishful for his Spanish ax. But now was not the time and place. Perhaps he'd get a chance to kill the lout later.

His train of thought was interrupted when the house door opened and a tall, lean man said, "Can I help you?"

"Yes, my good man," Clouston said. "And who might you be?"

"I might be anybody. But my name is Duncan Campbell and this is my house."

"Ah, then you must be Miss Judy's father."

"I am. And who are you?"

"My name is Dr. Thomas Clouston."

"Then you're the man who saved my daughter from an attack. She told me about you."

"I am honored," Clouston said. "That she would remember me so."

"Come in, man," Campbell said. "I'll have

one of the hands tend to your horse."

With a last glance at the lowering, thunder-torn sky, Campbell closed the door behind Clouston and himself and said, "Come into the parlor. I have a good fire going to keep away the dampness. Let me take your cloak and hat." Then, "You brought flowers I see."

"Yes. They're wilted, I'm afraid. Is Miss Judy to home?"

"She's in her room. Once I see you settled with a whiskey in your hand I'll fetch her."

Bound by his Scottish heritage and the code of the West, Duncan Campbell was duty bound to offer hospitality to a stranger. But there was an arrogance and coldness about Dr. Clouston that put him on edge. He just didn't like the man and he resented his calling on his daughter, about thirty years his junior.

Now that Clouston was freed of his cloak and hat, Campbell saw him as a tall, stately man with gray hair falling to his slight, narrow shoulders. But the doctor did not have a good face. The man's mouth was small and mean and hinted at cruelty, and his blue eyes were without warmth, as icy as his demeanor. Standing aloof and distant in the parlor, he looked more undertaker than suitor.

Campbell ushered Clouston into a chair by the fire, then said, "A dram of scotch?"

"Please," the doctor said. He sat stiffly, not a muscle in his body relaxed.

Campbell handed Clouston a filled glass, waited, and when he saw his guest had not tasted his drink, he said, "The whiskey is not to your liking?"

Clouston raised the glass to his lips. "It's adequate," he said. "My intention was to visit with Miss Judy."

"I'll get her," Campbell said. He was irritated that the man had damned his scotch with such faint praise. A fine single malt adequate indeed!

Thomas Clouston was stunned. Judy Campbell was even more beautiful than he remembered.

Her unbound hair fell in amber waves over her shoulders, and her peach morning dress revealed every voluptuous curve of her firm young body.

Clouston wanted her. He had to have her. Like an art connoisseur hoards a stolen great master, he'd lock her away for only him to enjoy. Such loveliness was for his eyes and his eyes only.

Clouston rose to his feet and bowed. "I hope I haven't come at an inopportune time, Miss Campbell."

"Not at all," Judy said. "The storm is doing an excellent job of keeping us all indoors." Her smile, though dazzling, was tentative, unsure. She hardly knew this man, yet she owed him her life.

Clouston picked up the bouquet that he'd dropped on the parlor table. "I brought you flowers," he said. "But I fear they are sadly wilted."

Judy took the bouquet and smiled again. "It's the thought that counts, and I love wildflowers. Please be seated."

Clouston waited until the girl sat and then he took his chair again.

Judy resettled the burning logs with an iron poker, then said, "A fire in the middle of summer. You must think us strange, Mr. Clouston, but this old house does get damp."

"My dear girl it's *Doctor* Clouston, and I don't think anything you do is strange. Au contraire, you are very sane. I observed signs of madness in one of your father's hired hands, but none in you."

Judy smiled. "Well, thank you, I think. What kind of doctor are you?"

"I am a psychiatrist. I make a study of the human mind."

"I rather fancy that there are few chances

to practice your profession in the Rattle-snake Hills, Doctor."

Clouston's smile had all the warmth of a grinning alligator. "You are correct about that, dear lady. But as of now I am resting from practice. All at once the manifold tensions of treating the mentally ill became too much of a burden, and I fled west to get away from it all for a while."

"But you will return soon, I trust," Judy said, trying to keep the hope from her voice. Clouston's eyes had already stripped her to her underwear, and he was working on the rest.

"One day, perhaps, with a beautiful bride at my side," the man said. "And, of course, that is the reason I'm paying court to you, my child."

The girl was thoroughly alarmed. "I don't think I'm ready for marriage," she said. "Not for a few years at least."

Clouston took a large S-shaped pipe from an inside pocket, stuck it in his teeth, and stepped to the window. Judy could only see the back of his head, which was a mercy because his face bore a furious expression that bordered on the demonic.

But his voice was level when he said, "The storm shows no sign of abating. I fear I will have a most unpleasant return journey, especially since my quest has apparently failed."

Trapped by the manners of her time and place, Judy said, "Then you must stay the night, Dr. Clouston. We have plenty of room."

Clouston let a triumphant smile flicker and die on his lips before he turned and said, "My dear young lady, that would be a most singular kindness. I'm a rather timid creature by nature, and the thought of a trail beset by thunder and lightning makes me most anxious. But pray you, will not your father mind a stranger under his roof?"

"No, he will make you most welcome," Judy said. "That is his way."

The girl's dress rustled as she rose to her feet. "I'm afraid I must leave you for a while, Doctor. I have some duties in the kitchen. But I'm sure you'd like to smoke your pipe, and my father will be in directly."

"I put you at a great inconvenience," Clouston said, bowing.

"Not at all," Judy said. She stepped out of the parlor feeling stark naked.

CHAPTER THIRTY-NINE

Dinner at the Four Ace ranch passed quite well, despite the baleful presence of Dr. Thomas Clouston and Duncan Campbell's growing dislike for the man. He saw how the white-haired man's eyes lingered on his daughter's breasts every time he spoke to her and his less-than-subtle innuendoes about returning east with a young bride.

The meal was saved by the presence of the new ranch foreman, a large, jolly man named Johnny "Big Boy" Harrison who was a former seaman, peace officer, army scout, and sometime stage actor. He had a fund of stories about his adventures and people he'd met, including the diva Lillie Langtry who'd once given him a kiss backstage in a New Jersey theater.

"On the lips?" Judy asked, drawing a rebuke from her puritanical father.

Big Boy grinned. "Nah." He pointed to his left cheek. "She laid one on me right here. I didn't shave for a month, well, at least until her lip rouge wore off."

Clouston didn't join in the laughter that followed, but when it ended he said, "Was she insane, this Lillie Langtry? All actors are, you know."

Big Boy was baffled. "No . . . I don't reckon so."

"What did she say? After she kissed you, what were her exact words?" Clouston said.

"She gave me some advice," Big Boy said.

"Ah ha! Now we reach the crux of the matter." Clouston, who had eaten very little, laid his fork on the plate. "Were they the words of a madwoman?"

The big foreman looked uncomfortable. "Good roast beef, boss," he said to Campbell.

"Come now, my man, Lillie Langtry's exact words," Clouston said. "I must hear them." His eyes were on fire.

"Well, near as I can recollect, she said, 'John, anyone's life truly lived consists of work, sunshine, exercise, soap, plenty of fresh air, and a happy, contented spirit.' Yup, I guess that's about it."

"Sounds like sane advice to me," Duncan Campbell said, chewing.

"Perhaps," Clouston said. "But the sanity of the female of the species is very suspect, especially when it comes to deciding what is good for them."

He stared hard at Judy when he said it, and her father said, "Big Boy, tell us about the starving feller down to the Texas Glass Mountains country who ate his mother-in-law that time."

"Do we have to?" Judy said, making a face.

"Sure you do," Big Boy said. "The cannibal's name was Hope Hooper and he was a rascal. His mother-in-law was the only Democrat in Brewster County and that's how come he ate her."

"Did you know him, Mr. Harrison," Judy said.

"Well, we weren't kissin' kin or anything like that, but since I was the feller who shot him, I guess we had a bond."

The talk continued and Judy laughed a great deal, but Clouston had dropped out of the conversation, sitting upright and morose in his chair. He didn't like Big Boy. The man was obviously mentally ill, and the doctor badly wanted to split the man's skull open with his battle-ax.

Shortly before eleven as Duncan Campbell and his daughter readied themselves for bed, Thomas Clouston excused himself with the pretense that he wanted to check on his horse.

"Please don't stay awake for me," he said. "I can find my own way to my room."

When he stepped outside, the rain had ended but lightning still flashed within the clouds and the night air smelled of a further downpour to come.

By the light of a single lantern, Clouston led his horse from its stall and saddled the sleepy animal with little haste. There was no rush. The plan he had in mind would take time to mature.

He turned down the lantern, led the horse to the barn door, and looked around outside. Good. There was no one in sight. The hands had already sought their bunks, and the only sound was the steady tick of rain from the barn roof and a distant rumble of thunder. The night was black as ink as Clouston tied his horse to the cast iron post outside the house. When he stepped inside a single candle burned in the hallway to light his way upstairs. He smiled. How just too, too touchingly thoughtful.

After he entered his room, Clouston blew out the candle and pulled a straight-backed chair to the window, sat, and stared out into the dreary night.

He was still there an hour later.

When the old grandfather clock in the hallway downstairs first chimed midnight, Clouston rose to his feet like an automaton. He checked the loads in his Colt, then shoved the pistol back into the holster.

From his pants pocket he took a large, blue and white polka dot bandanna and spun it into a sausage shape. Now was the time to proceed with stealthy tread, like a man tiptoeing through a graveyard on All Hallows' Eve.

Testing the tautness of the bandanna, Clouston slowly stepped to the door and let himself out into the hallway. After its chiming exertions, the grandfather clock now tick-tocked contentedly downstairs and patiently waited for the opportunity to strike one. Lightning shimmered inside the darkened house as he stood and listened, the bandanna stretched tight between his hands.

There were three bedrooms upstairs. Stentorian snores from behind the door at the end of the hallway marked Duncan Campbell's, so the one opposite Clouston's own must be Judy's.

On cat feet the man stepped to the door. The house was well built and the floorboard did not creak.

Clouston tried the door handle. It turned easily and he pushed. Excellent! It wasn't locked. Such sane, trusting souls. He smiled. Little did they know that they had a bogey-man in their midst.

Judy Campbell lay on her back, her hair spread across the white pillow like spilled red wine. Under the sheet her breasts rose and fell with every breath, and her long, shapely legs were outlined, slightly open in unconscious invitation.

Clouston licked his lips and advanced on the bed. Duncan Campbell still snored and that was good, very good. Clouston knew his merry men would have laughed to see how slyly he crept up on the sleeping girl, the bandanna a tight garrote in his fisted hands. This had to be done swiftly and without sound.

Like a crouching shadow in the darkness, Clouston bent over the bed for a moment. Then, like a predatory animal, he hurled himself on top of the sleeping girl.

Judy Campbell's eyes few open and she tried to scream, but Clouston gagged her with the bandanna, then knotted it tightly at the back of her neck. He dragged her from the bed and threw her over his left shoulder, aware of the firm shape of her body under the sheer silk of her nightdress.

The girl struggled, fighting the gag, but

Clouston rammed the muzzle of his colt into her temple and said, "Quit that or I'll kill you and then your father."

Suddenly the girl went limp. Because of his threat or the fact that she'd fainted Clouston did not know, nor did he care. She was quiet and had ceased to struggle, and that was all that mattered.

The girl was slender and Clouston did not feel particularly burdened as he carried her out of the bedroom and into the hallway. There was now no sound from Duncan Campbell's room, and he made haste to take to the stairs. But he grabbed his cloak and hat from the rack without undue hurry and stepped out the front door.

Despite the lightning and pattering rain, Clouston's horse stood placidly at the hitching post. Clouston threw Judy over his saddle and then mounted. He grabbed the girl and held her close to him and walked his horse away from the ranch house.

After a while, riding through murk, Thomas Clouston tilted back his head and laughed. It had all been so damned easy. He'd been a wolf among sheep and stolen a woman from them without their notice, just as nice as you please.

He figured his future plans would go even better. When he conquered Broken Bridle, the sheep would run, he'd drive the Chinese north, get rich, and take time to enjoy his new woman.

For Thomas Clouston life was good, and he reveled in it.

Judy Campbell had feared for her father's life and had feigned unconsciousness. Now she struggled again and said, "Where are you taking me?"

Clouston grinned. "To my home, of course. But first to my camp near the Rattlesnake Hills."

"My father will come after you," Judy said. "He'll find you and kill you."

"Is that right, my child?" Clouston said.

"You betrayed his hospitality."

"What a shame. But in doing so I've gained a bride."

"I'll never marry you," Judy said. She struggled and strands of wet hair fell over her forehead.

"Depend on it, my dear, you will. All women are whores at heart, and when you discover that you will live like a queen you'll gladly accept my ring and my bed."

"I'd rather die first," the girl said.

"That can also be arranged, and I assure you, you will find it a most unpleasant experience." Clouston scowled. "Now shut your trap and leave me to my thoughts."

The certainty came to Judy Campbell that this was the man who'd kidnapped Jane Collins. And if that was the case the poor girl was already dead . . . or wishing she was.

CHAPTER FORTY

Broken Bridle lay under a pall of mourning made more somber by the thunderstorms that came in flashing, roaring bands and threatened never to leave.

The blue-faced bodies arrived in a freight wagon that parked outside city hall, and when Oskar Janacek's four-hundred-pound wife saw what had happened to her husband she collapsed in the street. It took three men to lift her onto the boardwalk where smelling salts were administered and then brandy. But Andrea Janacek rallied when she saw the emotional state of the young widows. She insisted on getting to her feet, and then she hugged them to her ample chest and comforted them as she would crying children.

But in the end it did little good. People were already leaving town.

By midafternoon the hardware store was closed and locked after Mark Logan the proprietor loaded his wife and three children onto a wagon and left for places unknown. Carson's Rod & Gun followed. Big, laughing Andy Carson and his wife left in the company of the baker Lucas Mellon and his wife Agatha with their brood of seven.

More were preparing to leave the next day, filling wagons and even handcarts with supplies and a few sticks of furniture. They were determined to escape Broken Bridle as though it was doomed Sodom.

If nothing was done to stop the exodus, Shawn O'Brien estimated that Broken Bridle would be a ghost town within a week.

When Shawn said this to Sheriff Jeremiah Purdy, the young lawman stared at him, his eyes empty behind the owl glasses. The man was broken and seemed too dispirited to pick up the pieces.

"What do you want me to do, O'Brien?" he said. "You saw what happened when we tried."

"Organize the defense of the town," Shawn said, suddenly angry. "In other words, do your damned job."

Purdy glanced out the office window. "Will this rain never end?" he said.

Hamp Sedley, horrified by what he'd seen in the hills, was on a short fuse. He pulled his Colt and thumbed back the hammer.

"Purdy, git out of the chair or by God I'll shoot you out of it."

"Go ahead," the sheriff said. "You'd be doing me a favor."

"Hamp! Let it go," Shawn said. "Broken Bridle can't afford any more dead men."

Sedley hesitated, his finger on the revolver's hair trigger, and Shawn whispered, "I said let it go."

The gambler thumbed down the hammer and shoved the Colt back into its holster. To Purdy he said, "You make me sick. Go on, get out of here and become a politician and kiss babies. It's the only job you're fit for."

"I'm not fit for any job," Purdy said. He pulled the star off his shirt and hurled it into a corner. "Especially this one."

Shawn stared at the young man for a long time, saw nothing to reassure him, and said, "Hamp, let's go see if Burt Becker is awake."

"Why, Shawn?" Sedley said. "We came here to help Purdy. Well, he doesn't want our help and we can't go out there and stop the great skedaddle, so I say we cut our losses and light a shuck with the rest of them. I mean, while we still can."

"Before we do anything, we'll go see Becker," Shawn said.

Sedley let out a wearisome sigh. "Well, I

tried to warn you."

For cowboys coming in off the trail, Broken Bridle was a glittering metropolis, a mecca for sin and debauchery where sex and booze came easily but never cheap. But in fact it was a Frontier cow town like any other, small, dusty, fly-specked, the buildings huddled close, its only contact with the outside world and its reason for existing at all the slender thread of a single railroad track.

Thus it was that the weeping and wailing of widows and bereaved mothers in a close-packed town produced a keening noise, a low, nerve-scraping whine like an out-of-tune violin.

"Like lilies in the rain, aren't they?" Pete Caradas said when Shawn and Sedley stopped at his table. As was his habit, he sat in his robe at a table in the Streetcar drinking coffee with his morning bourbon. A sleepy girl with mussed hair sat next to him, her shift revealing too much leg and breast.

"We need Becker," Shawn said. "You saw what happened."

"I saw the aftermath of what happened. Funny, I was always told steady infantry would defeat cavalry. I guess that's all wrong."

"They were drunk," Sedley said. "They were mighty unsteady infantry."

"A massacre they call it," Caradas said.

"It was," Shawn said.

"You know the Chinese left in the night, don't you?" Caradas said. Shawn was shocked and the draw fighter smiled and said, "I can see you don't."

"They were mighty quiet about it," the girl said. "Usually they're the noisiest people God put on earth."

"The thunderstorm provided good cover," Caradas said. "And of course the town was busy with other concerns and didn't notice."

"Why would they just pull out like that?" Sedley said. "They scared of the crazy doc like everybody else?"

"I don't know," Caradas said. "The women and children are gone, so I reckon that means they don't intend to ever come back."

Shawn said, "This has something to do with Clouston, I'm sure of it."

"Seems like he's the main troublemaker around here," Caradas said. "So it's likely. Clouston makes Burt Becker look like an altar boy."

"Is the altar boy awake and taking nourishment?" Sedley said.

"I don't know. Sunny Swanson is up there

with him. Why don't you ask her?"

"I'll do that," Shawn said. He turned for the stairs, but Caradas said, "Folks pulling out, O'Brien."

"Seems like," Shawn said.

"You should go with them, O'Brien," Caradas said. "There's nothing for you here now."

"Some will stick," Shawn said. "And what about the widows and the orphans? How will they get out with their menfolk dead?"

Caradas smiled. "O'Brien, unlike you, Burt hasn't suddenly got religion. He couldn't care less about widows and orphans. There's no money in it."

"Maybe I can convert him," Shawn said.

"I wouldn't count on it," Caradas said. "I wouldn't count on that at all."

Sunny Swanson looked tired, but when she saw Shawn O'Brien she merely looked angry. "Are you here to gloat again?" she said.

"You know what's happened to this town, Sunny?" Hamp Sedley said.

"Should I care? I'm a whore and that's how this burg treated me . . . like a whore. I don't give a damn if the whole place burns to the ground."

"There must be people in this town who

never did you any harm," Shawn said.

"Name them," Sunny said. Then, "Burt is awake, but he's still not right in the head. He says he's being haunted by men with no skins and they scare him. It's hard to understand him because Dr. Walsh still has his jaw bound up tight. But he says there's gold in the Rattlesnake Hills and Thomas Clouston is trying to steal it from him."

Sedley snapped his fingers. "Damn it, now I remember something that's been bothering me. Shawn, you recall hearing the name Last Chance Pike, a prospector from over New Mexico way?"

"I think I heard my father or one of my brothers mention that name. Maybe it was Jake. He knows everybody."

"Pike had two simple sons and a wayward daughter. None of them came to any good, and I recollect that the youngest boy was hung. Or was it the oldest? I can't —"

"Hamp, where are you going with this?" Shawn asked, a tinge of urgency in his voice. "I have to talk to Becker."

"I'm sneaking up on it, Shawn. A few years back when I was dealing faro in Abilene I heard Pike tell another tinpan that if you can find yourself a belt of greenstone, you can find mineable gold. Then he talked about how much gold you can take from a good-sized seam."

Shawn opened his mouth to speak but Sedley silenced him with a raised hand. "There's a massive belt of greenstone in the Rattlesnake Hills. I saw it with my own two eyes."

"How come you noticed but nobody else did?" Shawn said. "I didn't see any green-colored stone."

"Pike gave me an eye for it. The seam is well hidden at the base of an overhung rock face, and that makes for mighty dangerous digging. If a man's not careful, the whole damn hill could come down on top of him. Now maybe others did see the greenstone, but to mine a worthwhile amount of gold, you'd have to shift thousands and thousands of tons of rock."

"How much gold would be in that seam you saw, according to what Pike told you?" Shawn said.

"From what I remember, I'd say at least a million ounces, maybe more."

Shawn stood in thought for a while, then said, "That's over thirty tons of gold, about twenty million dollars' worth. There are men who would kill for that."

"A man like Clouston would," Sedley said. "He's proved that already." He smiled.

"How did you calculate that tonnage so easy?"

"I've got a head for figures," Shawn said. Then to Sunny, "Does Becker know there's that much gold in the hills?"

"Sure he does," the girl said. "But he never thought it through like Clouston did. Why do you think Clouston moved the Chinese?"

"Of course. To work the mine for him," Shawn said.

"The Chinese work hard and they work cheap," Sunny said. "Clouston stands to get rich, even if he moves the ore out by train and pays to get it crushed somewhere else."

"And it has to be kept secret until the Chinese cut out all the greenstone. If the news of a strike got out there could be a gold rush," Sedley said. "That's why he wanted everyone gone from Broken Bridle."

"Seems like he got his wish," Sunny said. "The whole town is going to up and leave."

"Not if I can help it," Shawn said. "Now I want to talk to Becker."

"Follow me," Sunny said. "I moved his guns out of the way, O'Brien. He planned to shoot you on sight."

CHAPTER FORTY-ONE

Burt Becker, looking more than ever like a huge rabbit because of the bandage tied on top of his head, saw Shawn O'Brien and growled. He cast around frantically before Shawn removed a Colt from the big man's shoulder holsters and said, "Is this what you're looking for, Burt?"

Shawn spun the revolver, smiled, and shoved it back into the holster.

"Sunny moved the guns over here out of your way," he said. "She thought you might do yourself an injury."

"I'll kill you, O'Brien," Becker said, gritting out the words between clenched teeth.

"Don't get overexcited, Burt," Sedley said. "We're here to talk peace."

Becker's red eyes glared at Sunny and he gestured wildly to his guns on the table beside the door, an angry question on his face.

"Burt, you can't use guns," Sunny said.

"You're not ready yet."

Becker let out a frustrated wail and tried to swing his feet off the cot. But suddenly Shawn's Colt was in his hand and his face was stern.

"Burt, make a move toward your guns and I'll drop you right where you stand," he said. "Don't think about it, and don't try me."

Becker was mad clean through, but he read the writing on the wall and stayed right where he was.

"Did Sunny tell you what happened last night?" Shawn said.

"I haven't told him yet," Sunny said.

"The good citizens of Broken Bridle tried to drive Clouston out of the hills," Shawn said. "They lost thirteen men and now the folks who are left are pulling out. This town is dying, Becker."

Shawn saw in the big man's eyes that there was no point on playing on his compassion. He had none.

"Clouston plans to attack this town and kill everyone in sight," Shawn said. "And he will, unless you and your men are willing to stand up to him."

As he knew he would, Becker shook his head, and when he looked at Shawn his eyes were filled with murder.

"Becker, he's got the Chinese in the hills digging for him," Shawn said. He played his trump card. "If you don't stand up to him and stake your claim on the gold, you'll lose everything, including your life."

Greed is a powerful incentive. Becker's eyebrows lowered as he thought things through. After a few moments he waved Shawn away from him and lay on his back in the cot, staring at the ceiling.

"Leave him now, O'Brien," Sunny said. "You've tired him out." She saw the irritation on Shawn's face and added, "He's thinking about what you said. When he's made up his mind, I'll come for you."

"Don't take too long, Burt," Shawn said. "Time is running out for all of us."

"You still got big rats in there, Sunny," Hamp Sedley said. "They could eat ol' Burt alive."

Alarm flashed in the woman's face. "I'll take care of it," she said.

"You'd better make it fast," Sedley said. "Judging by the racket they're making."

"Hamp, right now we've got more to worry about than rats," Shawn said.

"I hate rats," Sedley said. "They give me the damned shivers."

■ ■ ■ ■

There was no sign of Pete Caradas or his girl when Shawn and Sedley left the saloon. Outside, rain fell from a low, leaden sky and the street and boardwalks were empty of wagons and people, as though the town had lost its will to exist and had come to a standstill.

The two men were about to cross the street to the hotel when they were hailed by Utah Beadles, who'd just stepped out of one of the few stores still open. He carried a pink-and-white-striped paper sack in his hand.

"Howdy, boys," the deputy said. "Got me some mint humbugs. You want to make a trial of them?"

Shawn refused, but Sedley eagerly shoved his hand in the bag. "I love humbugs," he said, sticking the candy in his mouth.

"How is the sheriff?" Shawn said.

"Right poorly, I'd say," Beadles said. His white eye looked like a piece of porcelain. "Fact is he fired me."

"How come?" Sedley said, talking around the huge candy in his mouth.

Shawn was easily irritated that morning, and Hamp and his humbug ruffled his tail feathers. "Stick that in your cheek or spit it out," he said.

"No. I'm enjoying it," Sedley said.

"Sheriff Purdy says there will be no one left in town to pay my wages," Beadles said, saving Sedley from harm. "So he said he was letting me go."

"Stay in town, Utah," Shawn said. "We'll need your gun."

The old man shook his head. "Hell, no. I'm too young to die. I plan to skedaddle like the rest o' them. I can tell you something though."

"What's that?" Shawn said.

"I know where Tom Clouston's camp is. The place where he keeps them damned drums."

"Why didn't you tell the sheriff?" Shawn said.

"I did. But he said to keep it to myself."

"You could have led Oskar Janacek's posse right to the camp," Shawn said.

"And they would have died just the same, me among them," Beadles said. "Besides, them boys wasn't inclined to listen to me, an old coot with one eye and a drinkin' man's reputation."

Sedley was noisily crunching now, and beside him Shawn gritted his teeth. "Where is the camp, Utah?" Hamp said.

"Due west of the Rattlesnakes, boy, about a mile," Beadles said. "It's hidden behind a rise, so even a long-sighted man can't see it from the hills."

"How do you know this, Utah?" Shawn said.

"Saw it on my way here, didn't I?" the old man said. "I steered well clear and that's why I'm standing here talking instead of being as dead as a doorknob."

Beadles extended his candy poke toward Sedley. "Have another," he said.

"No!" Shawn said, slapping Sedley's hand away. "Suck on another humbug, Hamp, and I swear, I'll rip it out of your mouth."

"Kinda touchy, son, ain't you?" Beadles asked.

"This morning? Yes I am," Shawn said.

"Every morning, seems like," Sedley said, miffed.

But the morning was about to get a lot worse for both Shawn and Sedley.

CHAPTER FORTY-TWO

Just before noon Duncan Campbell led six tired, dispirited riders into Broken Bridle, their horses plodding through fetlock-high mud churned up by the ceaseless rain.

The seven men, their wet slickers shedding water, looped their horses to the Streetcar hitching rail and stepped inside, their spurs ringing.

Campbell ordered his men to the bar, then looked around him. Long used to the ways of the West he tagged the tall, handsome man who'd just had his lunch served at a table as a fast gun, probably out of Texas.

There were a few other patrons in the saloon, but the mood was subdued and men sat with solemn faces as though all the cares of the world were on their shoulders. Even the bartender, a magnificent creature with pomaded hair parted in the middle, a brocade vest, and a diamond stickpin, had lost some of his grandeur, like the gilt off the gingerbread.

Campbell told his men to drink up, that they deserved it, then drained his own glass and laid it on the bar for another.

"I'm looking for a man," he said to the bartender. "He goes by the name of Dr. Thomas Clouston. That's what he calls himself."

Campbell was struck by the look of terror that fleeted across the man's face. Finally he said, "You're Mr. Campbell, right? You own a ranch west of here."

"Yes, the Four Ace."

The bartender nodded. "Seen you in town a time or two." He leaned closer to the rancher. "Steer clear of that man, Mr. Campbell, he's poison." Then, "Did you hear what happened in town last night?"

Campbell shook his head and the bartender told him.

When the man's story finished, Campbell looked like he'd aged twenty years in the space of a couple of minutes. His riders were grim-faced, drinking, but saying nothing.

"Oh my God," Duncan Campbell said. "He has my daughter."

"Miss Judy? She was friends with Jane Collins, the young lass that disappeared?"

Campbell nodded. "Jane Collins was my

daughter's best friend. Clouston kidnapped Judy from my house in the early hours of this morning. We searched the Rattlesnake Hills where Clouston is supposed to hang out, but found nothing."

The bartender seemed distressed. He served whiskey to the punchers, then returned to Campbell. "You came here looking for help to find your daughter."

Campbell nodded. He looked drawn and used up, a man at the end of his rope.

"Now you know there isn't any," the bartender said. "Them as would have helped are all dead."

"Then I'll go it alone," Campbell said. "Boys, get ready to ride."

"That's not a real good idea, Mr. Campbell."

The rancher turned to the voice. Pete Caradas had laid down his knife and fork and was looking right at Campbell with curiously dead eyes.

"You have my handle. And you are?" the rancher said.

"Name's Pete Caradas." He stood but did not offer his hand. He'd seen too many men who'd shook on it with their gun hand and died as a result. "Trust me on this, stay here in town and Thomas Clouston will come to you."

"How do you know this?" Campbell said.

"He's made his intentions clear," Caradas said.

"I must find my daughter," Campbell said.

"Your daughter is dead. Get your revenge on Clouston and mourn her later."

"Mister, that's mighty hard talk," Big Boy Harrison said, elbowing off the bar, a mean glint in his eyes.

"This town needs to hear hard talk," Caradas said. "Campbell, ride out to the hills again and I guarantee you'll be dead before nightfall."

"Maybe you and Clouston are in cahoots," Harrison said.

"There's no maybes about you being an idiot," Caradas said.

Harrison absorbed the insult like a punch to the guts and pushed his slicker back from his gun.

"Big Boy, leave it be!" Campbell yelled. "There's no call for gunplay here."

He'd summed up Caradas standing relaxed and confident and knew how it must end if his ramrod went for the iron. Thunder rolled across the sky like a boulder along a marble corridor, and the other saloon patrons sat stiff, eyes empty, waiting. The men of Broken Bridle were numb, beyond shock, content to sit silently as observers.

"Now I'll accept the gentleman's apology," Caradas said.

"Step around it, Caradas," Campbell said.

"The gentleman impugned my honor and it cannot stand," Caradas said.

This was Texas war talk. Duncan Campbell had heard its like before, and he cast around in his mind to end it without a killing. Finally, his options exhausted, he said, "Big Boy, apologize to the gentleman."

But Harrison had sand and there was no backup in him. He spat and said, "Caradas, I won't apologize to the likes of you so be damned to ye."

The unlikely intervention of Hamp Sedley saved Harrison's life.

He barged into the saloon holding Bobby Miller by the scruff of the neck, then shoved the boy into the middle of the floor.

"Caught the little runt trying to loot the general store," he said to the bartender. "He says he's hungry so feed him. You don't need to kick his ass. I've already done that."

"That boy is a nuisance," a man said. "He should be hung."

"Mister, hasn't there been enough killing for your liking?" Sedley said. "He got his ass kicked and that's all he needs."

"And grub," the bartender said. He had two half-grown boys of his own.

For Pete Caradas and Big Boy Harrison, the moment had passed and each in his own way was relieved. Harrison knew he couldn't match Caradas's draw and had hoped to outlast him. Caradas saw no profit in killing a bumbling cowboy, even if he was a ramrod, and his reputation might have suffered. He set his pride aside and sat at his table.

"Boy, get over here," Caradas said. When Bobby fearfully approached the table, he said, "Sit." Then glaring at Sedley. "If you can."

The boy sat and Caradas pushed his plate in front of him. "I've lost my appetite for lunch, eat this, and the bread rolls."

Bobby's eyes bugged. "Steak and eggs," he said.

Caradas nodded. "The steak is overcooked and the eggs aren't over easy the way I wanted them. But make a trial of them anyway."

Bobby Miller needed no further invitation and dug in as though he was missing his last six meals, which he was.

Sedley, with his gambler's instinct for atmosphere, looked from the bartender to the grim-faced Duncan Campbell and back again. "All right, tell me what I missed," he said.

Campbell spoke up. "My daughter was

kidnapped by Thomas Clouston. I came here looking for help."

"And found the cupboard bare," Sedley said.

"That would seem to be the case," Campbell said. "How is Shawn O'Brien?"

"He's doing fine," Sedley said. "He owes Miss Judy and you."

"We did our Christian duty," Campbell said. Then to his riders, "Finish up, boys," he said. "We'll take up the search again."

"Talk to Shawn first," Sedley said. "He always comes up with a plan."

"I'm all out of those," Campbell said. "I'll listen, but only for a few minutes."

"Then come over to the hotel," Sedley said. "Can you trust your boys to stay sober?"

"They know what's at stake," Campbell said.

"Miss Judy's life," Big Boy said.

"You can't attack Clouston's camp with six men," Shawn said. "You'd be like ducks in a shooting gallery."

"That is where my daughter is," Duncan Campbell said. "I won't sit idly by while she's in the clutches of a monster." He rose from his chair, a grim old Scotsman with a stubborn streak. "A mile due west of the

Rattlesnake Hills, you say?"

"That's what Utah Beadles told me. He said he saw the camp."

"Then that's where I'll go, Shawn," Campbell said.

"I can't talk you out of it?" Shawn asked.

"If you were in my position, what would you do?" Campbell said.

"I'd go after my daughter," Shawn said. "No matter the cost."

He rose to his feet and said, "I won't ride with you, Duncan. My place is here in Broken Bridle."

"You're not beholden to me or mine," Campbell said. He extended his hand. "But you can wish me luck."

"With all my heart," Shawn said, taking the old man's hand. "And I'll say a rosary for you."

Campbell smiled. "Ordinarily I'd have no truck with popery, but I reckon I need all the help I can get."

"Stay in town and wait for Clouston to attack," Sedley said. "Beads won't turn bullets."

"Stranger things have happened, Hamp," Campbell said. "Now I have to be on my way." He looked through the window that was running with rain. "I picked a nasty day for it, didn't I?"

■ ■ ■ ■

After Duncan Campbell left, Sedley said, "You'll never see him or his riders again, Shawn. You know that, don't you?"

"He knows what has to be done and he's doing it," Shawn said. "I won't stand in his way."

"He's a dead man," Sedley said.

"Before long, we might all be dead men," Shawn said.

Sedley shook his head. "You sure know how to cheer a man, don't you?"

Shawn O'Brien answered a rap at his room door and found Sunny Swanson, her cape wet from rain, standing there, her face tear-stained.

"He wants to talk to you, O'Brien," she said.

"Are you all right?" Shawn said. "You look like you've been crying."

"Burt won't leave," the girl said. "That means he'll stay in this cursed town and die with the rest of you."

Shawn buttoned into his slicker. "He wants the gold in the hills, Sunny. A man will risk all he's got, including his life, on the throw of the dice for twenty million dollars."

"Would you?" Sunny said.

"No, I wouldn't."

"That's because you're a rich man's son. Money doesn't mean anything to you."

"Maybe not. But if I was Becker and had a woman like you, I'd value her more than all the gold in the world."

"You're talking pretties to me, that's all," Sunny said.

"I mean every word, and some day if Becker has any sense, he'll think as I do."

"You give me hope, O'Brien."

"Good. Because right now it's in mighty short supply around this burg."

Burt Becker ground out each word slowly, like a blacksmith flattening out a chunk of iron. "I'll fight Clouston here," he said.

"Glad to hear it, Burt," Shawn said. "With you and Caradas we can make a fight of it."

Becker again made the effort to talk. "Pete speaks for himself. Coop Hunter, Uriah Spade . . . same thing."

Hamp Sedley said, "Those boys pulled out, Burt. Right after Shawn busted your jaw."

"Wrong thing to say, Hamp," Shawn said.

"Then it's up to Pete," Becker said. "Now

get the hell away from me. I don't want to talk no more."

"Becker, where is Jane Collins?" Shawn said. "You don't need her any longer."

"Ace in the hole . . . still," Becker said through jammed shut teeth. "I get the gold, Purdy gets his woman."

CHAPTER FORTY-THREE

Petsha and Milos D'eth were not in good spirits. The tarot cards never lie, and each time Milos had laid them out the result was always the same: The Death of Twins.

Now Milos picked up the cards from the space he'd cleared on the livery floor and shoved them into his bib overalls. With dread in his eyes, Petsha watched him closely.

"It is always the same," Milos said. "There is no way to change fate."

"Perhaps there are other twins," Petsha said.

"Perhaps," Milos said. "Thomas Clouston must still die. We took on a binding contract."

"Can we run from the cards?" Petsha said. "Ride far?"

"Death will follow. He knows us, Petsha. We bear his mark."

"Then we take the man Clouston with us

and fulfill our contract as we have done twenty-seven times in the past. Is that not so?"

Milos nodded. "Twenty-seven contracts, thirty-eight men that we marked for death. It is a career to be proud of, Petsha."

Petsha made no answer. He stared out the livery door into the rain. "There is the orphan boy who survived the massacre of the innocents," he said. "I want to talk to him. Do you have a silver dollar, Milos?"

After he saw his brother nod, Petsha called out, "You, boy! Come over here."

"Hell, no," Bobby Miller said. "The street's muddy."

"I'll give you a dollar," Petsha said.

"You're up to no good," Bobby said.

"I want only to ask you a question. But if you don't want the dollar, I'll ask it of someone else."

Bobby considered that, then said, "All right, I'll be right over."

As he high-footed it through the mud of the street, the boy nonetheless affected a swagger. Not everyone was invited to share a famous Texas draw fighter's lunch.

Bobby stopped outside the livery, standing in a slanting rain. "What do you want, mister?" he asked.

"You're a brave lad," Petsha said. "You'll go far."

"I know it. Now what do you want?"

"Those seven men who rode into town. Who are they?" Petsha said.

"Where's my dollar?" Bobby said.

Milos spun the coin to his brother and he in turn tossed it to the boy, who caught it expertly in mid-flight. He shoved it into the pocket of his ragged pants, then said, "It's Duncan Campbell the rancher and his punchers. Crazy Dr. Clouston stole his daughter and he wants her back."

"And he's going out to search for her?" Petsha said.

"That is his stated intention," Bobby said, parroting words he'd heard an older man say. Then, "Right now he's talking to Shawn O'Brien, the one they call the Town Tamer."

"Yes, I've heard of him," Petsha said. "But you have no town to tame."

"Well then, I guess that's his problem." Bobby looked beyond the D'eth brothers into the livery. "Did you see that?"

"See what?" Petsha said.

"A shadow back there. Big, real big. It moved fast," the boy said.

"I didn't see it," Petsha said.

"Looked like a spook to me," Bobby said.

"I mean, it was huge and blacker than anything."

"You have an active imagination, boy. Go now," Petsha said.

With a youngster's capacity to dismiss a disturbing happening from his mind, Bobby smiled and said, "Thanks for the dollar, mister."

He turned, waded back to the boardwalk, and vanished into an alley.

Petsha turned to his brother. "Milos, did you see it?"

Milos shook his head. "No, but I felt its breath and it was cold as ice. The angel of death is without mercy. It heeds no pleas, no prayers, no promises. It strikes, kills, then moves on."

"Then so be it," Petsha said. "We will meet our death like Romani as our mother taught us."

"And woe betide the one who calls himself Dr. Thomas Clouston," Milos said. "He will join us in hell."

"We'll follow the man Campbell and see where he leads us," Petsha said. "There is no time to fetch our horses, so we will ride the mount we have."

Milos nodded but was silent. There was nothing further to say. Whatever happened now was in the lap of the gods.

CHAPTER FORTY-FOUR

Dr. Thomas Clouston was so enamored of his new bride-to-be that he was reluctant to let her out of his sight even for a moment.

"You'll be quite comfortable there, my dear," he said. "Close to my chair."

In fact Judy Campbell was chained by one ankle to an iron staple driven into a two-hundred-pound slab of rock in what Clouston called his parlor. The stretched tarp that served as a roof kept out most of the rain, and logs blazed in the fireplace.

"Clouston, my father will kill you for this," the girl said. She looked up at the man from her place on the floor. "He'll hunt you down and hang you."

"You grow tiresome, Judy," Clouston said, smoke curling from the bowl of his pipe. "Be thankful that so far I've treated you with respect and that your maidenly honor is still intact."

"I'm a whore," Judy said, venom tight in

her voice. "I've lain with a hundred men, two hundred, I've lost count."

Clouston smiled, at ease in his chair. "If I thought that I'd loose you to my boys and let them have their way with you. But lucky for you, my dear, I don't believe a word you say."

"Believe that my father will come for me," Judy said.

"He might. But then there's no fool like an old fool, is there?" Clouston said. "Your father is quite insane."

A man coughed outside and Clouston said, "Come in, Hansen."

A big, bearded man stepped under the roof tarp, leered at Judy Campbell, then said, "Now they put tents up the Chinese have settled. But feeding them is going to be a problem, especially when they start digging tomorrow."

"There's a shipment of rice and dried cod coming down by rail from Casper with the mining equipment," Clouston said.

"I know, boss, but now I hear a derailment will delay the delivery for at least three days, maybe longer," Hansen said.

"Well, feed them from our own supplies," Clouston said. "Damn it all, man, tiny people don't eat much."

"Boss, we're low on coffee, flour, bacon,

and —"

"Hansen, don't make your problems mine," Clouston said. "Feed the coolies with whatever scraps come to hand, and send a man to the railroad depot. I want to know the minute the supply train arrives. We need that mining equipment. How are we now for horses and wagons?"

"We have just enough to keep the ore rolling from here to the railhead," Hansen said.

"Excellent," Clouston said. "Now find a clean slicker for my bride-to-be and fetch it here. We'll ride out to the hills and I'll show her the foundation of our marital fortune."

"I'm going nowhere with you," Judy said. She yanked at the chain. "And I'll die before I spend a night in your bed."

"Are you insane?" Clouston said. "You foolish child, I intend to make you a rich woman. You'll wear dazzling jewels, dress in the latest Paris fashions, dwell in stately mansions, and travel in fine carriages." He smiled. "Your little bumpkin head could never imagine the life I will give you."

"You may take my body, Clouston, but never my love," Judy said.

Clouston snorted. "Love! A fiction made up by the insane. You little fool, all I want is your body!"

■ ■ ■ ■

Duncan Campbell knew that no civilized Christian man should be abroad in such vile weather, but he was also aware that the thunderstorms were on his side. With a bit of luck Thomas Clouston and his bandits would keep to their tents.

He and his riders swung south of the Rattlesnake Hills, then looped north at Saddle Rock peak into hilly canyon country.

"The rain is keeping up, boys," Campbell said, water cascading from the brim of his hat. "We might catch them napping, like Bonnie Prince Charlie caught Johnnie Cope."

"Boss, is that feller kin to Andy Cope who shot the Fort Smith dentist that time and got hung fer it?" Big Boy Harrison said.

"No, I'm talking Scottish history and the Jacobite rebellion of 1745 against English oppression," Campbell said. Then in a deliberate attempt to build his riders' confidence, he said, "I'll teach you about Prince Charles Edward Stuart and the Lost Cause tonight at dinner."

"Boss," Harrison said, "no offense, but I reckon I'll pass on that."

Campbell opened his mouth to speak,

when his scout, a Southern puncher by the name of Coonan who'd been a captain of cavalry in the Army of the Confederacy, approached. He came on at a canter through the gray veil of the downpour, waving his hat.

The rancher waited until Coonan drew rein in front of him, then said, "What did you see, Lem?"

Lem Coonan's face registered shock. "Boss, an army. Clouston's got an army camped in a valley back there."

"Did you see Judy?" Campbell said.

"No, sir, I didn't. All I saw was tents, a sea of tents, thousands of men, women, and children in camp."

"You used the long glass?"

"Sure did. But I didn't see any better. There's a rain mist in the valley."

Loud enough for the others to hear, Campbell said, "You didn't see an army, Lem, you saw the tents of the Chinese railroad workers who left Broken Bridle."

Understanding dawned on Coonan's face. "So this is where they went," he said.

"Lock, stock, and barrel, every man, woman, and child of them," Campbell said. "There's a gold seam in the hills, and Clouston plans to have the Chinese mine it for him."

"Heard that in Broken Bridle, didn't believe it though," Harrison said.

"Well, believe it now," Campbell said. Then to Coonan, "How is the camp laid out, Lem?"

"Well, sir, it isn't the Army of Northern Virginia," Coonan said. "The Chinese are to the north and its seems like they pitched their tents anywhere they felt like. To the south the tents are better deployed, maybe thirty, forty of them, and there are horse lines and a wagon park."

"That will be the camp of Clouston's gunmen," Campbell said.

"Boss, there's only seven of us," Harrison said.

"I know that, Big Boy," Campbell said. "But up until now Clouston has had it all his own way. I think it's time we shook him up a little."

Harrison was wary, as were the other riders. Even Coonan, a man of proven courage, looked uncertain.

Finally Harrison said, "What do you have in mind, boss?"

"Nothing too complicated. We ride in, shoot up those tents, then hightail it out of there. I want Clouston to know he's in a fight."

"But . . . but what about Miss Judy?" Harrison said. "She'll be in danger."

"My daughter knows I can't let her kidnapping stand. She's a brave girl, and she bears an honorable name, and it's what she'd expect me to do." Then, "Gather round me, men."

Duncan Campbell turned in the saddle and pointed west.

"Lads, there lies the Four Ace ranch and the road to safety," he said. His Scottish brogue was very thick. "I will not hold a grudge against any man who does not wish to join me in this enterprise. He will be welcome at my table and may dwell free of harm under my roof."

The six Four Ace riders exchanged glances, then Big Boy Harrison spoke for all of them. "We ride for the brand, boss."

Visibly moved, Duncan Campbell nodded. "Then let us teach that Clouston dog a lesson he won't soon forget. We'll remind him that now he's dealing with men."

CHAPTER FORTY-FIVE

Heavy rain and a rising mist cut visibility to less than a hundred yards, and the Clouston encampment looked as though it lay behind a ragged gauze curtain. A covey of wet bobwhite quail, their eyes like black beads, huddled under a clump of sagebrush and watched Duncan Campbell's riders pass.

The old rancher moved his men to within two hundred yards of the valley, then ordered them to shake out into a skirmish line.

"Boss, may I have the honor of leading the charge?" Lem Coonan said.

Campbell smiled. "We have but a small force, Lem, but surely you've earned that honor." He put his hand on the shoulder of Coonan's wet slicker. "Lead the way . . . Captain."

"One thing more, boss," Coonan said. "In my trunk in the bunkhouse I have my uniform" — he grinned — "smelling of mothballs, I'm afraid, and the honored flag. If I fall, see I'm buried in one and that that the other drapes my coffin."

"I can say you won't fall," Campbell said. "But those would be empty words."

For a few moments Coonan's blue eyes studied the black sky, then he said, "It's been a long twenty years. Now it's time." He reached under his slicker and produced his old cap and ball Remington. "Shall we proceed, gentlemen?" Coonan took his place in front of the others and called, "Forward at the trot!"

The skirmish line lurched into motion and then took up the trot. After a hundred yards Coonan yelled, "Charge at the gallop!"

As Duncan Campbell kicked his horse into motion, words from the English poet Alfred, Lord Tennyson's "Charge of the Light Brigade" flashed into his mind . . .

Into the jaws of Death,
Into the mouth of Hell
Rode the six hundred.

Then, his six, not six hundred, riders screaming wild, incoherent war cries, Campbell was among the tents, the Colt in his hand roaring.

A man's remembrance of a gunfight does

not progress smoothly from first shot to last, rather it comes to him flickering and cartwheeling, bits and pieces of a few seconds of madness he must later piece together like a collage.

So it was with Duncan Campbell.

He rode through the tents and shot into two on his right. A big, bearded man emerged from the second tent, a gun in his hand, and Campbell leaned from the saddle and fired at almost point-blank range. The big man fell, triggering shot after shot into the air. Campbell drew rein and looked around him. He saw Big Boy Harrison, enormously strong, lift a man by the back of his shirt, haul him clean off the ground, and throw him head first into the side of a tent. The tent collapsed and men inside yelled and cursed. Other tents were down and his punchers fired into them. His riders scored hits because he heard men shriek, some in death, others from wounds. Amid the noise and confusion Lem Coonan received a mortal wound from the double blast of a Greener scattergun. A small, slight man, the impact lifted him from the saddle and sent him sprawling on his back. He died on churned-up, muddy ground with a slight smile on his face.

"Big Boy!" Campbell yelled. "The corral!"

"We've sure played hob, boss!" Harrison yelled, grinning, the light of battle in his face.

He swung his horse and rode for the corral, a cut between two hills fenced off at the front, its rear protected by a steep hogback.

Campbell ordered a retreat but failed to make himself heard above the din. Now the Clouston gunmen were getting organized, and in addition to Coonan, two of his men were down.

Waving to his surviving riders, Campbell rode toward the mouth of the canyon. Two more of his punchers, one with blood streaming down his left arm, followed. Then Campbell saw a sight that made him rein up his plunging horse. Set into the hill on his right was a ruined cabin, and standing outside, a steel ax in his hand, his maniacal face twisted, Clouston roared defiance. At that moment the eyes of Clouston's gunmen were on Big Boy, who'd dismounted and was pushing open the corral gate. He'd been hit and was making a slow go of it.

Clouston was beyond the effective range of a Colt, but Campbell two-handed the big revolver to eye level, centered on Clouston's chest, and fired.

He had time to see his shot go wide right, but he saw Clouston clutch his left arm and even above the noise he heard the man scream, a shrill shriek of outrage and terror.

A bullet thudded into Campbell's lower back, then a second took off the thumb of his gun hand and his Colt spun away from him and landed in the dirt. The old rancher knew he was done for. He swung his mount and galloped in the direction of Harrison, bullets splitting the air around him.

When he reached Big Boy, he fell out of the saddle, picked himself up, and laid his good hand on the gate. "Pull, Big Boy," he said.

"I'm shot through and through, boss," Harrison said.

Campbell smiled, blood in his mouth. "Me too. I hope the Pearly Gates are easier to open than this corral."

Now Clouston's men were only yards away, firing as they came. Shot to pieces Campbell and Big Body Harrison fell together. "I think this gate opens inward, boss," the big man said.

But Duncan Campbell didn't hear him. He was already dead.

Harrison staggered to his feet, tried to bring his revolver to bear, but was hit by a dozen bullets. He fell on top of Campbell and was dead by the time the Clouston gunmen reached him.

Dr. Thomas Clouston shrieked in pain and grasped his left arm, horrified by the blood that trickled down his fingers and spotted the ground where he stood. He'd been struck by a bullet! It was an atrocity, the wanton act of a savage. Bad enough that his person had been violated, but worse, it made him feel vulnerable, no longer invincible . . . no longer immortal.

Clouston screamed and ran inside and flopped on his chair.

Was he insane? Had the bullet that touched his arm also touched him with madness? He looked around and saw that his woman was gone. But that was a minor irritant compared to the assault on his sacred person.

The man called Hansen stepped under the tarp. "Boss, are you hurt?" he said.

"Of course I'm hurt, you fool," Clouston said. "Are you insane?" Then, before the man could answer, "Who attacked me?"

"Punchers looked like," Hansen said. "They seemed to be ramrodded by some old coot."

"Did we kill them? Did we kill every rotten last one of them?"

"We killed four, boss, including the old one, but a few escaped."

Clouston wailed, "My arm hurts. I need a doctor."

"Boss, you are a doctor," Hansen said.

"I'm a doctor of the mind, I need a doctor of the body, you idiot."

"Let me take a look at it," Hansen said. "I've seen some gunshot wounds in my time."

"Gently, you oaf." Clouston grimaced as Hansen took his arm.

The big man ripped apart the shirtsleeve, studied the wound, and said, "It's a flesh wound, boss. You got burned."

"How could this happen to me?" Clouston said.

"There was lead flying everywhere, boss. We lost five, and another three wounded. They took us by surprise, coming out of the rain like that."

"I said, how could this happen to me?" Clouston said. "I thought I was invulnerable, but now it seems I'm a mere mortal after all."

Hansen grinned, ever the frontier diplomat. "You'll live forever, boss."

"That is my intention." Then, casually, "Send a couple of men out to find my woman and bring her back. She can't have gone far in this rain. After I bandage my arm I will come down to inspect the enemy dead."

Thomas Clouston's rage was volcanic, erupting into violence. He kicked Duncan Campbell's lifeless body and screamed obscenities into the old man's gray face.

"He's the one who shot me!" he yelled to Hansen. "The insane pig took aim and shot me!"

More kicks followed, thudding into Campbell's face and chest, breaking bones. Finally spent, Clouston stared at Hansen, his eyes red, features twisted by anger and hatred.

"Have you sent the men out yet to find the woman?" he said.

"Not yet, boss. I was —"

"Send them out and tell them to use her like a whore and then kill her. Tell them to let her know she's dying, let her be aware of my wrath. I don't want the spawn of this pig anywhere near me. Do you understand?"

Hansen grinned, a brutish man savoring his thoughts. "Hell, boss, I'll go myself, me and Matt Simpson. After we get through with her you'll never see that little gal again."

"Make her pay for the sins of her father, Hansen," Clouston said. He fisted his hands and through clenched teeth snarled, "Make . . . her . . . pay."

CHAPTER FORTY-SIX

It was the opinion of the D'eth brothers that the forlorn attack on the valley where Thomas Clouston's men were encamped was driven by an old man's vanity. How else to explain seven men riding against five times their number?

Three of the seven, two of them wounded, had survived and had fled the valley, convincing Milos and Petsha that there was no advantage to be gained from the attack. To ride in after Clouston now when his men were on edge and ready would be suicide.

"Brandy, brother," Milos said, passing a silver flask to Petsha.

Petsha took a swig and glanced at the sky. "Will this rain never end?" he asked.

"It will end when next the sun decides to shine," Milos said.

"We must kill Clouston soon."

"We will. Never fear," Milos said. Then, his eyes on the hills, "Hello, what do we have here?"

Petsha, more far sighted than his brother, rubbed rain from his eyes and peered into distance. "Two riders," he said. "They must be the doctor's men."

"Then we will follow and see where they lead us," Milos said.

"And then kill them," Petsha said.

"That," Milos said, smiling, "is one of life's few certainties."

Judy Campbell was not hard to find. A scared, barefooted woman does not run far across brush and cactus country in a lashing rain.

She'd taken refuge in the thin cover of a struggling piñon, her sodden shift covering the curves of her body like a second skin. When the two riders approached her she recognized Hansen's bearded, grinning face and tried to make a run for it.

The big man easily rode Judy down and forced her to the ground. He jumped from the saddle and pulled her to her feet. Hansen pulled back her arms and showed her to Simpson. "Like what you see, Matt?" he said.

Simpson's tongue flickered over his top lip. "I sure do. Is there anywhere we can take her out of the rain?"

"Nah. We'll take turns here, then you can cut her throat. You like that, Matt. Don't you?"

"Always have," Simpson said. He was a small, thin, snake-faced man, an abuser of women who was lightning fast on the draw and shoot. He reached under his slicker and produced a silver dollar from his shirt pocket. "Heads I have first go," he said.

"Toss the coin high and let it fall on the ground where I can see it," Hansen said.

Simpson swung out of the saddle and grinned at Judy, "You ready?"

The girl struggled like a wildcat. "My father will kill you for this," she said.

"No, he won't. The old coot is dead," Hansen said. Then, "Get on with it, Matt. I'm growing mighty impatient."

Simpson flipped the coin high, the dollar spinning through rain — and Milos D'eth shot it out of the air.

"What the hell!" Simpson said. He turned and his eyes widened as he saw a couple of rubes step from the cover of thick brush, both with a Colt in hand.

They ignored the two men and the terrified girl.

"Good shot, Milos," Petsha said. "I could never do that."

"It's a party trick of mine," Milos said.

"It's very much easier than it looks."

"Well done, just the same," Petsha said.

Hansen was the first to recover from his surprise. "What the hell are you farm boys doing here?" he said.

"Do you work for a man called Dr. Thomas Clouston?" Petsha said.

"Sure we do, me and Matt there," Hansen said. "What of it? Now get lost and leave us alone to enjoy our woman."

Two shots, close together, fired by Milos. Two hits. Right between the eyes of Hansen and Simpson. Two dead men sprawled on the wet ground. All this in less than two ticks of the watch in Hansen's vest.

This time Petsha did not praise his brother's shooting. Hitting the silver dollar in midair had come as a surprise, but killing two men with deadly efficiency was a matter of routine.

The sound of the shots was still ringing in Judy Campbell's ears as Milos said, "Who are you?"

"My father . . . is my father dead?" she said. She was unaware of her naked breasts and shoulders where Hansen had torn her shift and of the rain that fell on her.

"A man with gray hair riding a gray horse?" Petsha said.

"Yes, yes. That was my father. Have you

seen him?"

"He lies in the valley with his dead," Petsha said. "It was his fate."

Judy buried her face in her hands and sobbed. Milos and Petsha exchanged glances.

Finally Milos said, "What do we do with her?"

"Kill her?" Petsha said.

"Why?"

Petsha shrugged. "It was a suggestion."

Milos held Judy by the shoulders and talked to the top of her bowed head. "What is your name, girl, and why are you here?"

Without looking up, Judy's broken, hesitant voice tumbled from between her fingers.

"My name is Judy Campbell. Clouston kidnapped me from my father's ranch. When . . . when my father attacked his camp I managed to escape."

"Why did he take you? For ransom?" Petsha said.

"No. He wanted to make me his kept woman."

"Then your father attacked him and he decided to kill you instead," Milos said.

"I don't know," Judy said.

"It seems likely," Milos said.

He bent, stripped the slicker from Simpson's body, and draped it over Judy's shoulders. She immediately threw it off. "I don't want to wear that. It's a filthy thing," she said.

"Then you will be cold and wet," Milos said.

"I don't care. He probably helped to murder my father and he would have murdered me."

"Eventually," Milos said. "Now you will come with us."

Judy dropped her hands from her tear-stained face. "Where will you take me?"

"Back to Broken Bridle," Milos said.

"Or we can leave you here," Petsha said. "When his men don't return, Thomas Clouston will send others to investigate. We must be gone."

Judy nodded and Petsha said, "You bob your head up and down. What does that mean?"

"It means I'll come with you," Judy said.

"Then you can ride our horse," Petsha said. "It is not a filthy thing like the slicker."

CHAPTER FORTY-SEVEN

Sheriff Jeremiah Purdy was on the street when the D'eth brothers led in a horse with a drenched, half-naked woman on its back. Most of the reflector lamps along the boardwalk were out, barely holding the night at bay, but Purdy recognized the slender form and tear-stained face of Judy Campbell.

The young lawman stepped into the street and grabbed the horse's bridle. The D'eth brothers flanked the animal, neither of them with any great liking for peace officers.

"What happened?" He asked the question of Milos.

"Let the woman tell you," the man said. He reached up and effortlessly lifted Judy from the horse. "She is cold," he said.

Milos turned his back on Purdy as Petsha turned the horse and headed for the livery.

"Wait," Purdy said. "I want to talk with you two."

"No," Milos said. "No talk. You will infect

us with your weakness."

Embarrassed by Judy's nakedness, Purdy pulled her shift up to her shoulders and led her toward the Streetcar, a place where there was bound to be womenfolk.

Milos D'eth's last comment still stung, but the sheriff knew that the insult was no more than he deserved and he had no answer to it.

Sunny Swanson sat by the piano located near the staircase where she could hear Burt Becker if he called out for her, or rather groaned for her. But when Purdy assisted Judy inside, she stepped quickly across the saloon floor and confronted the sheriff, a frown gathered between her eyes.

"That's Judy Campbell. What did you do to her?" she demanded.

Purdy was flustered. "I . . . I mean, I did nothing to her. The D'eth brothers brought her into town."

"What did those two freaks do to her?"

"Nothing," Purdy said. "I don't know what they did."

Sunny took the girl in her arms, called for brandy and a blanket, and led Judy to a table. She waited until the girl took a few sips of brandy and was wrapped in a white, red, and green trade blanket before she spoke.

"What happened, Judy?" she said. "I haven't seen you in months."

"You were always very nice to me, Sunny," Judy said, talking in a small, quiet voice.

Sunny squeezed Judy's hand. "We're both part of the sisterhood, honey. We may have our petty jealousies and our moments of backbiting, but when the chips are down, women help other women, and now I'm trying to help you."

Judy Campbell took time to gather her thoughts. Pete Caradas, ever the Southern gentleman, added brandy to her glass and said, "From the beginning, Miss Campbell. Take it slowly."

Judy gave the gunman a smile, then told her story, from her kidnap to her life being saved by the D'eth brothers.

"I think my father is dead," the girl said. "He was always a very headstrong man. He led six men into the valley and only three came out, two of those wounded."

"Don't give up hope yet, Judy," Sunny said. "Your father could have been captured."

"Yes, perhaps that's the case," Judy said, very little hope in her voice.

"You've been through a terrible ordeal and I'm not sending you to the hotel," Sunny said. "You'll stay in my room tonight here at the Streetcar. The brandy will help you sleep and now I'll help you upstairs."

Judy Campbell made no protest.

She woke to darkness. Somewhere in the Streetcar a clock chimed two, then fell silent again. Judy Campbell turned on her back and stared up at the mirrored ceiling. How tiny she looked in Sunny's huge brass bed, made for fun, not sleep. Slightly embarrassed by the thought, Judy sat upright on the billowing pillows and the memories of the previous day flooded back to her.

Her father was dead. She knew that with certainty. His loss hadn't quite reached her yet, but it would soon and she'd wear black for a year to mourn him. She'd been too young to remember her mother's death, but her father's hit her doubly hard.

Judy lay back and closed her eyes. Outside coyotes yipped, a hunting pair moving in close, and a dying fly buzzed on the windowsill. Somewhere a woman sobbed . . .

Judy sat upright, listening into the night. Her borrowed nightdress slipped, leaving her left shoulder bare and her hair, flattened by rain but now dry, fell in tight ringlets over her forehead.

There it was again, definitely a woman's sobs and from close at hand.

Could it be Sunny? Was she pining for a lost love? No, that couldn't be. From what she knew of Sunny she wasn't the type to sob over a man, or over anyone else.

Was it . . . ? No, it was impossible. A saloon girl would not grieve for Duncan Campbell. But she may be hurt and sobbing for herself.

Judy's instinct was to curl up in bed, mourn for her father, and put all else out of her mind. But the sound of the crying girl was insistent, demanding her attention.

Forcing herself to get up, Judy used a box of Lucifers to light the single candle by her bed. She then opened the drawer of the side table and found what she'd expected. Sunny kept a Sharps .30-caliber pepperpot revolver there to discourage drunk and abusive clients.

Judy opened her room door and stepped onto the balcony. A dark saloon empty of people is a gloomy, shadowy place, and the guttering light of the candle did little to banish the murk. The girl paused in the doorway, then determined the sobbing came from a room to her left. Holding the candle high, the revolver ready in her right hand, she stepped in that direction.

Her bare feet made no sound as Judy stopped at a door where a man groaned and turned in his sleep, the bed creaking under him. Was the girl in there? She tried the door handle, but the room was locked. Again she stood motionless and listened. Rain ticked on the roof just a few feet above her head. For a moment she imagined her father's body lying cold and blue in the downpour, untended, abused. Judy closed her eyes and banished the thought. The sobbing had started again.

But there was no room beyond that of the groaning man, just a sheer wall covered with flocked red and black paper. The sobbing came from behind the wall. But there was no apparent door, unless . . . was the entrance to the hidden room in the groaning man's quarters?

Judy tapped on the wall and determined that it was made from thin boards and seemed to be quite flimsy in construction. She put her mouth against the wall and whispered, "Who is there?"

There was a long pause, then a girl's faint answer. "I'm Jane Collins. I'm being held captive."

Judy's excitement spiked and she said, louder than she intended, "Jane! It's me! It's Judy Campbell."

A little squeal of delight from behind the wall, then, "Judy, I knew you'd come for me. I knew it."

"Step away from the wall, sister, and drop the stinger."

A hard, raw muzzle of blued iron pushed into the back of Judy's neck. "Do it now or I'll bury you beside your pa."

The Sharps thudded to the floor and Sunny Swanson tapped on the wall with the barrel of her Colt. "You in there, shut your trap or I'll put six through this wall."

Jane Collins hushed as though she'd just been gagged. She knew Sunny was capable of carrying out her threat.

"Back to your room, Miss Campbell," Sunny said, shoving her gun into the girl's side. "I'll lock the door so you don't sleep-walk again."

"What are you going to do to me?" Judy said.

"I don't know yet," Sunny said. "That's up to Burt. But if I was you I wouldn't make any big plans for the future."

CHAPTER FORTY-EIGHT

Dr. Clouston was angry, raving, foaming at the mouth mad.

He'd lost seven of his best men including the loyal Deke Hansen, and one of the wounded was not expected to live. But worse, the Chinese were now refusing to work.

"Boss, they say they haven't been fed since they got here and that undercutting the rock to remove the greenstone will be too damned dangerous."

A man named Lark Rawlings, a Cajun whom Clouston didn't particularly like, delivered the unwelcome news.

"Are they insane?" the doctor said. "Did you tell them that food is on the way and wagons to haul the ore to the rail depot? Did you tell them I'm increasing their wages to a dollar a day because of the danger of the overhang?"

"Seems they already know them things,

boss," Rawlings said.

"I want work to get started right away on cutting the greenstone so it's ready for loading," Clouston said. "Haul those Chinese off their lazy butts. Hang a few if you have to. That will make the rest pay attention."

Rawlings, a tall, unshaven man with black eyes and hair, nodded. "Sure thing, boss. I'll string up half a dozen of the ringleaders and let them dangle for a spell, make a big impression."

Clouston said, "I wish to attend the hangings," then waved his hand in dismissal. He'd thought earlier about cleaving a few heads, but six bodies dangling on a makeshift gallows until they rotted would be a potent reminder of his wrath.

He sighed, lit his pipe, and picked up his copy of Dr. J. C. Bucknill's brilliant treatise on the care and control of the insane. It was clear from the words he read that the Chinese were all demented and must be treated most severely, like naughty children.

In the end, Thomas Clouston hanged the five men and two women who were judged to be the ringleaders of the revolt.

The job was badly bungled by Rawlings and his assistant hangmen, and all seven Chinese strangled to death. Being small and light, their deaths had not been quick or easy.

Clouston, however, was very pleased. The Chinese had learned what happened to those who displeased him, and several hundred men and boys were already hard at work on the greenstone seam, despite the looming threat of the massive rock overhang that looked like a huge, curling wave about to crash onto their heads.

By right of his fast gun and ruthlessness, Rawlings had stepped into the boots of the late Deke Hansen and Clouston pulled him aside, the elongated shadows of the Chinese dead falling on them.

"Do you think six mounted riflemen are enough to keep the diggers in check?" he said.

"Sure, boss. The Chinese know what those six men can bring."

"Very well, then I'll leave that up to you," Clouston said. "But at the first sign of discontent and muttering, hang a few more, women preferably. I need the men as workers."

"You can depend on that," Rawlings said.

"How many men have you killed in gunfights?" Clouston said.

The man thought for a few moments, then said, "White men?"

"Yes," Clouston said. "Let's confine it only to those who matter."

"Seven white men, boss."

"Anyone of note?"

"Well, I kilt stuttering Willie Newsome down Ellsworth way. He claimed to be the fastest gun and hardest man north of the Red until I taught him the error of his ways."

"Good, then you are eminently qualified to supervise this enterprise," Clouston said. "Work the Chinese like slaves, Rawlings, dig, dig, dig, faster, faster, faster, dawn till dusk until they drop. Understand?"

"I got it, boss," Rawlings said, grinning.

"There's one other thing that's of the greatest moment," Clouston said. "I will attack Broken Bridle very soon and wipe that accursed town off the map. I want to hear plans from you and your men that I can use or adapt."

"I fit Indians when I scouted for the army," Rawlings said. "Wiped out a few Sioux and Cheyenne villages in my time. I know how it's done."

"Good, then we'll have a consultation soon," Clouston said.

He glanced up at the seven hanging bodies, the ropes creaking in the wind. "Building a gallows was Hansen's idea and it was a good one," he said. "All things considered

I'd say that our golden enterprise is off to an admirable start."

"There is one thing, boss, we need to fill the wagons quickly," Rawlings said. "I don't know how much longer the overhang will hold up, if you catch my drift. It's already dangerously undercut."

"At your present pace, how long before the entire greenstone seam is removed?" Clouston said, worry suddenly niggling him.

"Three, four weeks if the entire hill doesn't come down before then."

"We have a thousand Chinese men at the diggings, but we obviously need to increase the workforce. Get the women, children, old people, anyone who can use a pick, shovel, or load wagons."

Rawlings did a quick calculation and said, "That takes in everybody, say three thousand people. But if that cliff comes down . . ."

"Do you really care, Rawlings?" Clouston said.

"No, can't say as I do."

"Nor do I. Get them to work and shoot those who won't. One other thing, I want ten, not six, mounted men on guard with orders to shoot to kill. If you need to, step over Chinese bodies to get my wagons to the railhead."

CHAPTER FORTY-NINE

Coming up from the boom town of Medicine Bow, Deputy United States Marshal Saturday Brown thought of the Union Pacific smoking-car cushions with nostalgic longing as he rode south of the Rattlesnake Hills in a roaring rain.

His ass hurt from the McClellan saddle, designed to favor the horse, not the rider, and his rheumatisms punished him. At fifty-five, he knew he was too old for manhunts, but the law was stretched thin, and the army, their hands full with resettling Indians, had no interest in helping the civil authority.

In fact, Brown wasn't really on a manhunt; he was chasing wild rumors that had percolated down the southern trails as far as Medicine Bow and had ousted him from his cozy berth as the resident law and much sought-after raconteur.

A gray-haired man of medium height and

build, he didn't look like much, but Saturday Brown had stories to tell. In the course of a law enforcement career that spanned more than three decades, protecting himself and stopping fleeing felons, he'd killed twenty-eight men. Not one of them troubled his conscience or disturbed his sleep o' nights. A lifelong bachelor, he lived for his work; yet he'd never gained a reputation as a fast gun or found fame as a lawman, and he'd sought neither.

Now in the twilight of his career, the marshal contemplated retirement and a move to Detroit where his younger sister had a hat shop and a spare bedroom.

A man much addicted to a tobacco habit he'd picked up from Texas cowboys, Brown pulled his horse into the shelter of cottonwoods that lined a creek bank and with the steady hands of the gun-skilled built himself a cigarette. He smoked and gloomily stared out at the rain that moved in the wind like a glass curtain.

"It's an easy assignment, Sat," U.S. Marshal Cliff Miles had told him. "An afternoon's ride in the park. Gold is a hard-kept secret so believe me all you'll find in the Rattlesnake Hills are rattlesnakes. It's wide-open country with just one quiet town close by where the folks go to church on Sunday and the saloon serves cake and ice cream. You head up there, take a quick look around, then come back to Medicine Bow, make your report, and put your feet up."

"The word around this town is —"

"Rumor, Sat. And most times rumor is a kinder word for a damned lie. Men killed over a gold strike, drums beating in the middle of the night, and a crazy doctor leading a band of desperadoes." Miles smiled, his brown eyes bright with sincerity. "I've even heard a big windy that Pete Caradas is there, him and that other feller they call the Town Tamer —"

"Shawn O'Brien," Brown said.

"Yeah, him. What's a big-time hired gun and a millionaire's son doing in a burg on the edge of the civilized world. Huh? Answer me that."

"Well, it don't seem likely," Brown said.

"Damn right it don't seem likely," Miles said.

"Cliff, them hills are a fair piece, maybe eighty miles," Brown said. "I'm getting too old to sit on a hoss for that long."

Miles patted Brown on the shoulder and said, "You can do it, Deputy."

And that had signified that his talking was done.

■ ■ ■ ■

Saturday Brown had started on his second cigarette, rain staining the shoulders of his slicker, when he squinted his brown eyes and stared into distance. He was a long-sighted man who needed spectacles to read a newspaper. A rider emerged through the downpour angling to the west of him into rolling brush country.

Brown did some quick thinking.

No God-fearing white man would ride out on such a day under a sky as black as mortal sin. This wilderness was owlhoot country, filled with hardcases on the scout, and Brown saw his chance to return to Medicine Bow. If, as he suspected, the rider was a wanted man, he'd arrest him and take him back and there would be no wild goose chase into empty hills.

Brown flicked his cigarette butt into the rain, slid a Winchester from the boot under his knee, and kicked his horse into motion. He moved southwest crossing rolling country where prickly pear and bitterroot thrived among the sagebrush. The rider hadn't seen him yet. The man's head was lowered against the onslaught of the rain and he kept his horse to a steady walk. But every now and then he checked his back trail, and on the last of those occasions he caught sight of Saturday Brown. The man immediately kicked his horse into a chaps-flapping run and lashed the animal with the reins.

Brown was not close enough to shout, but he drew rein and snapped off a quick shot. His intention to put a warning round across the rider's bow, but he badly misjudged the speed of the galloping horse and his bullet smacked into the animal's shoulder.

The horse staggered, then cartwheeled into the wet ground, throwing the rider over its head. The man rolled clear of his fallen mount and sprang to his feet, hand clawing for the gun under his slicker.

Brown drew rein and yelled, "Stop that!"

The rider, a youngish man who'd lost his hat in the horse wreck, had a shock of bright red hair and a temper to match. He shouted an angry obscenity at Brown and his right hand come out from under the slicker with a hammer-back Colt.

It was his death warrant.

Brown triggered the Winchester and punched a hole in the redhead's chest. The man took a step back, cursing, and tried to level his revolver. Brown's second shot hit him low in the belly and the redhead was done. The Colt dropped from his fingers and he followed it to the ground.

Brown climbed stiffly out of the saddle and stepped to the dying man who said, "Why did you bushwhack me?" There was blood in his mouth and it trickled down his chin.

"I took ye fer an outlaw," Brown said. "Figgered that's why you ran."

"I ain't an outlaw," the man said. "I am . . . I was a puncher for the Four Ace ranch and I wanted to put a power of git between me and them Rattlesnake Hills." The man coughed up black blood. "Now I ain't anything but dead."

"Hell, boy, I'm sorry," Brown said. "I shot you under false pretenses." He took his badge from his shirt pocket and pinned it on his chest. "I'm a Deputy U.S. Marshal and right now I'm real sorry for what I done."

"Well," the puncher said, "I've never been partial to lawmen. Robbed me a general store one time and spent three years in Lansing mining coal. Damn the law."

Brown took a knee beside the man. "Son, your time is short and you best make your peace with God. Don't die with a cuss on your lips."

The puncher's bloody hand grabbed Brown by the front of his shirt. "Say a prayer for me," he said.

Brown took off his hat and held it above the dying man's face to shield him from the rain. "Sing this with me and the gates of Heaven will surely open wide for you, even though you're a general store robber and a bounder."

The deputy tilted back his head and in a powerful but tuneless baritone sang . . .

"There's a land that's fairer than day,
And by faith we can see it afar.
For the Father waits over the way
To prepare us a dwelling place there."

Then louder, warming to his task, Brown launched into the chorus . . .

"In the sweet by and by,
We shall meet on that beautiful shore.
In the sweet by and by,
We shall meet on that beautiful shore."

"Sing it, boy," Brown said. "Lift your voice . . ." He trailed off, aware that he talked to a dead man. After he replaced his hat, he said, "I don't know your name, feller, but I'm right sorry that I shot you by mistake. I'll make things right an' see that you're planted decent."

Despite the rheumatisms and a bad back

from years of long riding, Brown easily manhandled the dead puncher across the back of his bronc. Besides, the man was a wiry little feller, made only two ounces heavier by lead.

The deputy marshal regained his own saddle and sat head bowed in the rain for long moments. The man had said he was fleeing the Rattlesnake Hills. Did that mean there was a grain of truth in the rumors concerning the place? He should have questioned the man when he'd had the chance, but it didn't seem hardly polite after shooting him over a slight misunderstanding.

Brown glanced up at the leaden sky and then his shoulders slumped and he sighed loud and long. He was too softhearted. That had always been his trouble.

Saturday Brown picked up the wagon road that led to Broken Bridle and rode into town under a clear sky where a crescent moon horned aside the first stars. Mud lay in the street to a depth of four inches, and the marshal's high-stepping Morgan made a splashy show of it. Brown drew rein when he spotted two men smoking on the front porch of the hotel.

"Howdy, boys," he said. "Is there a law-

349

man in this burg?" he asked.

"You could call it that," Hamp Sedley said. "Some don't."

"What do you have there, stranger?" Shawn O'Brien said.

"Feller I shot by mistake," Brown said. "I took him fer a bandit."

"No shortage of them around this neck of the woods," Sedley said.

Brown opened his slicker and showed his badge. "Name's Saturday Brown. I'm a Deputy United States Marshal. Came up from Medicine Bow and regret every minute of it."

"So does the ranny on the yellow mustang," Sedley said.

"Afore he passed away, he told me he was a puncher, worked for the Four Ace ranch. Said he was hightailing it away from the Rattlesnake Hills. That was after I shot him, like."

"He was a wise man, at least until he met you," Sedley said. "Name's Hamp Sedley, a knight of the green baize. This handsome feller here is Shawn O'Brien. He's a mick, but we don't hold that against him."

"Pleased to meet your acquaintance," Brown said, touching his hat. "Heard of you, O'Brien. Your pa owns half the New Mexico Territory and they call you the Town

350

Tamer." He looked along the muddy street and the deserted boardwalks and said, "Well, seems like you sure tamed this burg."

"This town doesn't need taming, Marshal," Shawn said. "It needs saving."

Perhaps made restless by the near proximity of the dead man, the Morgan restlessly pawed at the street, sending up great gobs of mud.

Brown said, "I heard all the rumors. That's why I'm here."

Hamp Sedley said, "No rumors, Marshal. You just rode into hell."

"Been there afore, boys," Brown said. "Now where's that law dog?"

"Down the street a ways on the left," Shawn said.

"Don't expect much," Sedley said.

Brown touched his hat again, then kneed his horse into motion. "See you boys around," he said. He stopped again. "I plan to bury this poor feller tomorrow morning. It would be real neighborly of you to come pay your respects to another white man."

"I don't think —"

Shawn elbowed Sedley into silence, then said, "We'll be there, Marshal."

"I'm beholden," Brown said.

After the lawman rode away, Sedley said,

"Kind of long in the tooth for a peace officer."

"Maybe, but he's killed more than his share," Shawn said.

"How do you know?"

"I read it in his eyes," Shawn said.

CHAPTER FIFTY

"Name's Deputy United States Marshal Saturday Brown and I got me a dead man outside."

Sheriff Jeremiah Purdy had gotten up from his coat at the back of the office to answer Brown's pounding, and he looked tousled, his weak eyes blinking behind his glasses.

"What happened to him?" he said.

"My official report will say that I shot him in error, that I mistakenly took him fer a lawbreaker. Mistakes like that can cost a man his pension."

"What's the deceased's name?"

"I don't know. Afore he died he said he'd been working for the Four Ace ranch, said he wanted to put a heap of git between him and the Rattlesnake Hills. That's all I know about him."

"We all want to put a heap of git between us and those hills," Purdy said. "This town has already lost a third of its citizens."

"I figgered something like that. The wagon road was mighty churned up. Take a lot of wheels to do that."

"I reckon some of that was caused by Thomas Clouston's ore wagons. Seems he has more arriving every day."

"By nature, I'm a drinking man, Sheriff," Brown said. "You got any whiskey to wet my pipe, like?"

Purdy opened his desk drawer and produced a bottle of Old Crow and a couple of glasses. "Take a seat, Marshal," he said.

"Don't you want to see the dead man?" Brown said, his eyes measuring the young lawman. "Maybe you can put a name to him."

"You sure he's dead?" Purdy said.

"When I shoot a man that's the way he usually ends up."

"Well then he can wait."

Brown watched Purdy pour the whiskey, picked up his glass, then said, "All right, Sheriff, tell me what's going on with this town. I want to hear everything, so start at the beginning."

"It will be long in the telling," Purdy said.

"The night is young," Brown said. "It ain't really since it's past my bedtime, but I'm listening."

After many stops and starts and pointed questions from Saturday Brown, Purdy told the story of Clouston's arrival in the Rattlesnake Hills and the tragic effort of the men of Broken Bridle to oust him from his stronghold. He also mentioned his college education and the kidnap of his betrothed by Burt Becker.

It took Brown a while to answer, as he mulled over what Purdy had just told him. Then he said, "Clouston's a doctor, you say?"

"Yes. A psychiatrist."

"I've heard o' them. Never had much need for one though," Brown said. He shoved his empty glass across the desk. "Fill that, son," he said.

Glass in hand, the marshal said, "Clouston ain't stupid. He'll attack this town all right, but only when the Chinese dig the gold out of the ground."

"I don't catch your drift, Marshal," Purdy said. "I told you, Clouston fears a gold rush."

"Hell, you already said a third of the folks in this town have lit a shuck. Don't you think that the word is already out that there's gold in the Rattlesnake Hills? He'll work the Chinese to death, get all the gold he can in the shortest possible time, and then attack this burg. And do you know why?"

"No, why?"

"For a college boy you ain't too smart, are you, son?" Before Purdy could answer, Brown said, "He'll cut down on the number of shares. If Clouston has a score of men, he knows he'll lose half of them in an attack on Broken Bridle, especially with three big-name draw fighters in town. That's ten less fingers in the pie. Now do you catch my drift?"

"Pete Caradas won't fight for this town and neither will Burt Becker," Purdy said. "O'Brien might, but then, who knows?"

"What about you, Sheriff?" Brown said. "Will you fight?"

"I have no choice."

"You can run."

"I won't do that. How about you, Marshal?" Purdy said. He looked small and insignificant, blinking behind his round glasses, about as potent and dangerous as the .32 on his desk.

"I'll see this out," Brown said. "It's my job." He smiled. "This Clouston feller has never had to deal with the likes of Saturday Brown afore."

The marshal rose to his feet. "The gambling man with Shawn O'Brien says you ain't much, Sheriff."

"And what do you say?" Purdy asked.

"I don't think you're much, either," Brown said. Then, "There's a dead man outside."

"I'll take care of it," Purdy said. He sounded tired, defeated.

"I'll want his hoss an' traps," Brown said.

Purdy nodded. "You'll get them."

The big marshal stepped to the door, his spurs ringing in the quiet. He turned. "Sheriff Purdy, if my gal was kidnapped I'd tear this town apart board by board to find her, and I'd kill any man who got in my way, including Burt Becker."

Brown opened the door and delivered a parting barb. "For God's sake be a man, and be a peace officer."

After the marshal left Jeremiah Purdy buried his face in his hands. He knew he could no longer be either.

Saturday Brown rode past the hotel on his way to the livery. Shawn O'Brien was no longer there, probably in bed, but the marshal planned to wake him up later anyway.

As was his habit, Brown leaned from the saddle, opened the stable door, and rode inside. A couple of rubes lay asleep on hay to his right, but the Colt in the fist of the man to his left cost more than a farm boy could ever afford. A spotted pup lay curled up between them.

"I can drill you just fine from here," Milos D'eth said.

"You always sleep like a cat, Milos, or so I've heard," Brown said.

"I heard you were dead," Milos said.

"And I was told that you and Petsha there, pretending to be asleep, got hung over to San Francisco way," Brown said.

"You heard wrong," Milos said.

"And I ain't dead, either," Brown said. "At least not yet."

"You got a warrant on us, Saturday?" Petsha said, now standing gun in hand. His face was stiff, as hard as iron, and the pup sniffed around the lawman's boots.

"Nope. Shot a feller by mistake and brung him in is all. What are you two sewer rats doing in a burg like this?" Brown said.

"One day that kind of talk will get you shot, Saturday," Milos said.

The marshal smiled. "Not by you, Milos. You know I can outlast you."

"Nobody can outlast a shot between the eyes," Milos said.

"A truer word was never spoke," Brown said. He got ready to climb out of the saddle, but Milos said, "Saturday, you wouldn't be planning a fancy move, would you?"

"Me gettin' off this pony is never fancy," Brown said. He dismounted, then reached into his saddlebag. Milos said, "Easy does it, Marshal."

"Damn it all, you boys put away them irons," Brown said. "It's highly likely that I'll shoot you at a later date, but this isn't the time."

"We don't like you, Saturday," Petsha said. "Never did and never will."

"Well, that makes feelings kinda mutual all round, don't it?"

Brown produced a bottle of whiskey from his saddlebag. He took a swig and passed the bottle to Milos. "Here, wet your whistle, then tell me why you're here. Who will have the honor of getting his ticket punched by the D'eth brothers?"

Milos took a drink, passed the bottle to his brother, and said, "Somebody you don't know."

"I know everybody so try me," Brown said. Then to Petsha, "Hell, don't sip that whiskey. Drink it like a man."

"I'll kill you one day, Saturday;" Petsha said, his black eyes mean.

"Yeah? Well, until then quit drinking like

my maiden aunt Agatha. It surely irritates a man."

"Clouston. His name is Dr. Thomas Clouston," Milos said.

Brown decided not to show his hand. "What did he do? Saw off a wrong leg?"

"He killed our client's brother," Milos said. "He said he was incurably insane and starved him to death at his clinic in Philadelphia. Truth was, our client hadn't yet made his fortune and couldn't pay for his brother's treatment, so Clouston murdered him. Our client wants us to bring him Clouston's heart to see if it's made of stone like he believes."

"You boys are the best assassins in the business," Brown said. "How come you haven't done for him?"

"So far we can't get close enough," Petsha said. "But we will."

"You'll be close enough when Clouston digs out enough gold from the Rattlesnake Hills and attacks this town," Brown said. He took the bottle from Petsha.

"Clouston won't do that," Milos said. "He has no need. He's already killed half the men in Broken Bridle."

"I'll tell you what I told Sheriff Purdy —"

Petsha snorted. "Him? He's only half a man. Why tell him anything?"

"I can't argue with you there, but Clouston will attack to whittle down his numbers."

"Less shares," Milos said. "More money for him."

"When it comes to the killing for profit business you catch on quick," Brown said. He took a drink from the bottle and offered it to Milos, who refused, as did his brother.

"Saturday, we will take care of your horse in payment for the drink," Milos said. "We will kill you one day, and when that time comes I don't wish to owe you anything."

"Spoken like a white man," Brown said. His eyes flicked over the man's black hair and dark skin. "Well, a kinda white man. What will you do when Clouston attacks?"

"My brother and I will talk about it," Milos said. "It may be that Clouston will return east and we will follow him there. Or we will kill him here. Petsha and I will discuss what is best."

"Let me know, boys, huh?" Brown said. "By the way, your dog is biting my ankle."

"When we kill Clouston, you will know." Milos picked up the pup.

"Well, it's been real nice talkin' with you boys again after . . . what? . . . six, seven years," Brown said. "Do you mind that? The time you gunned the Yankee railroad millionaire as he kneeled by his bed a-sayin' of his prayers. I was sent after you, rode a hundred mile and more, but never seen hide nor hair."

"But we saw you," Milos said. "You were lucky on account of how there's no profit in killing marshals."

"Well," Brown said, "as my old ma used to say, let bygones be bygones. Now make sure my hoss gets a rubdown and a scoop of oats, all right?"

"We have no quarrel with your horse, Saturday," Milos said. "We will take care of him."

Whiskey bottle in hand, Saturday Brown slogged through ankle-deep mud to the hotel. Across the street the Streetcar Saloon was lit up but the silence behind its doors suggested a lack of customers. The marshal didn't mind, his business was with Shawn O'Brien. Besides he'd promised his wife that his lips would ne'er taste strong drink or linger on those of loose women. He'd been able to more or less keep the latter, but the former had so far eluded him.

When he reached the hotel porch Brown stomped the mud off his boots, an action that brought the night clerk hurrying outside with a warning that he would "wake the whole damned town."

"It's too early for Christian folks to be in bed," Brown said. "I'm here to see a feller named O'Brien."

"Mr. O'Brien is abed and cannot be disturbed," the clerk said. He was as fussy as a mother chicken and looked like one, too.

Brown was a straight-talking man, but he decided to let Sam Colt do his speechifying for him. The desk clerk suddenly looked cross-eyed at a gun muzzle shoved into the hairy bridge of his nose.

"Can I expect trouble from you?" Brown said.

"No, sir," the clerk said. "No trouble."

"Room number," Brown said. Heat lightning flashed in the sky and his face shimmered like a bronze bust in a furnace.

"Room twelve, upstairs, first door on the right," the clerk said. His knees shook.

"Good man," Brown said. "You're a credit to the innkeeper profession."

The marshal took to the stairs, making no effort to be quiet, and slammed his fist repeatedly into the door of Shawn O'Brien's room.

He waited a few moments and was about to pound again when a voice from inside said, "Mister, you better have a good reason for disturbing my sleep."

"I have good reason. This is Deputy United States Marshal Saturday Brown. Open up in the name of the law."

The door opened and Brown stared into the cold black eye of Shawn's Colt. The marshal ignored it. "Get dressed. We've got things to do."

"Do what?" Shawn said. He lowered the hammer of his revolver.

"What your town sheriff should have done weeks ago," Brown said. "We're going to take the saloon apart and save a lady in distress."

"You're talking about Jane Collins," Shawn said.

"The same. She's your sheriff's intended, or so he says."

"Then he told you about Burt Becker," Shawn said. "He says he'll kill the girl if any attempt is made to rescue her."

"I know. But we won't give him a chance to kill anybody. Now get dressed, O'Brien. I need that fast gun of yours."

"What's going on?" Hamp Sedley stood at the door in his underwear, a revolver in his hand.

"Get dressed," Brown said. "We're going

to rescue a gal from a fate worse than death."

Sedley echoed Shawn's question. "You mean Purdy's intended?"

Brown nodded and Sedley said, "I reckon Pete Caradas will have something to say about that."

"I know. That's why O'Brien is going with us."

"I didn't say I was going anywhere," Shawn said. "And Hamp is right about Caradas. He's drawing gun wages from Becker and he rides for the brand."

"I'll handle Caradas," Brown said. "But if he looks like he's about to draw down on me, kill him." The marshal seemed irritated. "I'm now the law in this town, and for a hundred miles around, so I'm ordering you two to get into your duds and follow me."

Suddenly Brown looked appalled. "Don't tell me there ain't a wire in this town."

"There's a telegraph at the railroad depot, bound to be," Sedley said.

"Good. We'll stop there first. No, second. Now quit standing there staring at me like a couple of sheep. Get ready."

"Shawn?" Sedley said.

"We'll do as the man says," Shawn said. "Maybe I can stop him getting killed."

"Been there afore, O'Brien, and I ain't been killed yet," Saturday Brown said.

CHAPTER FIFTY-ONE

"Where's the hardware store?" Marshal Saturday Brown said.

"Across the street," Shawn O'Brien said.

"Then follow me."

Shawn and Sedley exchanged puzzled glances, then stepped off the boardwalk. When they reached the other side, their boots dripping mud, Brown's face lit up. "Ah, I see the store," he said.

"It's closed," Sedley said.

Shawn tried the handle. "And it's locked."

Brown raised his boot, kicked the door in, smashing glass and splintering wood. His feet crunching on debris he looked around, then said, "Ah-ha! Just what we need."

The marshal selected a couple of axes for him and Sedley. To Shawn he said, "Nothing for you. I want your gun hand free. Now one more stop before the saloon, boys. Oh, wait a second." A jar of pink and white candy cane sticks sat on the counter. "Any-

body want one?" he said. "No? Well I do."
The candy stick jutting out of his mouth
like a cigar, Brown said, "Let's go."

Marshal Brown had not been gentle with
the hardware store's door, nor was he with
the train depot agent. He loudly woke the
man from sleep, frog-marched him to his
office after telling Shawn and Sedley to stay
outside on guard.

"Now set and send the wire I'm about to
tell you," Brown said to the agent, whose
sleeping cap was askew on his head. "Is the
line between here and Medicine Bow standing?"

"How the hell should I know?" the agent
said. "I have a medical condition. I can't be
treated this way."

"You better hope the line hasn't been cut,"
Brown said. "If it has I'll put a bullet in
you."

The agent, a small man with the furtive
look of someone who momentarily expects
a slap up the head, said, "What kind of lawman are you?"

"The worst kind," the marshal said. "I'm
all horns, rattles, and bad attitude, son." He
crunched on the candy stick and it shattered between his teeth, spraying pink and
white shrapnel. "And I bite like a female
cougar in heat. Now start telegraphin' . . ."

■ ■ ■ ■

Saturday Brown stepped out of the depot office and said, "Right, let's get it done, boys."

"Marshal, you're taking Becker and Pete Caradas too lightly," Hamp Sedley said. "They're both killers."

"I'm not taking them lightly, son. I already told you, that's why O'Brien's here."

"Your confidence in me is touching, Marshal," Shawn said.

"Is that right?" Brown said. "Well, just see you don't mess things up, huh?"

The marshal led the way to the Streetcar and halted outside the door. The saloon was in darkness and a brooding silence lay over the entire town. Moonlight glistened on the muddy street and cast mysterious shadows in dark places.

"Ready, boys?" Brown said. He stared hard at Sedley. "Son, you don't look too good."

"He always looks like that," Shawn said. "Got a gambler's skin."

"Well let's hope lady luck is on our side tonight," the marshal said. Then, a hint that he wasn't as cocksure as he seemed. "I got a feeling we're going to need her."

Brown kicked the door open and rushed inside.

"Where?" Saturday Brown yelled at Shawn.

"Up the stairs! Becker's room is straight ahead!"

With a spryness that belied the hard years on his back trail, the marshal ran up the stairs and stood on the landing, the ax clutched in both hands. Sedley stepped beside him, wondering why the hell he also had an ax in his grasp.

"Burt Becker!" Brown roared. "Show yourself in the name of the law."

A bed creaked inside the room and Becker's strained, tight voice said, "What do you want?"

"This is Deputy United States Marshal Saturday Brown and you know what I want, by God."

"Go to hell," Becker said, trying and failing to shout.

"Been there!" Brown yelled. He slammed the sole of his boot into the door that collapsed inward. The brass hinges burst apart and sharp shards of timber shredded into the room like shrapnel.

Becker roared and rolled out of bed in his underwear, his hand grabbing for the Colt on the table beside him.

Brown slammed the flat of the ax onto the big man's hand and Becker yelped in pain and fright.

"Where is she?" the marshal hollered.

In answer, Becker swung a right at Brown's chin and missed as the lawman dodged to his right. Brown shrieked like a banshee and raised the ax above his head, the honed blade ready to crash into Becker's skull.

"Nooo!" the big man yelled. His face contorted in fear, he pointed to the blank wall to the right of the ruined door. "In there, both of them!"

Brown kept the ax poised like the blade of a guillotine. "Both of them?" he asked.

Becker said nothing. He hung his head and the rabbit ears of his bandage drooped.

Sedley was already at the wall, his hand moving over the garish wallpaper. "There's a seam here, Marshal," he said. "Looks like it could be a hidden door."

"Then open it or chop it down," Brown said. He turned his attention back to Becker. "You made the right decision, son," he said, smiling. "I would have sure chopped you into kindling."

Becker's bloodshot eyes lifted to the lawman. "I'll kill you for this," he said.

"It's a door, all right," Sedley cried out

suddenly.

Now a woman's muffled voice called out, "Help us! Oh, please help us."

"Damn you, boy, get it open," Brown said. "Use the ax."

Sedley nodded and his ax swung.

Pete Caradas emerged from the darkness of the balcony. He wore his robe, but his feet were bare and he held a Colt in his right hand. Behind him Sunny Swanson looked as though she'd just wakened from sleep. Her eyes were free of makeup and her unruly hair was bound up with a pink ribbon.

Caradas could be almighty sudden and he had the drop, and Shawn O'Brien knew the danger he represented. "Sorry to wake you, Pete," he said.

For a moment Caradas was silent, listening to the crash of Sedley's ax, then he said, "What's going on in there?"

"Just a Deputy United States Marshal doing a little remodeling," Shawn said.

"Has he done anything to Burt?" Sunny said. "Let me past."

"No, stay where you are," Caradas said. "I'll go look." Then to Shawn, "If Becker is hurt, I'll take it hard."

"I'll take it hard if anyone else gets hurt,

Pete," Shawn said. He would not be pushed and was prepared to draw on Caradas, even though the man would get off the first shot.

Caradas knew that, too, and it gave him pause. O'Brien was fast and he'd go down with a gun in his hand. Caradas estimated the odds at slightly more than even in his favor, but the margin was way too slim for comfort.

The appearance of Burt Becker in his room doorway ended it for now.

The big man saw Sunny and said painfully, "He broke my hand, Sunny."

Shawn felt a spike of concern. "Your gun hand, Becker?"

"Yes, it's his right hand, O'Brien. Can't you see?" the girl said. She rushed to her lover and took his huge, bruised paw in hers.

"Is it broken?" Shawn said. "Can he move his fingers?"

"Burt, can you move your fingers?" Sunny said. She studied Becker's hand, then said, "Yes, he can move them."

"Good, it's not broken," Shawn said, relieved. He needed Becker's gun, probably real soon.

"Thank you for your concern, O'Brien," Sunny said, stabbing him with her glare.

Shawn smiled and said, "Keep well, Burt," to which Becker replied, "You go to hell."

From somewhere inside, Sedley's voice rose to a pitch of horror. "Oh my God," he said. "Marshal, git over here."

Then a moment later from Brown, "Don't just stand there, help them!"

Sedley and the marshal helped two women onto the balcony.

Shawn recognized Judy Campbell immediately. The girl shivered, whether from cold or fear he didn't know, but she seemed to be unhurt and the nightgown she wore was clean.

The same could not be said for Jane Collins. A torn, ragged cotton dress, much stained, hung on her emaciated body and her blond hair had been raggedly cut and was stiff with dirt. Her hazel eyes were huge in her pale, thin face and the stench from the hidden room where she'd been held spoke volumes about the horrible conditions of her captivity.

Jane tried to talk, say something, anything, but her tongue refused to work in her mouth. She clung like a leech to the fastidious Sedley, her dirty fingers clawed into his coat, an experience the gambler obviously was not enjoying.

"Becker!" Shawn said, his rage at boiling point. "Give me an excuse to put a bullet in you."

"Damn you, O'Brien, she was well treated," Becker said. "If she wanted to live like a pig, that was of her own choosing."

"You treated her like a caged animal," Shawn said.

He was aware of Caradas who seemed to be struck dumb, his face revealing only stunned horror. Shawn gave him the benefit of the doubt. It seemed that the gunman had been unaware of Judy Campbell's terrible ordeal.

"Judy!" the cry came from behind Shawn. He turned and saw the girl fling herself, sobbing, into Jeremiah Purdy's arms.

"I knew you'd come," Judy cried, clinging to him, not caring that Jane was his true love. "I knew you'd find me."

"Sedley, take her," Purdy said. He gently pushed the girl away from him. "I'll be back in a moment."

It was only then that Shawn noticed the shotgun in Purdy's right hand. He wasn't alarmed, didn't expect much. The sheriff would bluster, threaten Becker with jail or some such, and Caradas would soon run him off.

But it didn't happen that way.

The young lawman stepped up to the sneering Becker and swung the shotgun butt. The walnut crashed with a horrifying thud into Becker's broken jaw, and the big man went down shrieking. With snakelike speed, Purdy swung the scattergun and the muzzles gouged hard into Pete Caradas's right cheekbone.

"Give me your gun," the sheriff said. Then, "Now, damn you! Or I'll paint the wall behind you gray with your brains."

"Here, that won't do," Saturday Brown said. "I'm the law in this town."

"Shut your trap, old man," Purdy said. "I've already heard enough from you. Caradas, you've got two seconds. One . . ."

"Take it," the gunman said. He deftly turned the Colt in his hand and extended it butt-first to Purdy. "I never argue with a shotgun when it's stuck in my face."

The sheriff shoved Caradas's revolver into his waistband. To Sunny he said, "Were you in on this?"

"She was the one who put me in the hidden room," Judy Campbell said.

Sunny's face contorted in fury. "Yes, and I should have scratched your eyes out."

"Get Becker on his feet, Sunny," Purdy said. "I've got a jail cell for both of you. And you, too, Caradas." He nodded to Brown. "I thank you kindly for what you did."

"Should have done it yourself, boy,"

Brown said.

"Yes, I should have," Purdy said. "But I was too much in love with Jane to risk losing her."

"Well, you played the man's part tonight," Brown said. He smiled at Caradas. "Didn't he, Pete?"

The draw fighter gave an elegant bow. "I can't deny that."

"Caradas, help Sunny pick up Becker, or what's left of him, then come with me," Purdy said.

"I'd like to change first, Sheriff, if you don't mind," Caradas said.

"I do mind," Purdy said. "You're just fine the way you are. A jail cell doesn't give a damn how you're dressed. Now move!"

Hamp Sedley whispered in Shawn's ear, "The worm turns."

Shawn nodded. "I've heard of such once before, the consumptive Jim Riley kid who killed all those hardcases over to Newton, Kansas, that time. But I'd never seen it happen until now."

"There's a second time for everything, I guess," Sedley said.

CHAPTER FIFTY-TWO

Sheriff Jeremiah Purdy ushered his three prisoners out of the saloon into the boardwalk — and was greeted by a hail of gunfire.

Sunny Swanson took a bullet between her breasts and went down. Hit hard in the left leg, Purdy collapsed onto the walk. Becker dived to his right out of the way of flying lead, but Pete Caradas got down on a knee beside the fallen lawman and jerked his Colt from the young man's waistband.

Riders, about a dozen in number, had charged through the mire of the street, churning up mud like a stern wheeler stuck on a sandbank. They'd regrouped at the southern end of the street and now charged again. But this time the raiders met with disaster.

Caradas had his gun up and ready, and Shawn and Sedley flanked him. The riders crowded to the side of the street nearest the saloon, and for close-range draw fighters like Shawn and Caradas this was a perfect opportunity.

Slowed to a slogging canter by the mud, the leading riders met a barrage of rolling thunder from the guns of Shawn and Caradas. Sedley had his hands full with a man who charged his horse along the boardwalk, firing as he came.

Three men and a kicking, screaming horse lay sprawled in the mud of the street. The riders behind them had to swing wide, away from the mayhem, and their whole attention was directed at controlling their terrified mounts.

Sedley fired twice at the raider on the boardwalk, but scored no hits. The man came on at a fast gallop and kicked out at Shawn as he passed, sending him spread-eagled into the street, his face in the mud. The rider drew rein, his horse rearing, and fired a shot at Caradas.

"We got 'em, boys!" he yelled. He grinned, his teeth gleaming.

Such last words would have sounded noble on the lips of a dying Civil War general, but not from one of Thomas Clouston's thugs who was too stupid to realize that the fight was lost.

Sedley now informed him of that fact.

Standing with his back to the saloon wall,

he raised his Colt to eye level, sighted on the rider's chest, and pulled the trigger. Sedley got lucky. His shot was way too high but his bullet slammed into the man's temple, just under the hat brim. The rider threw up his arms and crashed onto the boardwalk so hard it shook under Sedley's feet. The horse galloped on until the drum of its hooves was lost in distance.

Caradas, stung across his right shoulder, stepped to the edge of the walk and, as an act of defiance, thumbed off the last round in his Colt at the departing riders. But a moment later gunfire roared from the direction of the livery stable, not the ragged fusillade of amateurs but the measured cadence of professional gunmen.

Then the riders were gone, swallowed by darkness.

Shawn O'Brien pushed himself out of the mud, his eyes and teeth white.

"You look like a gingerbread man," Sedley said, stepping to the edge of the boardwalk. It was a lame attempt at a joke and the gambler didn't put his heart into it.

Caradas had taken a knee beside Sunny, now he rose to his feet and said, "She's dead." Then, "How are you, Sheriff?"

"My leg's shot through and through," Purdy said. He stared through the gloom at

Burt Becker. "Are you hurt?"

"No. And I didn't have a gun," the big man answered. The bandage had fallen from his head and he slipped it under his chin again, pushed it back into place. "Jaw hurts," he said.

Dripping mud, Shawn stepped onto the boardwalk.

"You're a sight," Caradas said.

"I reckon," Shawn said. "My gun is in the mud somewhere." He brushed mud from his chest and found that he still had the rosary around his neck. He kissed the crucifix, then let the beads hang again.

"Three dead in the street and a wounded horse," Caradas said.

"I see that," Shawn said. Then to Sedley he said, "Let me have your gun, Hamp."

Sedley handed over his Colt and Shawn checked the loads. "One round left," he said.

Caradas tensed, an empty gun in his hand, but Shawn stepped into the street to the twitching horse, pushed the Colt muzzle against the animal's forehead, and pulled the trigger.

When he returned to the boardwalk mud had begun to harden on his face, as though he wore a black mask.

Dr. John Walsh, a coat over his night attire, kneeled on the boardwalk beside Sunny's body. He got to his feet and said to the grimacing Purdy, "Straight through the heart, Sheriff. She died instantly. Now let me take a look at that leg."

Burt Becker looked like a man consciously stifling grief. "Is that all there is? She died instantly?"

Dr. Walsh's austere face was chillingly bleak. "There's nothing I can do for her, Mr. Becker," he said. "My business is with the living, not the dead."

He turned his back on Becker and began to examine Purdy's leg.

The young sheriff winced as the doctor probed, then said, "Becker, get back to your room and consider yourself under house arrest. You, too, Caradas. O'Brien, take his gun."

"May I point out that I helped save your life tonight, Sheriff?" Caradas said. He handed his Colt to Shawn.

"Yeah, what about that, college boy?" Sedley said in the usual belligerent tone he adopted when talking to Purdy.

Purdy spoke directly to Sedley. "Mr. Caradas is still under the suspicion of aiding and abetting in the kidnap of two young women, a hanging offense."

He yelped in sudden pain and Dr. Walsh said, "The bullet is still in your thigh. I need to extract it." Then to the gaping people who'd gathered on the boardwalk, "A couple of you men help the sheriff to my surgery."

A pair of volunteers stepped forward, got Purdy to his feet; then, his arms over their shoulders, the young lawman limped away.

Dr. Walsh stayed where he was. "Mayor Bromley, the dead men and the horse should be removed from the street as soon as possible," he said. Then, a slight catch in his voice, "And take care of Sunny. Treat her with . . . kindness."

Hugo Bromley, a harried, middle-aged man with a magnificent set of gray mutton-chop whiskers that hung to the top of his chest, nodded. Then he said, "Deacon Dance says this is the apocalypse, that Broken Bridle is paying for its dalliance with demon drink and loose women. What do you think, Doc? Have the end times truly fallen upon our fair town?"

Walsh said, "The drums have told you all along that this town is in the way of a man's greed for gold. You have only two choices — fight or flee. Some have fled already but those who are left must pick up the gun. Tonight three professional gunmen did our fighting for us but we must be able to rely on ourselves."

Weakly, Bromley said, "But, Doc . . . what about strong drink and fancy women?"

Walsh smiled the day the War Between the States ended and now he did it again. "Taken in excess, they're both bad for the health," he said. "Now I must go to my patient."

Hamp Sedley said, "Seems you're still free to indulge in whiskey and women without the world ending, huh, Mayor?"

Bromley's wife, a shrew of a woman with a nose as sharp as a pen, glared at her husband, but the mayor gave a politician's professional "Harrumph," then ordered the menfolk on the boardwalk into the street.

"We've got some dirty work to do," he said.

Unnoticed, Shawn O'Brien left the others, Pete Caradas's reloaded Colt in his own holster. He walked to the end of the boardwalk, then crossed twenty yards of open ground that was now a river of mud.

He counted two men dead in the street and a third kneeling on hands and knees coughing up frothing pink blood. Shawn shot the suffering man in the head as he walked past. There was no recovering from a bullet through the lungs.

The D'eth brothers stood at the entrance

to the barn, each with a gun in his hand. Shawn, covered in a thick layer of mud from the crown of his hat to the toes of his boot, emerged from the gloom like a phantom.

Milos watched him come, then said, "Speak, thou apparition."

"Name's Shawn O'Brien. I want to talk to you."

"You ever hear of Jake O'Brien?"

"He's my brother."

"We like Jake."

"Everybody likes Jacob. All the ones who didn't are dead."

"Step inside, O'Brien," Milos said. "We'll talk."

Shawn walked into the barn and Milos introduced his brother Petsha. "Petsha doesn't like people but he cottoned to Jake, since they both play the piano."

"He plays Chopin well," Petsha said. Then, "You've come to talk about the dead men outside."

"They were Thomas Clouston's hired guns," Shawn said.

"We know," Petsha said.

"Then we have a common enemy," Shawn said.

"We have an enemy, but not in common," Milos said. "We told the marshal that we'll kill Clouston alone and in our own way."

"The attack tonight was to test our strength, and Clouston got his fingers burned," Shawn said. "Next time he'll plan his attack better."

Milos shook his head. "He wants as many of his men dead as possible. There will be fewer hungry mouths to feed when the gold is shared."

Petsha said, "But you are right, O'Brien. Next time he'll wipe this town out to the last man, woman, or child."

"I don't want that to happen," Shawn said.

"Then maybe you can stop it," Milos said. "But I don't know how."

"I can stop it," Shawn said. "I can stop it by helping you kill Clouston."

"We don't want or need your help," Milos said. "We've done more difficult jobs in the past."

"Even if I kill Clouston you'll have fulfilled your contract," Shawn said. "You've got nothing to lose."

"We don't like to depend on anyone," Milos said. "At a critical moment you could cut and run."

"Would my brother Jake cut and run?" Shawn said.

"No. He would not," Milos said.

"We're of the same stock," Shawn said.

Milos thought for a moment or two, then

said, "My brother and I will talk of this. Tomorrow we will let you know what we decide."

Shawn knew the D'eth brothers would not back away from that line, and he was forced to accept their terms.

"Until tomorrow then," he said.

Milos nodded. Then he said, "Tell the people of Broken Bridle to come collect their hurting dead."

Chapter Fifty-Three

"The ore cars aren't there, boss," Lark Rawlings said. "We got wagons backed up along the rails with nowhere to unload."

"What does the depot agent say?" Dr. Thomas Clouston asked, anxiety spiking at him.

"He says his request for a dozen ore cars was approved by the railroad and that he doesn't know why they're not here. He says they should arrive any day now."

Clouston leaned forward in his chair and took the pipe from his mouth. He'd been happy at the slaughter inflicted on his men by the resident gunmen in Broken Bridle, but this news banished his good mood and left him sullen and angry.

"When the ore is finally moved I'll hang that damned, incompetent depot agent from his own telegraph pole," he said.

"There's something else, boss," Rawlings said, his brutal, hangman's face worried.

"More bad news?"

"I reckon so."

"Then tell me and be damned to you for spoiling my morning pipe."

"Sometime last night a crack appeared on the overhang and the whole rock face is starting to creak," Rawlings said. "I reckon if the undercut gets much deeper it will bring down the whole shebang."

"How much of the greenstone have we removed?" Clouston said.

"I estimate about half," Rawlings said.

"Then get the Chinese to work faster."

"Boss, it looks like an ants nest at the undercut, men, women, and young 'uns. If the overhang falls we'd lose a thousand people, maybe all fifteen hundred of them. Do you want to come see for your ownself?"

"Are you insane? No, I won't come. How many Chinese die digging out greenstone is unimportant to me so long as we get all of it," Clouston said.

"Sure, boss, sure," Rawlings said, uncomfortably aware of Clouston's growing anger. "I do have some good news."

"Tell it," Clouston said.

"The railroad did deliver food, sacks of rice, and salt cod."

"Good. Then distribute it when you can." Clouston took time to relight his pipe, then said, "Use some Chinese, women and boys preferably, to unload the greenstone along the railroad spur. We need those wagons back here at the diggings. When the ore cars get here the Chinese can reload the stone into them."

"I'll get that moving, boss," Rawlings said. But the man stood where he was, hesitant, as though he wished to say something but was afraid to talk.

Clouston was irritated. "What is it, man? Speak up."

"Boss, the boys are pretty down in the mouth about what happened last night in Broken Bridle," Rawlings said. "Six men missing, probably dead, and Jesse Pender is gut shot and ain't likely to last until nightfall."

"I should have led that raid myself," Clouston said. "I won't make that mistake again."

"Maybe if you talked to them —"

"I don't feel inclined to talk to anyone, Rawlings. Make sure the men get plenty of whiskey and throw a few Chinese women to them. They'll feel just fine tomorrow."

Loop Eakins was familiar with the seven deadly sins because he'd committed all of them at one time or another. He was fifty and his résumé was extensive . . . bank robber, shell game artist, lawman, hired gun, lawman again, hotel doorman, and finally a top gun for Thomas Clouston. He'd killed three men and it didn't bother him none, nor did the drunken roar of men and the shrieks of Chinese women in the tents trouble him.

But the growing remoteness of Clouston and his complete unconcern for the lives of his men convinced Eakins it was time to throw the coffee on the fire and move on. He had two hundred dollars in his pocket, a good horse under him, and he could go anywhere. But he decided the safest place, at least for now, was Broken Bridle.

While everyone was otherwise engaged, he threw together his gear, saddled his bay, and rode out under cover of the falling darkness. He checked his back trail often, but no one followed him.

The night was still young when Eakins rode into Broken Bridle. He had not been part of the raid the night before and little evidence of it remained except that the muddy street seemed more churned up than was usual in a small town.

He left his horse at the livery, stared at by a couple of strange-looking rubes who were dark enough to be breeds, and then made his muddy way to the Streetcar.

Loop Eakins had many faults, but he wasn't stupid. He told the men standing at the bar that he'd fled Thomas Clouston and his thugs because of their attack on their town.

"That was something I could not abide and I decided it was time to quit," he said.

That sparse statement earned him the approval of the good citizens of Broken Bridle, and a few offered to buy him a drink. But when in his cups Loop Eakins was a talking man. And Pete Caradas sat at his usual table and listened to his every word.

"I tell you," Loop said to a respectable-looking man in gray, "that whole damn hillside is gonna come down and bury them Chinamen. I told Clouston that back at the hills but he wouldn't listen to me."

"He's digging for gold, I understand?" the respectable man said.

"Yeah, and he's got a whole cliff face undercut, maybe for a half mile. Part of the overhang showed a crack this morning." Eakins shook his head. "Damn it all, when it comes down it will bury a thousand Chinese miners under a mountain of rock, or I'm not standing here drinking this whiskey."

Eakins looked around the saloon to sample the reaction to his dire prophecy. When his eyes fell on Caradas they lingered a moment, long enough for the graceful draw fighter to crook a finger in his direction.

"Come here," he said.

Loop Eakins had seen Texas draw fighters before, and this one with his strange, dead eyes bore the stamp. He crossed the floor as the men behind them talked among themselves, then he said, "That's the honest truth, mister. Them Chinese are doomed, every man, woman, and child of them."

"Did you take part on the attack on this town last night?" Caradas said.

"No, sir, I sure didn't," Eakins said. "I was guarding them Chinese I told you about."

"Is your glass empty?" Caradas said.

Eakins drained his whiskey and grinned. "It is now."

"Good," Caradas said. "Then get on your horse and leave town."

"Now see here," Eakins said. "I've got friends in this saloon."

"Can you tell time?" Caradas said.

Eakins glanced at the clock above the bar. "Sure, it's ten minutes till midnight."

"If you're not gone by the time the hands meet, I'll kill you," Caradas said. "And think yourself lucky. If you'd been with the trash who rode through Broken Bridle you'd be dead by now."

Eakins was ashen. He spread his arms and appealed to the men at the bar. "Gentlemen, this won't do," he said. But every back was turned to him and he read the signs.

Caradas, an exclamation point of danger, rose to his feet.

Eakins's eyes got big and he turned, slipped on the floor, picked himself up, then ran for his life. When Western men are asked about the Eakins Streetcar scamper, a few say Loop dropped out of sight and was never heard from again, others that he died of yellow fever in 1889 while working for the French as a laborer on the construction of the Panama Canal. But most say, "Who gives a damn?" And that's where the matter must end.

Chapter Fifty-Four

"You came here at this hour of the night, pounding on my door, to return my gun?" Shawn O'Brien said. He examined the Colt. "After you fished it out of the mud you cleaned it real well and I'm much obliged." Then, apologetically, "I'm sorry I didn't clean yours."

"No matter," Pete Caradas said. I very much doubt if you'd have cleaned it to my satisfaction anyway."

Shawn let that slide and said, "Drink?"

Caradas nodded. "Make it a large one, O'Brien. I ran a bluff with an empty gun tonight and that wears on a man."

Shawn handed Caradas a brimming glass, ushered him into the hotel room's only chair, then said, "Tell me about this Eakins ranny."

"About him, there's not much to tell," Caradas said. "He says he quit Thomas

Clouston, then he told me about the Chinese."

"Let me hear it," Shawn said.

Caradas repeated what Eakins had said, then he added, "The bottom line is that if half a mile of overhanging rock decides to come down, it will kill a lot of Chinese."

Shawn was silent for a while considering the implications of what he'd just heard, then he said, "What do you expect me to do about it?"

"I don't expect anything," Caradas said. "I'm just telling you."

"What if I rode along the bottom of the overhang and tossed dynamite into the undercut?" Shawn said. "The whole thing might come down."

"Yeah, on top of you, O'Brien," Caradas said. "And there's half a mile of cliff. You'd need to carry a heap of dynamite."

"I came here to help this town, and that includes the Chinese," Shawn said. "Hell, I can't turn my back on them."

Caradas took a long sip of his whiskey. "They're only heathen Chinamen, not Christian white folks."

Shawn smiled. "You don't believe a word of that."

"No, I guess I don't," Caradas said. "What about Saturday Brown? He's the Deputy

United States Marshal, maybe we can let him work it out."

"Brown is a loose cannon," Shawn said. "He'd deputize what's left of the men in this town and go charging into the hills to save little yellow people. He'd only get himself and everybody else killed."

Caradas sighed. "Well, if we don't get the Chinese out of Clouston's grasp they'll all die. But if there's nothing we can do, then there's nothing we can do."

"Not with a gun or dynamite . . . but just maybe . . . just maybe . . ." Shawn said, his forehead wrinkled in thought.

"Don't keep it to yourself, O'Brien. Let's hear it."

"Pete, where do you get those fancy shirts of yours washed and ironed?"

"Right here in town. The Chinese lau—" Stunned, Caradas shook his head. "No, O'Brien, no! You can't send an old man, his wife, and three daughters into those hills to rescue their countrymen."

Shawn smiled. "Of course not, but the old man speaks Chinese and we don't. Suppose he infiltrates the camp and tells his people what's about to happen to them, explains the danger of a rock fall."

"Don't you think the Chinese already know that?" Caradas said. "They're being forced against their will into the undercut by Clouston's gun hands."

"Well, it won't hurt to talk to the laundry man," Shawn said. "What's his name?"

"I call him Sammy Chang," Caradas said. "And I guess everybody else does."

"I'll get dressed," Shawn said. "Let's go talk with him."

"Now?" Caradas said, surprised. "It's after midnight."

"You're right, Pete. The clock has already struck midnight for Broken Bridle and I'm willing to try anything."

"Hell of a job for a Town Tamer," Caradas said.

"Hell of a job for anybody," Shawn said.

It seemed that the Chang family were light sleepers because the patriarch himself answered the door at the first knock. He looked to be about fifty and was fully dressed in indigo-dyed pants tucked into knee-high boots and a matching loose-fitting shirt. He recognized Pete Caradas immediately.

"Your laundry not ready, Mr. Caradas. You come back afternoon," the man said.

He made to shut the door but Caradas stopped him. "We need to talk with you, Sammy," he said. "It's urgent."

"What about? Shirts?"

"No. About Thomas Clouston."

Recognition dawned on Chang's face. "Then you'd better come in," he said. He led the way into his dark home, situated just behind his laundry business. A hallway that smelled of incense and vaguely of boiled rice ended in a locked door. Chang produced the key, opened the door wide, and he walked inside, telling his two visitors to follow.

The room was in pitch darkness, but Chang felt around and lighted a lamp that spread an orange glow into every corner. Shawn's eyes were immediately attracted to the two huge Tranter revolvers on the table in the middle of the floor. Beside them lay a double shoulder holster rig and a supply of .577 ammunition. The cartridges looked like miniature artillery shells, and Shawn had seen their like before. When he lived in England an army officer returning from India had a pair of such Tranters, though his were highly engraved and plated with gold. The powerful revolvers were strange weapons to find in the home of a man who washed shirts for a living.

Chang's shrewd black eyes noticed Shawn's interest in the guns and said, "In China I had the honor to number among the imperial bodyguard of the noble emperor Xianfeng. These were my weapons." He smiled at Shawn's slight look of puzzlement. "Yes, we also carried swords, but the British and Germans soon taught us that firearms kill much more efficiently."

Chairs were placed around the table like a conference room, and Chang asked Shawn and Caradas to sit. The door opened and his wife, pretty but now graying, entered with a tray bearing a teapot and tiny china cups. Chang registered no surprise at the entrance of his spouse, as though he'd expected it. The woman poured pale green tea into the cups and handed them first to the guests and then her husband.

When she left, Shawn introduced himself, then asked Chang if he was familiar with the mining going on in the Rattlesnake Hills.

Chang said he was and added, "I am aware that the man called Clouston forces the Chinese to work like slaves and has hanged many as examples to those who would refuse. There were leaders among the Han, but they have all been killed. But I, who was bodyguard to an emperor, can lead them."

"That's why you have the revolvers on the table?" Shawn said.

"Yes. For the first time in twenty years I

will buckle on my weapons and help my people. In the service of my emperor I killed eighteen men. Soon I will kill more."

Chang was a small, intense man, well-muscled as a bodyguard should be, but he had the eyes of a poet, deep as black pools in moonlight, and when he spoke his voice was as soft as a nun's Act of Contrition in church.

"Sammy, do you know about the green-stone undercut?" Shawn said.

"Yes, and about the fault in the overhang," Chang said. He smiled. "The Han are a small, dark people; we come and go in the night and no one notices us. There is nothing about the man called Thomas Clouston that I haven't learned. Why do you think that the ore cars have not arrived? North of us many Chinese work for the Fremont, Elkhorn and Missouri Valley Railroad. It was a simple matter to disable the ore cars."

"Mr. Chang, you have devious ways," Shawn said, grinning.

"Ah yes, the Chinese are a wily people," Chang said. "Now, you have finished your tea? Good. You gentlemen have been an enlightening distraction, but I must be on my way."

He picked up an old Union Army knapsack, laid it on the table, and loaded his holstered revolvers into it. The ammunition followed and then a greasy paper sack of corn cakes.

"You need a horse, Mr. Chang?" Shawn said.

"No, I will walk so the dark will better conceal me. If I leave now I can reach the Rattlesnake Hills before dawn." He placed a conical, bamboo straw hat on his head, then said, "I must go."

Realizing he had little time, Shawn said, "Tell us your plan."

"It's simple. I will lead the Han in rebellion against their slave masters."

"But when? We can help."

"I don't know when. As soon as possible. Within a few days. It depends how quickly I can organize my people. They are not gunmen, Mr. O'Brien, and I don't want to lose any of them."

Chang stepped to the door but Pete Caradas stepped in his way. "Sam, just have them get up and leave, say about this time tomorrow under the cover of darkness. They did it here."

"They were not guarded by riflemen here," Chang said. "But it is a thought and perhaps I will find a way." He nodded. "Farewell, gentlemen."

CHAPTER FIFTY-FIVE

Dr. Thomas Clouston decided the trembling depot agent was criminally insane and a danger to civilized society.

"What do you mean, the ore cars are broken?" he said.

"Broken. That's what I heard. I telegraphed back up the line for a hundred miles and the word I got back from the other agents is that the cars can't be moved until they get a repair crew down from Casper."

His face black with anger, Clouston stared out at the tumbled heaps of greenstone dumped beside the track. Another wagon had just pulled in and a couple of Chinese women sullenly added to the pile. Millions of dollars' worth of ore lay next to the rails as far as the eye could see, a useless pile of rock unless it could be loaded and sent to the crusher.

The Rocky Mountains normally protect

Wyoming from severe weather by blocking air masses from the Gulf of Mexico, North America, and the Pacific Ocean. But around the Rattlesnake Hills summer thunderstorms are frequent and now another threatened, adding to Clouston's angry state of mind. To the north the sky was deep purple, almost black, and behind that smoky white clouds rose in massive ramparts, as though somewhere a great swath of the world was burning.

Fat drops of rain ticked around Clouston as he ordered Lark Rawlings to bring the depot agent closer. Rawlings, grinning, pushed the little man nearer. "You gonna hang him, boss?" he asked.

"No. I want this gentleman to do something for me," Clouston said.

Thoroughly frightened the agent wrung his hands and said, "I'll do anything. Please don't hurt me."

"I have no intention of hurting you," Clouston said. "Do you see the rails stretching away in the distance? I can tell you do, smart fellow. Now, you walk those rails north until you find my ore cars and then you expedite their repair. Understand?"

"But . . . but I could walk for a hundred miles," the little man said.

"Then you'd better get started, hadn't

you?" Clouston smiled. "Make tracks as they say."

"Please, mister, I'll work the telegraph . . . I'll . . . I'll find the cars. I could die out there."

"No doubt, but if you don't start walking I'll" — Clouston's tone changed from almost bantering amusement to the harsh whisper of a man possessed — "chop off your head."

The agent backed away from Clouston, his hands in front of him as though he warded off evil, his face stricken with horror.

"Mr. Rawlings, see our envoy on his way if you please," Clouston said.

Rawlings grinned and mounted his horse. He rode between the rails and hoorawed the little agent like a puncher cutting a steer out of brush. The railroad man turned and ran, tripped and fell, and then ran again.

Finally Rawlings drew rein and watched the agent go as fast as his short legs could carry him. He rode back to Clouston and said, "How long do you think he'll last out there, boss?"

Clouston shrugged. "Who knows?" Then, with a straight face, "May God go with him."

■ ■ ■ ■

Thunder crashed and beyond the shelter of the rock overhang rain drummed on the hat and slicker of the mounted rifleman who stood guard on this section of the diggings.

Sammy Chang swung his pick into the greenstone seam and levered free a large chunk. Here and there the stone was rotted and crumbled easily to the touch, and the hillside was dangerously undercut, the terrifying weight of the creaking cliff ready to crash to ground. All along the half-mile length of the undercut, hundreds of men picked away at the rock and women and children lifted up the ore and carried it to the waiting wagons. Once every two hours the diggers were allowed a fifteen-minute break when they bolted down a few rice cakes before returning to the menacing undercut. Their guards looked bored and uncomfortable in the teeming rain but held the butts of rifles upright on their thighs, and their cold, uncaring eyes were restless.

Talking on the job was an offense that called for a vicious beating, but the man working next to Chang whispered out of the corner of his mouth, "It must be soon. Six dead men in the tents this morning."

Chang nodded. The Han were being systematically worked to death in the cut and as the work and danger increased so would the death toll.

"It will be soon," Chang said. "The suffering will end."

A rifle roared and a bullet chipped rock inches above Chang's head. "Quit that blabbering," the guard yelled. "Or the next one goes through your head."

"It will be soon," Chang whispered without turning.

CHAPTER FIFTY-SIX

Deputy United States Marshal Saturday Brown wanted to send another wire to Medicine Bow demanding confirmation that his first message had been received. But there was no sign of the depot agent and that irritated him considerably. But perhaps he was already in the telegraph office.

"Damn rain," Brown muttered as he slogged through muddy ground to the flat-roofed cabin that passed for the train station. A tin sign on the wall nearest him advertised the benefits of Mrs. Fannie Tyler's Elixir for the Ague and All Female Ailments. The marshal thought he saw a shadow pass across the darkened window to the right of the sign and pegged it as the missing agent's. He took a couple of steps, then stopped again as the heaps of greenstone beside the track caught his eye. Brown walked closer to the rails and saw that the rock piles continued for a considerable distance along the track. At that time there were no freight wagons in sight.

Saturday Brown pondered the greenstone. Apparently it had been dumped here for a later pickup by ore cars. But why not unload the stone directly from wagons into the cars and save many hours of backbreaking work? Then Brown knew what had happened: The freight train hadn't shown up and Thomas Clouston had no way to transport his ore.

The marshal looked in the direction of the Rattlesnake Hills, then studied the terrain around the depot. In the distance rolling hill country but closer brush flats, wide open, made for rifle sights. Brown did a joyous little jig. Hot damn! This is where he would fight Clouston, right here, on ground of his own choosing.

"Hey you!" A tall, bearded man with a life-hardened face stood at the door to the office and glared at Brown. "What the hell are you doing here?"

The marshal played the doddering old codger. "I was looking for the agent. I want to send a wire to a dear cousin who's been keeping poorly."

"The agent is lost somewhere up the track," Lark Rawlings said. "And now I advise you to get lost with him."

"Well, thanks for the advice, but I think

I'll look around for a spell," Brown said. Then, looking Rawlings up and down, he said, "By your surly demeanor, I'd say you work for Thomas Clouston. Am I correct?"

Rawlings, a man on a short fuse, came down the steps from the depot and walked toward the marshal. He stopped when he was about seven feet from Brown and that made the lawman smile inwardly. It was the draw fighter's comfortable distance.

"Maybe you didn't hear me, pops, but you git," Rawlings said. "I won't tell you again."

Saturday Brown dropped the old coot act like soiled pants. "Not too bright, are you, son?" he said. "Your slicker is buttoned. Now see mine, it's closed in front of me, but it ain't buttoned. Know why?"

Rawlings was suddenly uneasy. His gun was under the slicker and this old-timer didn't scare worth a damn.

"I'll tell you why," Brown said. "It's so I can get to the iron real easy. He pushed the slicker away from his holstered Colt. "See what I mean?"

Rawlings was caught flatfooted and he put the tip of his tongue to his top lip, his brain whirling.

"Well, don't just stand there, son," Brown said. "Say something."

Rawlings undid the top button of his

slicker. "You go to hell, Methuselah," he said.

Brown shook his head. "Oh boy, did you say the wrong thing."

He drew and fired, fired again.

Two bullets crashed into Rawlings's chest, immediately staining the front of his slicker bright red. The big man's knees buckled and his face registered shock at the time and manner of his death.

Brown watched Rawlings fall, then said to dead ears, "Son, any friend of Thomas Clouston is no friend of mine."

"I'm sorry it had to end this way, but he was a mighty threatening man," Saturday Brown said to Sheriff Jeremiah Purdy. "And name-calling and low down."

Purdy, leaning heavily on a crutch, a fat bandage around his wounded leg, stared at the body, then looked at Brown. "His gun is still in the holster."

"Is that a fact?"

"You didn't give him much of a sporting chance, did you?"

Brown looked stunned, his eyes filled with disbelief. "Hell, no, I didn't. I had the drop on him. In a gunfight you don't give the other fellow a sporting chance. It's a good way to get yourself killed. Son, I declare that sometimes you sound like you went to West Point."

Purdy turned away from Brown and watched as a couple of wagons pulled in, each piled high with greenstone. Two young Chinese women were up on the driving seat, and when they saw Rawlings's sprawled body, they exchanged words that the sheriff did not understand. The older of the women climbed down from the wagon. She grabbed a large chunk of greenstone and without a glance at Brown or Purdy stepped beside Rawlings's body. Her beautiful face expressionless, she raised the rock above her head, then threw it down with all her strength into the dead man's groin. She stood motionless for a moment, then spat on the bloody corpse. The girl turned and regained her place on the wagon seat.

Saturday Brown smiled at the girl and said, "Not one to hold a grudge, are you, honey?"

But she made no answer. She turned the horses and drove north along the track, the second creaking, overloaded wagon following.

Brown said, "Sheriff, call a town meeting for tonight. I got some speechifying to do."

Purdy said, "Brown, I'm still considering a charge of murder against you."

Brown said, "For what?"

"For the murder of the man lying at your feet."

"That wasn't murder, it was self-defense," Brown said. "I don't want any grief with you, son, so don't give me any. Just call that meeting like I told you."

"What do you plan to say?" Purdy said.

"That I need fighting volunteers to battle Thomas Clouston. I won't ask you, Sheriff, since you've already volunteered."

"You know what happened last time. The widows and orphans are still crying and our town lost a third of its population in just a couple of days."

"This time it will be different," Brown said.

"How can you be so damned sure?" Purdy said.

"Because this time I'll be the feller in command," Brown said. "Oh, an' send the undertaker for the body, makes the place look untidy."

Chapter Fifty-Seven

" 'I'll be the feller in command' . . . is that really what he said?" Hamp Sedley asked.

"Yeah, his exact words," Jeremiah Purdy said. His wounded leg was straight out in front of him, the crutch leaning against a wall.

Sedley said, "Then we're headed for another massacre."

"Where is Brown now?" Shawn said.

"I left him at the restaurant," Purdy said. "He says killing a bad man always gives him an appetite."

"I'll go talk to him," Shawn said. "See what he has in mind."

He crossed the floor of the hotel room and took his slicker from the hook behind the door. "If I leave you gentlemen here can I be assured that you won't drink all of my bourbon?" he said.

Purdy smiled. "I'm going. I have to check on Jane. She was at Sunny Swanson's funeral this morning. Although they hated each other, Jane said it seemed like the right thing to do."

"A right-thinking little gal," Sedley said. "You got a keeper there, college boy." He pointed at Purdy's wounded leg. "If that don't kill you."

"The only one that shed tears for Sunny this morning was Burt Becker," Shawn said. "Surprised me. I didn't think he was capable of grief."

Purdy said, surprised, "You were there?"

"It seemed like the right thing to do," Shawn said. "Sunny was a pretty woman who deserved better than she got." Then, "I knew another woman who died way too young. I reckon she would have expected me to attend the funeral." He shrugged into the slicker. "Ah well, it's hard to let go of old memories, huh?"

"Want me to come with you, Shawn?" Sedley said.

"No, I can handle this by myself. Why don't you go speak to Judy Campbell? She's living with Mrs. Flood, the blacksmith's wife. Ask Judy if she plans on heading back to the Four Ace. If she does, we'll arrange an escort."

Sedley said, "Sure, but why don't you do it yourself. I always figured she was sweet on you."

Shawn said, "I think she is, but I don't want to give her the impression that it works both ways. Those memories I talked about are still on my back trail, and right now they feel awful close."

Saturday Brown sat back in his chair. He had a piece of apple pie the size of a dime stuck in his mustache. "Well, what do you think, cowboy?"

"There's no guarantee he'll come after the greenstone," Shawn said. "He might attack Broken Bridle instead."

"When he hears that the stone had been confiscated by a marshal, he'll come after it all right."

Shawn said, "I wish I was as certain as you are. Provided there are any volunteers, and that isn't a cinch, the town would be unprotected."

"Not if the draw fighters, you, Pete Caradas, Burt Becker, and Sedley, are here to protect it," Brown said. "I need riflemen, boys who fought in the war or are hunters. Fast guns aren't the berries for what I got in mind."

"Brown, I think your guitar ain't tuned right, but I can see logic in what you say, and that means I must be as crazy as you are."

"O'Brien, did you know that some folks spend their entire lives sane?" Brown said. "You any idea how boring that must be?"

Shawn smiled and then said, "What did you ask for when you sent the wire to Medicine Bow?"

"An army, O'Brien! The entire city militia! Hell, I don't know, maybe a hundred men."

"They'd be handy if they get here in time," Shawn said.

"I reckon, but I don't know if there was an answer to my wire, so we may have to do it with what we have. And I won't know what we have until after tonight's town meeting."

Shawn said, "You know that any man who takes a message to Clouston to tell him that a federal marshal has confiscated his greenstone will end up dead? And don't look at me. I'm not real inclined to do it."

"And I'm not doing it, either. I can't ask a man to do what I won't."

"So how does Clouston get the word?" Shawn said.

"I'll show you," Brown said. "Come with me to the sheriff's office."

"By the way you've got a piece of pie stuck in your mustache," Shawn said.

"From this town or another?" Brown said, laying money on the table.

"It's fresh. I'd say this town."

Brown wiped off his mustache with the back of his hand. "Then it ain't worth saving for later," he said.

"Well, what do you think, O'Brien?" Saturday Brown beamed. "Ran up this little beauty all by myself."

The marshal stood beside a crudely painted sign about the size of a house door. It read: THIS PROPITY CONFISKATED BY ORDER OF FEDRAL MARSHAL.

"I used red paint so Clouston can see it real good from a ways off," Brown said.

Shawn nodded. "That spelling will scare him, all right."

Brown said, "Make him mad is what I want."

Shawn said, "It's sure to do that."

"Crackerjack!" Brown said. "Now help me carry it to the rail depot."

In a pouring rain, Saturday Brown propped up his sign with greenstone where it would be seen from the flat. He handed Shawn a ship's telescope and said, "You see a wagon with a white man at the reins, give me a holler. You understand that, son?"

Shawn, feeling like a fool for giving into the old lawman's crazy notions, allowed that he did.

"Good. And then give me room. I need plenty of room when I'm about to do some serious shootin'." Like a man peering through a waterfall as rain ran off his hat brim, Brown frowned and said, "You ain't sharing my excitement, O'Brien."

"Standing here in the rain looking for a white man driving a wagon just isn't that exciting, Marshal," Shawn said.

"You just wait. Hell, son, they'll write about us in a dime novel afore this is done." Brown tried to build a cigarette, but the rain-battered paper and tobacco dropped out of his fingers. "Keep the spyglass to your eye while I get under shelter for a smoke. When you see the white man —"

"Holler. Yes, you already told me," Shawn said.

"You catch on quick, O'Brien. Must be all that fancy education you got as a youngster."

Three wagons driven by Chinese women came and went, their greenstone dumped farther up the track. Then after an hour Shawn saw what he wanted, a fully loaded wagon with a white man up in the seat, a couple of Chinese men walking alongside the beautiful Percheron team.

"Marshal!" Shawn said.

"Yeah. I see him," Brown said.

"Then why have I been —"

"Just giving you something to do, son, while we waited," Brown said. Then "Let him get closer and hope he has good eyesight."

The wagon drew nearer, coming straight ahead. That amused Brown. "He's a white man all right. Gonna dump his load right here and then get out of the rain." The marshal looked at Shawn. "I seem to recollect hearing that you have a fine singing voice, O'Brien. Or was that one of your brothers?"

"No, I'm the only one who sings," Shawn said.

"Good," Brown said. "So git out there and sing out to that feller to mind the sign. He's close enough now."

"Damn it all, Marshal, why don't you do it?" Shawn said, irritated.

"Because I don't have a fine singing voice, son. Now go and do what I told you."

Shawn angled Brown a look, but the marshal was oblivious. He kept his eyes fixed on the wagon, a Winchester propped upright on his hip.

Shawn stepped over the piled greenstone and then yelled to the wagon driver, "Hey, you!"

The man drew rein. The collar of his slicker was up around his ears; his hat was pulled low and Shawn couldn't see his face.

"Point to the sign, O'Brien," Brown said. "And then holler, 'This here is Federal property.' "

Shawn did as he was told. The wagon driver craned forward in the seat and peered through the rain at the sign.

"Now say, 'Git the hell away from here,' " Brown said.

"Git the hell away from here!" Shawn yelled.

The driver's only answer was a rude, one-fingered gesture. He slapped the reins and the Percherons lurched into motion.

"He doesn't seem to be very impressed by your sign, Marshal," Shawn said. "Now what?"

"Now I plug him," Brown said. "Make him pay attention."

"Huh?" Shawn said, turning. But he was too late. Brown's rifle roared.

Shawn saw the wagon driver jerk in the seat, and blood spurted from a hole in his right shoulder just under the collarbone. The two Chinese men threw themselves flat on the muddy ground.

Brown levered a round into the chamber and said, "Now I'll clip both his ears."

"No!" Shawn yelled. "Damn it, Marshal, he's had enough."

Brown stood still for a few moments and watched the wounded driver frantically turning the wagon. "Yeah, you're right, son," he said. "I reckon he's had enough. But mark me, one day Saturday Brown's good nature will be his undoing."

The marshal absently fed shells into the Winchester, his eyes on the retreating wagon. "This will make Clouston good and mad. I'm counting on the rain keeping him to home until I can get my riflemen in place on this ground."

Shawn said, "Broken Bridle has already paid a high price battling Clouston. I don't think you'll find many volunteers. Hell, what am I talking about? There aren't that many men of fighting age left."

"Then I'll pray that the Medicine Bow militia arrives in time, and if the worst comes to the worst I'll recruit draw fighters." Brown stared at Shawn, a slight smile on his lips. "They're better than nothing, I guess."

Shawn let that go without comment, then said, "Clouston always does the unexpected.

He might attack in the depot in the rain."

"I suspect he might get up to some dev-ilry," Brown said. "That's why you'll stay here, son, and I'll send Sedley with your hoss. Keep the glass and if you see Clouston and his men coming, ride hell for leather to the Streetcar. I'll set up a defense in the saloon with Becker and Pete Caradas and any other fighting men I can round up, maybe even them two D'eth assassins and the sheriff."

Saturday Brown frowned. "Son, look at me. Are you understanding all this?"

"I got it, Marshal," Shawn said. "I don't like it, but I got it."

"Then I'll leave you to your duties," Brown said. "And if Clouston comes this way afore the militia gets here, God help us all."

CHAPTER FIFTY-EIGHT

"I smell madness here," Dr. Thomas Clouston said. "I can sniff it out like a terrier sniffs out a rat. One of the men got shot, you say?"

The short, stocky man who'd brought the bad news nodded. "Uh-huh, Len Baxter took a bullet in the shoulder."

"And they have a sign saying my greenstone has been confiscated by a federal marshal?" Clouston said.

"That's what Len read, before he got shot."

"Then there's lunacy afoot and I must stamp it out like a contagion."

Clouston set his S-shaped pipe on the table beside him and rose from his chair. Moodily he watched the slanting rainfall. The air smelled fresh as the downpour washed the dusty land clean. Thunder rumbled in the distance and lit up the steel-blue clouds.

"How many men showed up for roll call this morning?" he asked.

"Seven," the stocky man said. "And nine on guard and wagon duty."

"Now down to eight," Clouston said.

"Len Baxter is out of it, boss. He can't shoulder a rifle or lift his arm to shoot a revolver."

"Then get rid of him," Clouston said. "He's of no use to me any longer."

"You mean pay him off?"

"I mean pay him off with lead." Clouston studied the stocky man. "What's your name?" he said. "It's slipped my mind."

"John Smith, boss." The man looked uncomfortable. He had the broken-nosed, scarred-eyed face of a bareknuckle club fighter.

"Well, John Smith, I fear that Lark Rawlings has been either killed or captured, so you are now my new second in command, and that means a double share of the gold we dig out of this hellhole."

Smith's dark eyes glittered, reflecting the oil lamp that hung above his head. "Well, thank'ee, boss," he said, grinning.

"Prepare the men. Tomorrow we will occupy the depot, take back my property, and then destroy the town. I want every man I have on the attack. The Chinese can remain unguarded for a few hours. If they try to escape we can round them up later."

"Sure thing, boss," Smith said, playing the good soldier.

"And, Mr. Smith, take care of that bit of unpleasantness."

"You mean Baxter?" Smith slapped his holstered gun. "I'll take care of that right now."

"Good," Clouston said. "It seems that you and I will get along just fine, Mr. Smith."

Thomas Clouston thought riding in the rain uncivilized and a possible sign of madness, but he nevertheless saddled up and headed toward the rail depot to take a look for himself. There was no sound of thunder, but a gloomy rain sheeted across the brush flats driven by an east wind.

Clouston halted when he was still out of rifle range and put his ship's glass to his right eye. He swept the telescope over the depot office and then to the rails where his greenstone lay piled. The glass was of good quality, made for the Prussian army, and brought the land closer and in fine detail. Beside the painted sign — an outrage, Clouston told himself — stood a solitary figure in a tan-colored slicker. He didn't recognize the man, but he might be the federal marshal. It was clear the lawman didn't expect anyone to contest his confiscation of the greenstone, at least that day.

Clouston contemplated the wisdom of riding over there and gunning the marshal. But as members of such a risky profession, many of those men were good with a gun and he'd be putting himself at too much risk.

The failure of the ore wagons to arrive and the loss of his bride weighed on Clouston, and he felt a little weary. He decided matters could wait until tomorrow when he felt more refreshed and in a better mood for the day's killing.

CHAPTER FIFTY-NINE

Shawn O'Brien figured the man he saw in the rain, long, white hair spilling from under his hat, had to be Thomas Clouston. If he'd had a rifle, he'd have taken a pot at him, keep him honest.

He told as much to Hamp Sedley who'd arrived with his horse, beef sandwiches, a bottle of cherry soda pop, and some news.

"You'd have missed him anyway," Sedley said. "Who the hell can shoot in this downpour rain?" He glanced at the dark sky. "Let's move to the office and show Clouston that we got enough sense to get in out of the rain."

After they stepped inside, Shawn stood at the window and looked out at the now empty flat. Chewing on a sandwich he said, "What's your news?"

Sedley shook his slicker, scattering water everywhere. "Sheriff Purdy, if you'll forgive that expression, decided to call the meeting earlier. Right now somebody's punching holes in the air with his forefinger and saying nothing that makes a lick of sense."

"Is Brown getting any volunteers?" Shawn said.

"I don't know. I didn't stick around. But I can tell you this, those two weird D'eth brothers were in attendance and so was Pete Caradas."

"Burt Becker?"

"No. I heard he's keeping to himself, still grieving for Sunny Swanson."

Sedley joined Shawn at the window. "What are we looking for?" he said.

"Thomas Clouston marching an army toward us," Shawn said. "Then we skedaddle and spread the good news. At least, that's what Saturday Brown says."

"He says he killed a man and wounded another today," Sedley said.

"He did. Both of them were Clouston gunmen."

"Got a bad attitude that feller," Sedley said. "I don't know if he scares Clouston but he scares the hell out of me."

"He's old school, Hamp, doesn't take any sass."

Sedley took a bite from his sandwich. "Clouston isn't coming this way today. Great generals don't like to fight in the rain.

Napoleon didn't."

"Waterloo was fought in a rainstorm."

"Yeah, and as I recall he lost that one."

Footsteps sounded on the stairs outside and Shawn drew his Colt.

But the visitor was Saturday Brown. Judging by his muddy boots he'd walked all the way from town.

As Shawn holstered his gun, Brown said, "Meeting's over. I got eighteen volunteers, dismissed those who were too young, too old, or too sick, and ended up with seven men. Three of them were in the war but none of them were fighting soldiers, a teamster, a quartermaster's clerk, and a medical orderly." The lawman shrugged. "Ah well, a man has to do his best with what he has."

"And what's your best, Marshal?" Shawn said.

"They will man this redoubt and repulse the enemy, even though their womenfolk are agin it."

Shawn's heart sank. Seven volunteers, none of them fighting men, up against Clouston's hired guns. He didn't like the odds.

"What about Caradas and the D'eth brothers?" he asked.

"Who knows?" Brown said. "They didn't

volunteer, just sat warming their chairs when I asked for a show of hands."

"Clouston looked the place over a short time after you left," Shawn said. "He sat his horse a ways off where I couldn't get a shot at him."

"He'll attack here tomorrow, take down my sign, and then destroy the town," Brown said. "At least that's his intention."

"When do your volunteers get here?" Shawn said.

"As soon as it gets dark," Brown said. "They all have rifles and I can guarantee Clouston and his men a warm reception. Look out there, O'Brien. They'll charge across the flat and we'll catch them in the open."

"Clouston's men will be in the open for a couple of minutes at most, and then they'll be among you," Shawn said. "Will your men stand against trained horseback fighters?"

"That's a question I can't answer until it happens," Brown said. Shawn saw doubt in his eyes. "But no matter what happens I'll live or die on this ground. It's my job."

CHAPTER SIXTY

By evening the rain was a memory kept alive by the muddy street and the washed-clean air. The moon was just beginning its climb into the purple sky as Shawn O'Brien and Hamp Sedley stepped into the Streetcar.

Four men sat at a table, a pot of coffee and cups in front of them.

Shawn was suddenly interested. When draw fighters forsook whiskey for coffee it meant they anticipated gun work ahead.

Pete Caradas lounged in his chair, his elegant self. Burt Becker regarded Shawn with an almost psychotic hatred, and the D'eth brothers sat upright, their dark faces empty of expression.

Sedley, not the most diplomatic of men, grinned and loudly said to Shawn, "Well now, there's four rannies you don't want to ever meet in a dark alley."

Caradas smiled. "Sedley, I'm willing to overlook your little faults since we're both members of the gambling fraternity, but sometimes you really do push your luck."

"Only a jest, Pete. No offense intended," Sedley said.

"And none taken," Caradas said. "This time." Then to Shawn, "The stalwart sons of Broken Bridle marched out an hour ago. You missed a grand sight."

"I was at dinner," Shawn said. "All seven of them, huh?"

Caradas said, "Eight, if you include Marshal Saturday Brown. But I would value him pretty high. He's probably worth three or four of us ordinary mortals."

Shawn ordered a beer, then holding the glass in his left hand he said, "Why the meeting, Pete?"

"Oh, just settling our differences," Caradas said.

Becker, a clean bandage tied around his chin, looked more than ever like a belligerent rabbit. "You weren't invited, O'Brien," he said.

"Try not to talk too much, Burt," Shawn said. "You must give the jaw I broke some rest."

Caradas said, "Please, Mr. Becker, let us not be inhospitable. You're welcome to join us, O'Brien, but you're too late to take part, since we just passed a resolution."

"And that was?" Shawn said. The saloon was empty and the sheet music open on the piano was the soulful ballad, "A Soldier's Farewell to His Dear Old Mother."

"We resolved that we would support Marshal Brown in his endeavors against our mutual enemy, Doctor Thomas Clouston," Caradas said. He poured coffee into his cup, then added, "But lest you think us too noble, we are not singing 'John Brown's Body' and fighting to free the slaves. The D'eth brothers sitting next to me like twin sphinxes are contracted to kill Dr. Clouston, a commission they are most anxious to fulfill. And Mr. Becker here wants the Rattlesnake Hills and all the gold contained therein."

"And you, Pete, what do you want?" Shawn said.

"Me? Just craving a little excitement is all. I've grown more than a little bored with this hick town. And, I might say, with Dr. Clouston. He's caused enough mischief and it's time for him to go."

"How do you plan to play this?" Shawn said.

"We'll join the marshal's merry band sometime in the night and wait Clouston's attack," Caradas said.

"Suppose he attacks Broken Bridle?"

Shawn said. "There's only old men and boys to defend the place."

"Sedley, tell Mr. O'Brien what we're doing," Caradas said.

"Rolling the dice," Sedley said. "Hoping we make the right call."

"There's your answer," Caradas said. "And what about you, O'Brien. Will you fight?"

"That's why I'm here," Shawn said.

"Then you will join us at the barricades?" Caradas said.

Shawn nodded and smiled. And he was still smiling as he said, "Pete, we'd better pray that we've made the right call. I heard the banshee crying over dead men in the hills last night."

Shawn and Sedley had just stepped out of the Streetcar when the Medicine Bow militia showed up, trudging through mud as they emerged from the darkness . . . three old coots leading four mules burdened with the various parts of a small cannon.

The man in front, wearing a ragged blue coat with tan facings and brass buttons, halted his caravan outside the saloon and said to Sedley, who was closer to him, "Colonel Jeb Calhoun of the Medicine Bow Dismounted Mule Militia at your service.

435

I'm looking fer Deputy United States Marshal Saturday Brown, late of our fair city."

"Are there more of you?" Sedley said, horrified.

"No, just us. Me, Major Dan Sheehan, and Captain Tom Delaney, plus four mules and a twelve-pounder mountain howitzer, model of 1841."

"Hell," Sedley said, "how old are you fellers?"

"Right impertinent question to ask, sonny," Calhoun said, bristling. "But if you must know I'm eighty-one, Major Sheehan is two years younger nor me, and Captain Delaney is only seventy-five."

Shawn stepped to the edge of the boardwalk and said, "My friend means that we thought there would be more of you."

"This is the militia, sonny, all of it," Calhoun said. "The younger fellers all quit to go strike it rich in Cripple Creek, Coloraddy." The old man had a beard down to a brass belt buckle engraved with the words, NUMQUID AUT MORI, as had his two companions. "Now point the way to Marshal Brown and don't let me hear no more sass."

Shawn directed the colonel to the rail depot, then said, "Call out when you get close. Those boys up there are a might touchy."

After the old men and their mules disappeared into the night, Sedley said, "If Saturday Brown never had a heart attack before, he'll have one now when he sees his militia."

Shawn said, "Who knows? Maybe they can hit something with that old peashooter."

Sedley said, "Not even the side of a barn. And if they're lucky they'll get one shot off before Clouston's boys are among them."

"Well, let's hope they make it count," Shawn said.

CHAPTER SIXTY-ONE

It was on the owlhoot side of midnight when Shawn O'Brien and Hamp Sedley joined Saturday Brown and his volunteers at the rail depot. To Shawn's surprise Pete Caradas, Burt Becker, and the D'eth brothers were already there.

Deputy United States Marshal Brown was not impressed.

"I thought I told you rannies to stay in town," he said, his shaggy eyebrows joining over the bridge of his nose like an old angry bull. "What if Clouston attacks there first?"

"Marshal, we're rolling the dice," Shawn said.

"Well, I hope you call it right," Brown said. "Man the defenses. The boys already there will make room. And don't step in front of that damned cannon."

"That's not the way to play it," Shawn said. "Becker's jaw is broken and he can't shoot a rifle and I'm not real good with a long gun."

"Same goes for me," Caradas said. "And I'm sure our silent friends here feel the same way." He grinned at the stone-faced D'eth brothers. "Ain't that right, boys?"

Milos and Petsha remained silent and Caradas said, "See, they don't want to grab a musket, either."

"Then how do you want to play this, O'Brien?" Brown said.

"We'll be your reserve, Marshal," Shawn said. "If Clouston breaks your line, we'll join the fight. By then it will be close work and rifle skills won't matter."

"O'Brien, who made you general?" Becker said, his throat working as he formed each torturous word.

"He makes sense, Burt," Caradas said. "In this outfit, that qualifies him as a general. What do the D'eth brothers say?"

"We'll go our own way, Caradas," Milos said.

"Then make sure you're pointed in the right direction," Caradas said. "I'd hate to shoot you boys as deserters."

"Big talk. Empty talk," Milos said.

"Well, now that's settled," Shawn said, smiling. "All we have to do is hunker down and wait. It's going to be a long time until dawn."

"Where the hell do I go?" Sedley said.

"You're in the reserve," Shawn said. Then, "It will be close, Hamp. Just take your time and use the sights."

"Or haul off and chunk your piece at somebody," Caradas said.

Sedley frowned. "We sure got no shortage of funnymen around here."

A couple of hours later when the night was as dark as pitch, Sheriff Jeremiah Purdy showed up with his crutch, his rifle, and his woman.

Saturday Brown was incensed, boiling with rage.

"Why the hell did you bring a woman here?" he said. Despite his anger the quiet of night hushed his voice. "Git her back home."

Purdy shook his head. "Jane insisted on coming. She's taken a set on it."

"I'm staying right here, Marshal," Jane Collins said. "If you want to get rid of me, you'll have to shoot me down like a common criminal."

Watching her, Shawn was surprised at how pretty Jane was. He'd only seen her once before when she was released from Becker's dungeon, and then she hadn't been at her best. And it seemed that with so much on his mind Saturday Brown was not in the mood to tangle with a stubborn woman. "Then you'll stay in the depot office and not come out until I tell you to. Understand, missy?"

"I can take care of myself, Marshal," Jane said, her little square chin set and obstinate. She reached under her hooded cloak and produced a Remington derringer from the pocket of her dress. "My intended gave me this."

"Purdy, I'm holding you responsible for your woman," Brown said. "See she doesn't get in the way."

"I'll take care of her," Purdy said. "After I get Jane settled, where do you want me?"

"You got a rifle, so I want you in the firing line. Find yourself a berth among the others." Brown glared at the girl. "Why in God's name does a pretty little gal want to be here? Is it to be close to Purdy?"

Jane Collins shook her head. "No. It's not that."

"Then what is it, ma'am, if I ain't out of place in askin'?"

"I want to watch Burt Becker die," Jane said.

CHAPTER SIXTY-TWO

Just before dawn Dr. Thomas Clouston's gunmen ordered the Chinese to remain inside their tents and that anyone caught outside would be shot on sight.

Something big was afoot, and Sammy Chang knew that the time was approaching when he must raise the Black Dragon flag of revolt that the women had been secretly sewing for days. He heard Clouston yelling orders, and the whinny of horses and the clank of weapons and equipment told him the oppressors were mounting up to do battle.

He readied his Tranter revolvers and bided his time . . .

Thomas Clouston was pleased. He'd touched a hunchback for good luck and now it was high time to settle with Broken Bridle and wipe that vile pestilence off the map. But first he would take back what was his. It was a matter of pride, not necessity, but he could not allow such an affront to stand. The marshal who confiscated the greenstone would pay for his crime on the gallows, and Clouston planned to watch him kick.

Dressed in his cloak, astride his great horse, Clouston puffed on the S-shaped pipe clenched between his teeth and studied the defenses in front of the rail depot. He swept his telescope across the greenstone barricade and counted eight, perhaps nine, men. But then, behind the pathetic fortifications he spotted something that gave him pause — a small cannon manned by three graybeards.

Clouston removed the glass from his eye, slammed it shut, and studied the terrain between himself and the enemy. He calculated the cannon could get off a single shot, effective enough if it was loaded with canister and the old geezers could shoot. Somehow he thought that unlikely since they were obviously not regular army artillerymen. But in any case, he'd touched the old Chinese hunchback so all the luck in the world would be with him.

As a precaution, Clouston gave the order that his men should shake out into a loose line, leaving ten feet of space between the horses to reduce the effect of grapeshot. He had lost men through death and desertion but could still field eighteen gun-savvy horsemen, more than enough for the task at hand.

Six conscripted Chinese boys carrying large kettledrums, the very drums that had terrorized Broken Bridle for so long, stepped in front of the mounted men.

In that moment Thomas Clouston imagined he was a frontier Napoleon.

He turned to the man at his side. "Mr. Smith, we will advance at a walk. Order the drums to set the pace."

Smith barked out the orders and the line advanced. The horsemen drew their Colts and held them up beside their heads and the kettledrums pounded.

After a hundred yards, Clouston yelled, "Music to the rear! Advance at the trot!"

Horse harnesses jangled as the gunmen kneed their mounts into a fast trot.

"Damn you! Keep your line!" Clouston roared.

He placed his pipe in a coat pocket and grabbed his steel battle-ax. Ahead of him he saw a puff of white smoke, and then a cannon shell shrieked high over his head. He heard a dull *Crrrump!* as it exploded harmlessly somewhere in the hills.

"Forward at the canter!" Clouston yelled. Then, "Charge!"

CHAPTER SIXTY-THREE

"Here they come, boys!" Saturday Brown roared. "Let 'em have it!"

The men among the greenstone fired a ragged volley. Watching from the window of the depot office, Shawn O'Brien saw no hits.

Thomas Clouston's men came on at the gallop, firing their revolvers.

The window where Shawn stood shattered as a bullet hit the glass high up, and behind him he heard Hamp Sedley curse as the ricocheting bullet nicked him.

"Damn! Look at that!" Pete Caradas said. Three men left the firing line, tossed away their rifles, and headed for town at a run. "We better get down there."

"No, not yet," Shawn said. "When the greenstone slows them we'll play our hand."

Below them Sheriff Jeremiah Purdy stood, his crutch under his left arm. Unable to work his rifle, he fired his .32 steadily but to no apparent success.

Clouston's men, yipping like savages, were less than a hundred yards away . . . ninety . . . eighty . . . seventy . . .

The Medicine Bow militia gallantly tried to service their howitzer and get off another shot. But Colonel Jeb Calhoun took a bullet in the head and fell, sprawling across the barrel. Clouston's men targeted the cannon. Major Sheehan and Captain Delaney fell in quick succession and then a man who rushed to their help went down, screaming, his right leg shattered by a bullet.

"O'Brien!" Caradas called out. "For God's sake!"

"Get ready," Shawn said.

"You boys stay right where you're at," Burt Becker said. "You, O'Brien, let go of the iron or I'll drill you square."

For a moment Shawn thought about going for it and Becker read it in his eyes. He reached out, grabbed Jane Collins, then threw her violently on the floor. "She gets it first. Now drop the gun."

"Do as he says, O'Brien," Caradas said. "He means it."

As contract killers, the D'eth brothers mentally took a step back. This was no part of why they were in Broken Bridle. It was a time to wait and see. Outside guns banged and men roared their battle anger.

"What happened with the jaw, Becker?" Shawn said.

The big man removed the bandage. "It would take a better man than you to bust my jaw, O'Brien. As long as I made as though it was broke, I didn't have to answer any fool questions about missing women and the like."

"What's your game, Becker?" Shawn said.

"Game? No game. I surrender you to Thomas Clouston and then me and him cut a deal. My gun protection for a share of the gold."

"He doesn't need you, Becker," Shawn said. "He'll kill you."

"No, he'll need me after today," the big outlaw said. "He's losing men down there."

But the sound of the gunfire suddenly changed. It slowed down, ended, and was replaced by shrieks of terror and primitive screams of rage from many throats.

Alarmed, Burt Becker took a quick glance out the window. It was a reaction that came and went in a split second. But it was all the time Shawn O'Brien needed. He drew in one fluid, graceful motion and fired.

Becker was fast. He took the shoulder hit and shot back. His bullet ripped a gouge across the top of Shawn's shoulder and burned like a red-hot iron. But Shawn's second bullet hit true and slammed into the center of Becker's chest. The big man staggered back, his eyes wide and in shock. Shawn fired again, a second hit, this time to the base of Becker's throat. Some stubborn, inner strength kept Becker on his feet, but he was gone and Shawn could see it. His gun fell from his hand and he went to his knees. He stared at Shawn and managed to say just one word: *"Fast."*

Then Becker's eyes clouded and he fell flat on his face.

His anger up, the roar of gunshots ringing in his ears, Shawn swung on Pete Caradas. "Damn you, make your play," he said.

Caradas lifted his hands. "Your friends need help, O'Brien."

"Shawn!" Hamp Sedley's voice seemed to travel from far off. "Your enemy is outside."

Shawn forced himself to come back, out of the tunnel that stretched between him and Pete Caradas. After a few moments his Colt dropped by his side and he walked past Caradas to the door and then stepped outside . . . into carnage.

In the moment of victory, Thomas Clouston lost.

A thousand Chinese men swarmed over his mounted men and dragged them from the saddle. Clouston, his massive horse rearing, roared and laid about him with his battle-ax splitting heads and cleaving off hands, but the Chinese swarmed over him and hauled him to the ground. Clouston's battle cries turned to screams of terror as he was carried above the heads of the crowd in the direction of the Rattlesnake Hills.

Shawn, followed by Sedley and Caradas, waded into the brawl, their guns drawing. But they found no targets. Despite huge losses, the Chinese had overpowered all of Clouston's men and hacked them to pieces with whatever weapons they'd carried from their camp, knives, picks, shovels . . . and their bare hands. There was no longer anything human about the Clouston gunmen; here and there bloody remains spread across the ground like cherry pies dropped to the stone floor by a careless baker.

Shawn watched the D'eth brothers run in hot pursuit of the Chinese who'd taken Clouston. They still had their contract to honor.

"O'Brien!"

Shawn looked around the battlefield at the hurting dead and dying. The air was thick with gun smoke and the hot iodine smell of blood.

"Over here! You ain't very bright, son, or

you're deef!"

Saturday Brown lay under a pile of bodies, white and brown tangled together, united only by blood. The old lawman's face was ashen.

"Are you hurt?" Shawn said.

"All shot to pieces, son. Now git me to my feet."

Shawn and Hamp Sedley helped the marshal stand. Sedley looked Brown over and said, "You're shot through and through."

"Yup. Noticed that my ownself," Brown said.

"We need to get you to the doctor," Shawn said.

Brown said, "There are others here who need a doctor. See to them first. Then bring me the butcher's bill."

The bill was steep. Six dead, including the militiamen, and all the rest wounded, one of them, Brown, seriously. Clouston had lost three men during the charge and one more at the barricade. The Chinese had done for the rest.

Dr. John Walsh did the best he could, but Deputy United States Marshal Saturday Brown, shot four times, died within an hour of the battle's end.

Shawn O'Brien took his death hard.

■ ■ ■ ■

"What the hell happened?" Hamp Sedley said. He stared at the body of Dr. Thomas Clouston hanging by its neck from the gallows noose. "His whole damned chest is open. Man, look at the damned flies. Hundreds of them."

"I'd say the D'eth brothers took his heart," Shawn said. "I guess it was a clause in their contract." He turned to Sheriff Jeremiah Purdy who had his wounded left arm in a sling. "You sure you know how to work that thing?"

"I watched Colonel Calhoun do it," Purdy said. "She's all set and ready to go."

"What do you think Pete?" Shawn said. "Will it shoot?"

"Yeah, it will shoot. If it doesn't blow up first," Caradas said.

A townsman with a fat bandage around his head nodded, his face wise.

"Seen a cannon blow up once, but it was double-shotted. Killed the gun crew though."

"Is that thing double-shotted?" Sedley said, stepping away from the howitzer.

"No," Purdy said. "One ball ought to be enough to bring down the overhang."

452

"Aim for the crack, Pete," Shawn said.

"Easy," Caradas said. "Like looking down the barrel of a Colt."

Shawn eyed the overhang, the great fissure like a terrible scar.

"Let her rip!" he yelled.

The howitzer roared and its wheels bounced a foot in the air. Rancid smoke enveloped Shawn, but he heard a loud explosion and the crash of the collapsing rock face. When the smoke cleared there was no longer an overhang, just a pile of rubble at the bottom of the cliff.

"Didn't take much, did it?" Caradas said. Temporary deafness from the blast made him shout.

Shawn waved away smoke and dust from the front of his face and said to Purdy, "How much shot do we have left?"

"Enough to bring down the whole cliff face," Purdy said.

"Then that's what we'll do," Shawn said. "The greenstone has caused enough death and disaster. Let's bury it forever."

He felt worn-out, used up, and depression hung on him like a wet cloak.

EPILOGUE

Depression, the Celtic malady, ran rife in the O'Brien family, and at one point had driven Shawn's brother Jacob into a monastery. It was a black dog that lurked in dark corners, always ready to spring.

For a month, Shawn retreated to the hotel and saw no one but Hamp Sedley. During that time Jeremiah Purdy and Jane Collins got married, then left Broken Bridle never to return. Pete Caradas rode out for places unknown, and Judy Campbell sold the Four Ace to another rancher and took up a teaching post in the Arizona Territory.

Broken Bridle could not survive the deaths and exodus of so many of its citizens, and the town began its long dying process that would last until 1926 when the Streetcar Saloon burned down.

Shawn O'Brien blamed himself for all that had happened. He'd promised to help Sheriff Purdy tame the town and make it a fine place for American families to live. But instead, he'd destroyed it.

Sedley pointed out that it was a great evil that had devastated the town and that Shawn had defeated a monster and saved the lives of many women and children, both white and Chinese.

But Shawn would not be convinced and sank deeper into blackness.

Alarmed, Sedley wrote a letter to *Colonel Shamus O'Brien, Dromore, New Mexico Territory,* begging for his help.

It took the best part of the month before Jacob O'Brien arrived by train to take his brother home.

"Jake, I failed this time," Shawn told him. "I destroyed the very people I'd come to save."

Jacob said, "It's a long way to Dromore, Shawn. We'll talk about it."

And Sedley said, "Can I tag along?"

Jake, tall, gaunt, and grim, looked the gambler up and down with his icy stare and said, "Suit yourself."

"Thank'ee," Sedley said. "This is shaping up to be a fun trip."

The employees of Thorndike Press hope you have enjoyed this Large Print book. All our Thorndike, Wheeler, and Kennebec Large Print titles are designed for easy reading, and all our books are made to last. Other Thorndike Press Large Print books are available at your library, through selected bookstores, or directly from us.

For information about titles, please call:
(800) 223-1244

or visit our Web site at:
http://gale.cengage.com/thorndike

To share your comments, please write:
Publisher
Thorndike Press
10 Water St., Suite 310
Waterville, ME 04901